sin.net

Sam looked like a boy-band manager's wet dream: muscular and strong with lean legs; a neat little bottom clad in white cotton and broad shoulders that had a pale freckled tan. I didn't feel like I deserved this boy; I wasn't beautiful enough. He was too good for a mousey type like me, surely.

He fixed his gaze on me. He silently, seriously, watched the tiny, tentative movements of my hand over my pussy. His eyes were fixed, full of wonder tinged with desire, and I saw that I was more than good enough for him. I was a dream come true for him. To Sam I was Dominique – a thirty-year-old woman with great tits and ass who had come all the way to London to play Cowboys and Indians.

I was beginning to like being Dominique a lot.

D0625519

Other books by the author

STAND AND DELIVER

BOUND BY CONTRACT

sin.net

HELENA RAVENSCROFT

Black Lace novels contain sexual fantasies.
In real life, make sure you practise safe sex.

First published in 2001 by
Black Lace
Thames Wharf Studios,
Rainville Road,
London W6 9HA

Copyright © Helena Ravenscroft 2001

The right of Helena Ravenscroft to be identified as the
Author of this Work has been asserted by her in
accordance with the Copyright, Designs and Patents Act
1988.

Typeset by SetSystems Ltd, Saffron Walden, Essex
Printed and bound by Mackays of Chatham PLC

ISBN 0 352 33598 X

*All characters in this publication are fictitious and any
resemblance to real persons, living or dead, is purely
coincidental.*

This book is sold subject to the condition that it shall
not, by way of trade or otherwise, be lent, resold, hired
out or otherwise circulated without the publisher's
prior written consent in any form of binding or cover
other than that in which it is published and without a
similar condition including this condition being
imposed on the subsequent purchaser.

Contents

1. the spider to the fly   1
2. caught in the web   7
3. dominique talking   19
4. hanging on the telephone   34
5. cubicles at dawn   52
6. tales of the riverbank   72
7. midnight cowboy   87
8. two birds in the hand   101
9. treat him like a lady   115
10. something for the weekend   130
11. having the whip hand   141
12. the virgin and the shoemaker   159
13. storm clouds   172
14. the snow queen   179
15. fire and ice   192
16. my naughty angel   205
17. a salve for every sore   219
18. decision time   238
19. home   256

with thanks to all the internetter crew
especially
fancy, sam nmex, tough guy, tdh, pandora,
myst & muf, alexxs, and jasper – who went
way beyond what duty demanded . . .!

Chapter One

the spider to the fly

'*I*'m online now, Carrie. Why don't you come and join me?' murmured my sister-in-law, Eva, her voice silky-soft and alluring. She was temptation personified. I cradled the telephone receiver against my ear and sighed.

The flesh is weak, so they tell me. And none more weak than mine. I was a weak-willed, weak-fleshed girl. Easily led. Open to suggestion.

Eva is only ten years older than me, or so she claims. But in terms of experience she is a hundred years my senior. She does things that I don't even dream about. Eva had been doing Internet chat – or more specifically Internet sex – for almost a year. And now she'd dragged me kicking and screaming into the twenty-first century with a first-hand display of what a computer and modem might do for a non-existent sex life.

But wait. Rewind.
It doesn't start here. It started last night.

Once a month, on a Friday, I have dinner with my brother and his wife. Leon and Eva. We have nothing in common. Nothing to say to each other. And because of

1

this, they always make sure that there's a third party present so that we don't have to sit in awkward silence for the evening. Sometimes – rarely – these third parties ask to take me home. I always refuse. And Leon then mutters that it's no wonder I couldn't make my marriage last if I'm so frigid.

Happy families.

The previous evening had ended predictably enough. Max Armstrong, a visiting American businessman who'd been chosen as that night's third party, had offered to take me home. I had politely declined, and then watched while he shrugged his muscular shoulders into a light summer jacket. As he straightened his collar with wide, blunt fingers, he'd glanced up and caught me looking at him. I had blushed a fierce red and stared mutely down at the polished wooden floor, silently trying to convince myself that Max Armstrong was not my type. He had then shaken hands with Leon and taken his leave. My brother, once the door was shut, had regarded me with a look in his puffy eyes that spoke volumes of derision, impatience and contempt.

'I'll call Carrie a cab in a while, sweetie,' murmured Eva, pressing a kiss to his pale, fat cheek. 'We're going to have a girly chat. You go on to bed.'

I started to speak but Eva, all angular cheek-bones and glossy black hair, had raised one carefully pruned brow and silenced me with inscrutable blue eyes.

'Carrie,' she murmured, her New York accent twisting the 'a' of my name. 'Come with me.'

I meekly said goodnight to Leon and then followed Eva to the spacious study at the far end of the hallway.

'Didn't you like Max?' She closed the door behind us and leaned against it.

'He seemed very nice,' I said, wondering why I had been brought to her inner sanctum. I glanced around at Eva's tastefully furnished study with its pale walls and dark crimson flooring. Long shadowy curtains –

undrawn – framed the tall windows and a single lamp with a slender shade glowed on the bookcase. A vase of orchids was placed near the corner of her desk; the blooms were past their best and some of the petals had fallen on to the gleaming glass surface. The room was elegant and restrained with an undertone of suppressed decadence. Rather like its owner.

I was tired and I wanted to go home, but part of me was intrigued as to why Eva felt the need for what she termed 'a girly chat'. Girlishness was not her style. And cosy chats were something she almost never indulged in, especially not with me. I watched as she pushed herself away from the door and walked across the room, her fingers toying with the onyx bracelet that clasped her wrist.

'Well, I could eat our Mr Armstrong for breakfast.' She almost purred as she spoke, and I felt a twist of irritation. She probably already had eaten him. For lunch and dinner as well as breakfast. Eva was a predator, and the fact that Max Armstrong was doing business with her husband would be unlikely to count as an obstacle to the fulfilment of her desire. 'Unfortunately, though,' she murmured, 'it seems that I am not his choice of dish.' She leaned against the edge of her desk and reached sideways to run a light finger over her computer screen before holding it up as if to check for dust. Her eyes met mine suddenly, her gaze wry but serious. 'Maybe you are.'

'I doubt it,' I said.

She looked me quickly up and down. 'No,' she concurred. 'I doubt it, too. But, Carrie, it is time you started getting out there again. It's been two years since you broke up with Patrick – although why you had to do that still puzzles me.'

I felt a cold prickle finger my hairline. I wondered what she'd say if I told her the truth about Patrick, but then decided not to go near that particular can of worms. She probably wouldn't have believed me anyway.

Eva, one slender hand stroking the smooth casing of the computer beside her, looked me critically up and down. I cowered for a moment, wondering what she was going to say next. Then she smiled.

'Anyway,' she said gaily, 'I haven't brought you in here to lecture you about the way you run your life.'

'Really?'

'No. I'm going to show you something. Something wild. You're going to love this.'

She started up her computer and beckoned me over. I went to stand at her side and watched the screen flicker into life.

'Come into my parlour, said the spider to the fly,' she murmured with a low laugh.

I don't know quite what I had expected, but in Eva's study, that hot summer night, something was unleashed that swept me up, tossed me around, and spat me out a different person.

But wait. Fast forward. Back to where we started.

Weak-willed and weak-fleshed. Easily led. Open to suggestion.

Eva had rung me to tell me exactly where she was on the net, and how to get there. Last night, adult chat rooms had seemed fantastic: the safest way to have sex with a person you'd only just met; the ultimate way to communicate. What I had done had been tantalisingly erotic. But having had a night to sleep on it, I thought I might have changed my mind. This was a computer thing. It was geeky, wasn't it? And weren't all those other people tapping on their keypads just sad losers with no life? Rather like me in fact.

I told Eva what I was thinking.

'Oh, sure,' she conceded, 'it's just like real life. You get losers everywhere, but on the Internet they're easy to spot. You just ignore them. The people I choose to talk to

4

are articulate and fun. Most of them do it because the TV is boring, or they don't feel like going out tonight. Or they're horny, and their partner's working and they want to get their rocks off with a real person instead of a centre-fold. And . . . Carrie?'

'Yes?'

'Most of them do it for fun. For pleasure. So lighten up.'

'Maybe you're right.'

'You know I'm right.' She gave a low, sexy laugh. 'Besides, there wasn't much of the loser about Tough Guy last night, was there? Just think of what he did to you, and you to him. Doesn't it make you feel hot just remembering? It sure does me, and I was only sitting next to you reading it. You were the one getting thoroughly fucked.' Her voice dropped an octave to that deep, sensuous American drawl that was beginning to give me tingles at the nape of my neck. 'Come on. Get online and have a good time. What else're you gonna do tonight? Are you telling me that you'd rather watch TV all alone than have sex? Everybody needs sex.'

I leaned forward against the hall table and stared at myself in the mirror that hung above it. My eyes were wide and clear under heavy lids, my normally pale lips a sensual curve of plump, raspberry pink. I certainly looked like someone who needed sex, and Eva was offering me exactly that. On a plate.

'I don't know,' I prevaricated. 'It doesn't go anywhere –'

'Of course it does!' she cut in impatiently. 'It goes where you want it to go. It can go to your fingers inside your little panties as you sit at your computer, and some fantastic masturbation. Or it can go to phone-sex, which – take it from me – can be incredible.' Her voice became breathy with suppressed excitement. 'Or it can go to real life follow-through. You could do a sex-tour of the British Isles, or even the world. Believe me, it happens!' She laughed softly. 'The choice is yours, Carrie.'

Her soft, deep voice lingered over my name. The hushed sound of her breathing took me straight back to last night and made my pulse skip a beat. In her study, by the soft glow of a single lamp, I had leaned over her narrow shoulder and watched her fingers fly over the keypad.

The boy she'd seduced had been thrilled, his words getting misspelled in his excitement as he described to her how hard he was, how turned on he was, how he was sitting there slipping his trembling fingers over his rock-hard cock . . .

'Oh God.' I pressed my palm to my feverish forehead and silently cursed my weak flesh. 'I'll do it. Where are you?'

Chapter Two
caught in the web

I reached for a pen and scribbled down the web address, then unplugged the phone. Three minutes later the computer was on, and I was dialling up my server.

'Where are you, Eva?' I murmured, sitting forward on the edge of my seat.

There were around two hundred other people logged on to the site. I ran through the list which supplied the name Eva had told me she was using: Sapphire. The list was split up alphabetically and it didn't take me long to find her, or which of the many rooms she was in.

Sapphire – Sex Talk

I chose a name that sounded as far from my own meek personality as possible. Then I hit Go-To-Room, and jumped in.

Sapphire: you took yr time.
Dominique: I'm not used to this, remember?
9-inch: any ladies wanna swap pics?
Sapphire: if you see anything come up in red, then it's a private message that only you can see. You can ignore if

you like. But if you want to answer then click on the sender's name and send a PM back.
Dominique: OK, thank you.
Sapphire: and u don't have to be all accurate with yr spelling and grammar, the quicker u type the better the sex is, so something has to go and its usually spelling, lol.
Dominique: lol?
Sapphire: laughing out loud.
9-inch: laughing out loud . . .
SamUK: Laughing Out Loud!

I laughed out loud myself as the last three messages all came up at once, and then scanned the list at the side of my screen. There were five other people besides Eva and me in Sex Talk. They could all see what we were saying and join in, unless we sent PMs like 9-inch had.

SamUK: a/s/l, Dominique?
Dominique: oh help . . .
SamUK: age/sex/location.
Dominique: oh, lol, thanks. 30/f/UK . . . you?
SamUK: 23/m/London . . . lol, so a fellow countryman, makes a change, its usually State-siders in here at this time, lol, the time difference means they are going online in their lunch break . . . wanna chat here? Or I could call you . . .

I wasn't ready to talk to a complete stranger on the telephone. Not yet. Learning to talk dirty on the Internet was new enough. Besides, if I talked to SamUK on the phone then it would be obvious that I was not the vivacious Dominique, and I couldn't imagine him wanting to talk to the real me.

Dominique: stay here for now please. I'm new to this.
SamUK: sure. Want to go private?

8

Dominique: sapphire?

Sapphire: still here, just watching . . . go on, go private with him . . . you'll love it.

9-inch: come private with ME Dominique, I'll show you a good time.

HornyFiremanNYC: dominique, I was hoping to put out yr fire myself . . .

Dominique: lol . . . maybe next time, NYC. I like a man in uniform.

HornyFiremanNYC: Just doing my job, ma'am!

Dominique: Sam, help me, I don't know how to get to a private room.

I bit my bottom lip and watched the type turn from black to red as SamUK spoke to me privately. It was strange how different I felt about myself when I was called Dominique. Dominique was confident, funny, provocative. And wildly attractive: I had decided that straight away. And she wasn't a coward who couldn't answer back. I liked her a lot, and I knew she was who I would have been if I had made some different choices in my life. Like not marrying a bully. Or moving out of town away from a brother whose every word was law. Dominique – unlike me – had no history. She had any future I wanted her to have. And right now I wanted to have a try at calling the shots.

Smiling with anticipation at that thought, I squinted at the screen and read what Sam was saying.

SamUK: call it 'coolroom' (it's so damn hot tonight, we can imagine we're somewhere with huge fans and open windows) . . . then click Go-To-Room . . . see ya there?

Dominique: sure . . . going now, I hope. If it doesn't work for me will you come back to Sex Talk?

SamUK: I'll find you . . . don't worry.

9

I did what he said.

And there I was. In a completely private room. Sam's computer was obviously a bit slower: his name wasn't showing yet. I used the waiting time by sprinting out to the kitchen and grabbing a half-finished bottle of wine out of the fridge and finding a clean glass. The dirty crockery was piling up, as usual. I knew I'd have to get on to it sooner or later, but right now I had more pressing things on my mind.

By the time I got back to the computer with the bottle in one hand and a hastily rinsed glass in the other, Sam had bounced in and been talking to himself for a few moments. I watched his words come up on the screen and wondered briefly what he was like – what he looked like. He was 23, or so he said. Young, quite a bit younger than me, but then who cared? It wasn't as if I was ever going to meet him in real life. And if I was going to have Internet sex then surely it was better to do it with people who were young; switched on; familiar with the technology.

SamUK: hi . . . you made it. Good.

SamUK: Dominique . . . u here?

SamUK: PM me if you are here and cant talk . . .

SamUK: (whistling and putting hands in pockets) trust me . . . get myself a girl and then scare her off . . . are you ok dominique? TALK TO ME!

I grinned, poured myself some wine and decided to put him out of his misery.

Dominique: sorry, went to get some wine. Coming to stand close to you and pour you some chilled white.

SamUK: mmmm, tastes ok but i prefer beer myself, you don't have any do you?

Dominique: lol, no. don't drink beer its no good for yr belly, lol.

10

SamUK: nothing wrong with my belly, come here and feel it . . . its a real 6-pack.

Dominique: yeah right, like i believe you . . . you could look like Rab C Nesbit and I'd never know!

SamUK: that's true enough. Why don't we swap pics? send me a photo – my e-mail addy's sambronson78-@surfermail.com.

78, I thought, biting my bottom lip with amusement. That must be the year he was born. He was so young. Young and sweet. Ripe for plucking by bad-girl Dominique.

Dominique: i haven't got a picture to send. I'm new to this, I only tried a chat room for the first time last night. Send me yrs though: i'm mail@horton.u-web.com.

SamUK: I'm just sending you my picture. Why don't you describe yrself for me if you don't have a picture yet?

Dominique: well, i'm 5ft 6 inches, curvy, with shoulder length chestnut hair and a nice smile.

I winced a little as I read back what I had typed. It wasn't strictly true. Shoulder-length hair, yes. But chestnut? That was stretching a point. I sighed, then remembered that Dominique wasn't actually me. She was someone else, and she could be whatever I wanted her to be. So tonight I would be chestnut and gorgeous, and blow SamUK away. He'd never know.

SamUK: you sound like a wet dream, dominique . . . so . . . slipping my arm around yr waist i pull you in close and bury my face in that shoulder length hair . . . mmm you smell good . . . will you let me help you out of those clothes? I want to see that curvy body naked . . .

Reading what he typed, I felt a sudden rush of hot blood to my sex, a wicked heat that swelled and flared inside me at his words. Oh wow, I thought, if this was real life, what fun we'd be having. The Internet seemed amazingly full of possibilities: just meet a guy, ask him for sex, and get on with it. No preamble, no time-wasting. Just straight in with the hot sex. Cut to the chase.

I wriggled forward in my chair, aware of the pressure of the polished timber against the backs of my thighs. I could feel the stickiness of my cotton knickers as I spread my legs a little and pressed myself down against the hard surface. This was going to be better than curling up with a sexy book and an itchy trigger finger.

I pulled up my inbound mail and let his picture download.

Sam was definitely 23, and very sweet. Not Mr Right. Not Mr Sexy. Nor even Mr Fit. Just a nice-looking Mr Average with a baseball hat, lovely eyes and great grin. He looked fun. I decided to come on a little stronger. After all – I was Dominique, and I could do what I liked.

Dominique: there, nice bare tits swelling out at you . . . just aching for the touch of your hands. Grabbing yr wrist and pulling you closer. I press yr hand on my breast.
SamUK: oh yes. I like that. You feel so good, so firm.
Dominique: rubbing one hand up yr thigh. Mmmm, big package there, mister. So. Tell me what you want to do if you saw me in Real Life?
SamUK: oh God, in RL I'd want . . . to kiss and suck and hold your tits.
Dominique: mmm . . .?
SamUK: and a whole lot more things.
Dominique: like what? go on tell me more. Tell me what kind of person you would want to be if you could be anyone, and where you'd take me to fuck me.

There was a pause as he thought about it. Then his next words came up on my screen.

SamUK: lol, since i was a kid i always wanted to be a Cowboy. The stetson. The neckerchief. The fringed trousers, lol. And the rodeo skills too! Then I could lasso you . . . take you to my ranch. Kick open the door of my hay barn. It'd be cool in there, in the shade. I'd toss you down in the piles of fresh hay.
Dominique: oh yes, Sam, sounds good . . .
SamUK: I'd press you down in the biggest, softest pile of hay.

A cowboy! Oh, how nice. How sweet and old-fashioned he was. I could just imagine Sam when he was a little boy, watching cowboy movies and dreaming of being one himself one day. And here, online, he could do exactly that: indulge his fantasies. He was an escapist, just like me.

Dominique: mmm . . . the hay smells really sweet. Sam, have you got a cowboy hat on?
SamUK: yup. A black one like the bad cowboys wear. What're you wearing?
Dominique: oh, I'm all dressed up like Jane Russell in that 1950s movie poster: bare shoulders and tits because you already took off my shirt! A skirt tumbled up around my thighs. Little lace up boots. Tightly laced corset.
SamUK: Oh, man! I'm pulling zip down and getting my hard tackle out. I want to fuck you. Come here . . .

I was surprised at the tangle of emotions that zipped through my mind. And equally surprised by my own response to his words. I felt a rush of adrenalin in my stomach as I typed some more:

Dominique: I'm on all fours. I press back against you, I can feel you sliding your finger across my clit.
SamUK: stroking your clit, rubbing it hard and getting your juices all over. mmmm dominique you are so wet, so wet and warm, you feel really nice. Can we fuck soon?

I watched as his words came up on the screen and he began to tell me how he was pushing his hard cock into me, that I felt so tight, so sweet and sticky, that I smelled so fresh. I could feel my breath get a little faster as I read his words, and my pulse skipped along, drumming a steady rhythm in my veins. I went one-handed with my typing as I got more and more turned-on, letting my other hand drift down to the hem of my skirt.

SamUK: and pull out all the way to the tip and slide it all the way in. Oh you're so juicy. Slipping out and then in again. All the way in.
Dominique: feels so good . . .
SamUK: such a tight pussy – fucking you hard and fast now.
Dominique: pushing my ass up and back at you to let you in deeper.

I slowly slipped the silky fabric of my skirt up over my thighs so that I could touch myself; so that I could do with my hand what Sam was telling me he was doing with his cock.

SamUK: reach around and pinch your nipples
SamUK: as i fuck your sweet little pussy, tight pussy
SamUK: in and out
SamUK: in and out

I arched my back, taking a deep breath and letting my hands smooth over my breasts briefly before putting my fingers back to the keypad.

14

Dominique: mmmmmmm, fuck me really hard, sam. Drive it in, like a pile-driver . . . fast and HARD.

SamUK: pull all the way to head again. Then slam all the way to my balls. Fuck you as hard as you want it.

SamUK: Slam in again . . . doing this over and over, gripping your tits and holding them tight, leaning over you and ramming home deep inside yr honey-wet pussy.

Dominique: slipping my hand down and rubbing my clit while you slam me, love the feel of your balls against my pussy lips as you fuck me . . .

SamUK: feel my balls slap you, oh yeah right. You feel so sweet.

Dominique: oh yes. . .

My finger was hard against my aching clit and my eyes were narrowed as I sat back in my chair. A sweet sensation of desire washed over my body and I could feel tingles zinging from the tips of my toes all the way up my body to the top of my head. My hand worked a little faster, and a fresh juicy gush soaked my cotton knickers.

Dominique: love the way you fuck me . . . I'm reaching behind and holding your thighs with my hands

SamUK: . . . yes fucking you as hard as i can

Dominique: I'm pulling you in really close, can feel the coarse hair on your thighs, gripping your muscular legs tight with my fingers, can you feel my long nails digging in, pulling you in, getting your rhythm, oh God, yes, Sam . . .

My fingers worked quicker, my thumb curling around the warm wet gusset of my knickers.

SamUK: push my cock as deep as i can and grind it into you.

Dominique: sighing tiny little breathy sighs in time with your thrusts.

15

SamUK: can feel pussy pull on the head as i stroke you . . .
Dominique: mmmmm stroke me some more . . .

'Oh yes, stroke me some more, Sam,' I murmured, stroking myself and letting my eyelids fall lazily down over my eyes. I could just see the screen, just read his words: I was in a semi-conscious state of surrender and I loved it.

SamUK: pull back to head and push all the way in again
Dominique: and feel my hard clit, like a pearl under your fingers as I grab your hand and crush it against my clit
SamUK: yes its hard, a sweet little bud. I press it hard and you arch yr back more
SamUK: fucking you hard and deep now

This was dirty talk at its finest, at its most direct. And it was almost better than real-life dirty talk because there was no heavy breathing to get in the way: just impure, sexy words appearing on the screen. The fact that the spelling was bad seemed to make the sentences doubly urgent.

My knickers were soaked. Hot and damp, they clung to my pouting sex and began to feel like a hindrance as I sat in the chair, one foot braced against the desk-leg and the other planted firmly on the carpet. My knees were so far apart that they almost ached, and my typing was getting slower and slower as I let sensation take over and rubbed myself faster.

SamUK: you've stopped typing. Are you touching yourself in RL?
SamUK: Oh Jeez you are aren't you? You're so hot dominique. Touch yrself more. Take your underwear off for me . . . can you do that?
Dominique: yes. lol, sam, tell me – are you hard in RL?

SamUK: as a rock. I'm busting the fly on my jeans here, lol. Oh Dominique, tell me you've taken off your knickers. Tell me what you feel, how wet you are, how good you smell.

I wriggled out of my knickers and scrunched them briefly in my hand, enjoying the heat of my body that still clung to the light fabric, then dropped them on the floor under my desk.

Dominique: I feel warm, and very wet . . . inside I'm so smooth, and quite tight, but I can slip my finger in easily.
SamUK: yes Dominique, do it with yr fingers, fuck yourself . . .

I shuddered with pleasure and anticipation. Rubbing lightly with my forefinger, I circled my hard clit with a slower, more hypnotic rhythm and gazed at the screen, watching what he wrote.

One finger became two. I let them slip wetly over my sex, feeling the vivid heat of my lips, and velvet hair that brushed briefly and then was crushed under the heel of my hand. I was far, far more turned on that I'd ever have imagined I could be just by talking to someone on a computer.

My body arched and trembled and I let myself slide further down in the chair. My sex felt so open, so greedy, so hungry. I was desperate to be filled. I pictured Sam, somewhere in London, sitting at his computer, helplessly buttoned into his tight jeans – maybe even wanking – his young face as flushed as mine and his eyes fixed on the words that scrolled relentlessly down the screen.

Dominique: pushing myself on to you really hard, grinding my cunt on to you
Dominique: I rub myself really hard against your iron-hard cock

17

SamUK: oh yes . . .
Dominique: harder
Dominique: and harder

I thrust my hard fingers deep into myself, imitating his cock. I was so ready: I could feel a pressure like a depth-charge just waiting to explode somewhere deep in my body. Pressing my thumb hard against my clit, I fucked myself with my fingers, thrusting deep inside and arching my body off the chair so that my pussy came up to meet my hand. My hand moved faster between my wide-spread thighs; my fingers slipped and slid in my own juice, and I could hear my own breath coming in gasps.

I could hardly get my words on to the keypad.

Dominique: oh it . . . feels so good. I might come here. Oh, Sam . . .
SamUK: yes, ride me, fuck me hard, you feel so good on me now, so hot and gripping me so hard –

The heavy brass knocker pounded against my front door and cruelly interrupted every sweet sensation that shimmered along my nerve-endings.

I left it for a minute, my sticky fingers motionless between my legs and my eyes fixed on the computer screen. But whoever was at the door wasn't taking no for an answer.

I swore and typed:

hold it, Sam, someone's at the door.

I pushed my skirt down and smoothed it along my thighs. Frowning, and hoping that Sam would wait for me, I stamped through to the hall and wrenched the door open.

Chapter Three
dominique talking

'*H*i, Carrie.'

Max Armstrong glanced up from a piece of paper. I could see that it had my address written across it in my brother's familiar scrawl. 'I hope you don't mind me dropping by unannounced.' He gestured with an abundant paper-wrapped armful of irises, passion flowers and feathery green fern. 'These are for you. To say thanks for last night.'

'Oh dear.' I winced at my own lack of enthusiasm and tried to smile as I took the flowers. They smelled beautiful, of sun-drenched meadows and dewy grass.

We both stood motionless for a few moments. I frowned at the third button on Max's shirt front, wondering how I could get rid of him. He, meanwhile, thrust his large hands deep into his trouser pockets and watched my face. There was an awkward silence, then he lowered his intense grey-eyed gaze, bit his lip, and nodded slowly.

'OK.' he conceded, stepping back. 'I'm sorry. I – I'll catch you another time.'

Flicking my eyes briefly up to his face, I was torn.

He looked genuinely disappointed by my underwhelmed reaction; but I had SamUK hanging on my every word in my study. I wanted to get back to him.

Then Max smiled. And the smile was the thing that did it for me. Lop-sided. Rueful. Very self-deprecating. It was the type of smile that didn't stop at his lips, but made his whole face light up and his dark eyes shine. I swallowed hard and wondered why I was keeping him on my doorstep. He was a nice guy and I was being rude.

'Come in, Max. Please.' I stepped back and opened the door wide. 'You'll have to help me put these in a vase. I never know what to do with flowers.' I closed the door and smiled up at him. He was so tall that his unruly black hair brushed the bottom of my lampshade. 'Eva's good at things like that.'

'Yes, she has many talents.' I thought I detected a slight dryness to his tone as Max followed me into the kitchen. He politely pretended not to notice my inadequate housekeeping as we looked for a vase. Eventually we had to make do with a big ceramic jug, and I cleared a space in the over-full sink so that he could get to the tap.

I remembered that the Internet connection was still on, so I left him unwrapping the blooms and snuck back to my desk. My white knickers were still crumpled on the floor and I kicked them hard to make them disappear behind the waste-paper basket.

Dominique: sam? still here?
SamUK: yeah, what's up? you've been an age . . . I'm dying here!
Dominique: sam I have to go. I'm so sorry, something's come up. But I'd love to chat with you again.
SamUK: are u SURE you can't stay? you got me at boiling point!
Dominique: sorry . . . I'll mail you.

20

'You were working when I rang your bell, weren't you?'

It was Max. He had followed me through from the kitchen, and was standing in my dining room holding the freshly filled jug of flowers. 'Darn it, I should have realised, Carrie. I'll get out of your way.'

After clicking 'Quit' on my keypad, I turned to smile at him.

'No, not work. I was just playing around on the Internet. Trying out a chat room. Listen, thanks for these. You shouldn't have.' I reached out and took the jug from him. 'I know you were probably bribed to be my date last night.'

'Bribed?' I watched him casually shove one hand into the pocket of his trousers and use the other to push his black hair into spiky points. 'I wasn't bribed,' he said. 'Well, maybe just a little, Leon kind of has me in his pocket at the moment. I nearly didn't come last night, though. I thought you were going to be just like Eva. But when I met you, I was so glad I did. You were so . . . so . . . normal!'

'Oh.' I didn't quite know what to say. Being called normal was hardly a great compliment, so I smiled back at him and carefully placed the flowers on my desk. I wondered how I could make it easier for him to leave. He obviously wanted to: he was twiddling his earlobe with one hand and jingling the loose change in his pocket with the other. I frowned as I gave him the exit line I thought he was looking for.

'Well, thank you. And I guess I'll be seeing you then.'

There was a long pause.

'That's what I was hoping actually. To see you again, I mean. I'm going to be in the UK for most of the summer, and I wondered – would you come out for dinner with me sometime?' His question was so direct, and so unexpected, that it caught me by surprise. I stared at him. His serious, dark grey eyes were fixed on mine with an intensity that almost took my breath away.

I found myself wishing that I was different. Prettier. Thinner. Sexier. Whatever.

I stalled for time by picking up the bottle of wine I had been drinking.

'Would you like to stay and have a drink?' I asked.

'Thanks, I'd love one. But, Carrie . . .' my stomach did a backflip as he directed that lop-sided smile at me again, '. . . that bottle's empty.'

'Oh.' I blushed. He must think I was a sad creature sitting in the dark drinking alone and talking to people in a chat room. I gave an embarrassed smile. 'So it is. Um, I'll just get another one.'

'Oh, don't do that just for me. I wouldn't want to put you to any trouble.' He took the bottle from my hands. His fingers brushed mine, but he seemed insensible to the sudden tingle that ran through my hands at the contact. He carefully placed the empty bottle on the surface of my desk. 'Look, maybe I should go.' His eyes met mine briefly, then he began to turn away. 'You don't really want me hanging around here; you probably have much better things to do.'

'Actually I haven't.' I took a deep breath and made a decision: better things to do than entertain Max Armstrong, with his stormy grey eyes and his lop-sided grin that made my belly do weird gymnastics?

'I want to open another bottle. With you. Right now.'

And so, for the first time, I heard Dominique talking.

'OK.' He smiled that smile. 'I'll give you a hand.'

Two hours later his wide, skilful fingers were spreading my thighs wide and kneading the soft, smooth skin there. I lay back on the pillow and let my eyelids flutter shut as his forefinger stroked my sex and made a wet, sticky sound as he sampled my thick juices. Pleasure coursed through my body like hot oil: soothing me, warming me, and sending my senses swirling.

'Touch yourself,' he whispered in my ear, his breath

warm and wine-scented against my neck. 'Touch your pussy. Make yourself really wet. I want to see you pleasure yourself with your fingers. Yeah, like that, that's good. That looks really good.'

'You like that?' I smiled and arched my back a little, and let my fingers play across my hard, bulging little clit. The sensations that rippled across my skin were almost too much to bear. I was already very wet, my hormones raging after the unfulfilling clinch with SamUK. My sex felt thick and fluid, like honey under my fingers. My flesh bulged out at the touch of my hand, and the cream that slicked from deep inside me was warm and smooth on my skin. I could smell my own scent – so fragrantly strong that I could almost taste it on my tongue – and I could see by the tortured look in Max's grey eyes that he wanted nothing better than to dive down and try for himself the juice that gleamed on my fingers.

I ached for him to do that. But a detached part of me wondered what Dominique would do if she was in this situation. She'd keep him in suspense. She'd control the game and make him wait. So – I resolved that I too was going to make him wait.

I fluttered my eyelids closed and began to rub my fingers smoothly over my own pouting pussy lips, feeling them swell and bloom under the insistent movement of my hands. Opening my eyes slightly, I saw that Max had reached for his discarded trousers and was digging in one of the pockets. I heard the sound of a foil envelope ripping and peeped again so that I could watch him roll the condom down the impressive length of his dick.

Well, there's making him wait and there's cutting off my own nose to spite my face, I thought. Forget Dominique controlling the game: I want him in me now. I reached out with trembling fingers and clasped his cock briefly in my hand. He smiled and I felt a blush warm my cheeks as I relinquished my hold and lay back against the soft pillows.

His prick was big. And wide. And his body was so incredibly hairy that the thick, lush, black curls shadowed all his skin and made it darker than it actually was. I shivered with anticipation as I watched him kneel between my thighs again and gently slide his hands over the curve of my hip. It was as if he had flames at the tips of his fingers, fire in his touch. I could feel my skin flickering beneath his caress and I breathed deeply, slowly, savouring that tiny moment of stillness as we breathed the same air.

'Sure you want to do this?' he asked in a whisper – his voice low and soft, almost velvety – as he lay his hard body over mine and slid his arms beneath my back, one at my waist, the other at my shoulders.

'Oh yes,' I whispered back. 'But don't stop afterwards. Let's make it last all night.'

'You really mean that?' he murmured, his body weight pressing the mattress down as he leaned on his arm. I turned my head slightly and watched the way his thick musculature twisted and knotted just above his elbow. 'I mean really? You aren't just faking it? Doing it out of some sense of duty or something. Because of our date at Leon's, I mean.'

'No! My goodness, no.' I was astounded that he should think that. Me? Feel a sense of duty about him? He must have got it all a bit mixed up somehow. 'No, definitely not duty. I'm doing this because I want to. You make me feel nice. And look, I'm not faking this one little bit . . .' I slipped my hand down to my juicy sex and then held my soaked fingers up to his mouth. 'That's real, not fake,' I breathed, then gasped as his soft lips enveloped my fingertips. As he sucked hard my sex throbbed and my heartbeat accelerated.

'Carrie,' he whispered, as his mouth moved from my fingers to my breast. Then his lips covered mine with a breathtaking hunger. I could feel the hard, clean ivory of his teeth against the tip of my tongue. I drank him in,

24

feeling the pressure that had gathered in my head beginning to seep out and down my body in tiny electric
shimmers. My legs were spread wide and crooked
around the rough-haired hardness of his upper thigh and
buttocks. I could feel his hand sliding down between our
bodies to guide himself into me.

Moving my hips slightly, urging him with my thighs, I
arched and wriggled, supple as a bow beneath him, until
he was poised at the hot, sticky mouth of my sex.

'Is this OK?' he whispered, his lips tight to my ear.

'Oh, yes, Max. It's more than OK,' I murmured, feeling
the blood rush from my head to make me feel faint with
pleasure.

He pushed into me, almost burying himself in the
juiciness of my ready cunt. It was a long time since I'd
been fucked, and I grunted out loud at the absolute, gut-
wrenching ecstasy of being stretched again. The sudden
fullness made me throw my head back against the white
linen pillow and press my hips hard against his, urging
him with little movements of my hands on his back and
tiny, pleasure-slurred words of encouragement.

He moved quickly, driving all the way in and then
withdrawing – with a delicious, juicy sound – then
jerking his hips and impaling my sex in one hard movement. Again. Again. Rhythmically in and out. Then great
pile-driver thrusts. Hard and fast and then faster again
until I could no longer match his movements and was
able only to reach up and grab the bedstead, clinging to
the iron bars to steady myself while, finding his rhythm,
he fucked me until I cried out again.

'More! Oh, Max!' I felt wild and abandoned, with
sensuous pleasure rippling through my skin. I felt my
cunt expand for him, and sensed his throbbing response
as he pumped deep into me.

Then his fingers were between us: exploring, pressing,
rubbing. He made tiny, skilful, circular movements on
my hard, swollen little clit that sent me wild. I arched my

25

body, feeling barely under control as his smooth fingertip slipped faster across the little muscle and made me gasp. Almost sobbing, I begged him to stop.

'Oh, please,' I sighed. 'No more. Stop. Oh, please stop.'

But then when he obeyed me and halted his delicious hand movements, I shook my head, laughing.

'Oh God. Don't stop. Don't stop, Max!'

He didn't stop after that. His long fingers carried on doing their delicious dance against my clit, making the muscular button lengthen and swell and become so engorged that it felt as if my whole body and all sensation was centred there. Little white stars danced in my head and I felt a hot wave of desire drag across my bare skin, sucking my nipples to erectness and making the hair on the nape of my neck feel like it was standing on end.

'Oh, you feel so good!' Max's hands were tight on my waist, squeezing, compressing, and I gasped to catch my breath as he slid his delicious length out of me. 'Turn over for me. Can I fuck you from behind? I want to see your neat little ass under my hands. Oh, Carrie.'

I loved the way he said 'ass'. His American accent deepened and lengthened the word so that it sounded like the sexiest piece of anatomy in the world. I stared up into his eyes, and felt myself drowning for a moment in their stormy grey depths. He was so strong, so considerate, so hot, and his cock had stretched me so wide.

I could feel the fresh sticky residue of my cream clinging to his length as I closed my hand on to his cock for a moment. Then I had to let go so as to wriggle and twist until I was on all fours. I felt open, and vulnerable, as if my whole cunt was gaping and begging to be filled. Then Max's palms felt cool on my fevered skin, and his touch infinitesimally light on my spine as he pushed me gently forwards until my face was crushed into the soft pillow.

I held my breath as he slipped his fingers across the

aching, swollen flesh between my legs; parting me, opening me again, then dipping his forefinger quickly into the hot depths as if to ready me for his cock. There was a pause, and I felt him shift on the mattress behind me, then he seemed to lean in towards me, sinking on to my body, as the head of his shaft pressed and poked and – finally – slid home. His crisp body hair crinkled against my bottom, and his balls were pulled up tight under him, pressing sweetly against my plump pussy.

Thrusting into me, his length sank deep inside and his thighs pressed hard against the backs of my legs. The realisation dawned that I was enjoying something that my sister-in-law would give her eye teeth for. I had somehow, against all the odds, succeeded where she had failed, and it gave me a warm glow deep inside my body that didn't go away. Eva wanted Max, and Eva always got what she wanted. But Max wanted me. And the thought made me close my eyes and thrust back against his powerful body.

Max's fingers left my waist and snaked round to my belly. He stroked my tummy softly, almost lovingly, then thrust his fingers downwards, deep into my curls, seeking my clit.

'Oh, yes,' I moaned, and buried my face deeper into the pillow so that I could hardly breathe. His hands were magic, working softly at first, then with greater insistence against my straining clit until I could feel a familiar heat spreading through my sex. The luscious feel of his forefinger – slick now with my copious juice – and his hard cock rooting deep up inside me, pushed me on until I could feel my climax growing, gaining pace, tingling and throbbing at the edges of my consciousness.

'Oh, Max. Yes. Oh, yes. Harder, Max. I'm coming! Oh, God I'm coming.'

'Come. Come on to me. I'm right here. I . . . I . . . oh, you're beautiful, you look so good, feel so good. Oh, yes.' Max reached round with his other hand, gripping one of my tits and imprisoning it in his fist, while he thrust hard against me. I could feel the heat of his exhaled breath on my shoulders, my neck and my back. The controlled power in his single taut fist, and the intense sensations that caught and exploded in my stomach, finally pushed me over the edge and I found myself biting hard on the pillow: shoving back against his body, thrusting hard with him so as to have him deeper inside me while I came.

A white hot pulse beat somewhere behind my eyelids and my warm skin began to quiver. Great muscular waves of pleasure coursed through me, tightening the succulent flesh of my sex on to his thick cock and making my nipples pucker suddenly into tiny, hard, rosy nubs. I could sense Max holding me tight and still, his fingers pressing firmly on my clit as I came: his body tense and his muscular thighs hard behind me. I cried out, a long, harsh, guttural cry that was partly absorbed by the wedge of pillow between my teeth.

He moved as I finished, easing himself down so that his chest was on my back, letting his weight rest gently while his mouth caught at my earlobe and toyed with it, his lips firm then soft as I closed my eyes to prolong the last flutters of orgasm while they shivered through my body.

'Didn't you come?' I whispered, puzzled by the hard rod which I could feel sticking to the moistness on my inner thigh. He shook his head, lightly rubbing the soft skin of my shoulder with his bristly chin.

'Not yet. We've got all night.'

'Was I OK?' I was suddenly worried, afraid that I might not have turned him on enough.

'You were . . . fantastic. Gorgeous. You look so beautiful when you're fucking, Carrie.' He scrunched up a handful of my hair and twisted my face towards his so that his mouth could brush mine. 'I love the way your eyelids flutter when you come.'

Relaxing a little, I wriggled under him so that my back was flat on the bed and I could see him properly. He smiled, and then bent his head to kiss me and I was reminded of a wolf: his eyes were grey and hungry, his brows thick and black, his jaw dark with stubble. Max was hairy on the outside. Just like a good wolf should be.

Smiling against his mouth, I arched beneath him and reached up to kiss him, my touch delicate at first, exploring the hard ivory of his teeth and the honey-sweet warmth of his tongue. He tasted delicious: the bottle of claret we had opened had given him a piquant smokiness, while the juice that he had sucked from my fingers had given his lips a dark, fresh, oyster taste. Kissing him was like sinking into a glass of mulled wine at Christmas: darkly comforting, warming, spicy. I just wanted to drink him all up.

Aware that he hadn't come yet, I slipped my hand down between our bodies and encircled his rock-hard tackle with my thumb and forefinger. He was very erect, stimulated almost to flash-point, and I felt the jerk of his shaft and the sudden, sharp intake of breath as I curved my whole hand around him. I circled his cock with my fingers and slipped them slowly up and down, my gaze fixed on his.

Groaning slightly, his eyelids fluttered briefly, then he rolled back on the bed so that he lay flat beside me. I leaned on one elbow, my hand still clenched around his dick, and – by the light of a single candle – I inspected the goods that Eva had unwittingly sent my way: his body was stocky and fit, muscular but not heavily so; his skin gold but darkened by the mass of his body hair; his knees were bent so that his thighs – muscular and coarsened with dark male fuzz – flexed and curved outwards away from his body. For a powerful man, he looked vulnerable and trusting, offering me his sex with almost total abandon.

I leaned forward and kissed the rapidly beating pulse in his neck, enjoying the feel of his crisp chest hair as it flattened under the weight of my breast. Alternately squeezing and stroking, I relaxed into caressing him, my fingers first squeezing tight, then becoming softer against his steely shaft. His balls were big but tight, and kissed right up under him, and the dark male scent that came up from his sex in hot waves made me feel like letting him go and just climbing on top of him again to find my own desperate pleasure.

Instead, I kneeled up beside him and let my mouth descend to his chest. I nibbled at the pinkish-copper discs of his nipples, teasing the tips into steel peaks which felt like little chips of dark sugar between my probing lips. I felt as though I couldn't get enough of him, as if I could stay here like this all night with my knees buried in the soft down of the mattress and my hands full of throbbing cock, my nose flared around the scent of seashell musk, and my body aching with lascivious desire.

I was hot, breathless, intent on the job in hand, aware only of the darkened room with its flickering light, the snow-white bed linen and the dark gleam of the body stretched under me. The scent of sex filled my nose, making me flare my nostrils to catch more of the fragrance of my own body, and that of the man who stretched across my crumpled sheets. Max's head was thrown back, his hair jet-black against the pillow, and I took a deep, shuddering breath as I moved my hand more urgently up and down the length of his straining prick.

Sliding downwards, I cupped his balls with my left hand, massaging him with my right. Then I sank my lips and mouth on to him. Max gasped, bucked once, then groaningly subsided into the bed as I sucked him deeply into my throat. I moved my tongue against the rigid veins that bulged under the latex that encased his cock, revelling in the salty taste of my own juice which rimed him.

I sucked him hard and long, stroking him with my right hand while my left curled around his balls and massaged them gently. Max groaned again, his fingers twisting sideways on the pale sheets and grabbing a handful of bed-linen as he jerked his hips up to my face.

I let my eyelids droop lazily as I slipped my mouth all the way down, tightening my lips around him, my fingers gripping firmly. My nose was suddenly and deliciously full of his peppery scent.

I slipped a forefinger easily round from his balls and into his puckered anus, instantly finding that precious gland which would send him into orbit. I sucked and fingered, wallowing in him, feasting on his cock as I eased my finger deeper into his bottom. I could feel the coiled tension in his body, and I marvelled at the way he held on. He was so controlled. Then suddenly he was barely controlled. And when I pressed lightly on his prostate I felt all his hard-won control sweep forward under the muscular onslaught of his orgasm.

He came suddenly. His hot spunk filled the tip of the condom so violently that I thought it would burst under the strain. Sucking hard, I gave him as much of my mouth as I could, revelling in the feel of the strong, muscular jerks of his thick cock as it beat against my tongue. It was a feast of the senses for both of us, and I could feel my nipples puckering to erectness as I listened to the low animal growl that emanated from Max's throat.

He grunted twice, then moaned loudly, his ecstasy apparent in the deep, hoarse – almost feral – noise. I could feel his hand digging into my soft hair, catching my head and forcing me further on to him so that he pulsed against the back of my throat again and again until he was spent.

* * *

Max and I spent Saturday night and all of Sunday deep under the sticky covers of my bed. By the time Monday morning came I knew I was going to have to practise the housewife skills I had left behind when I moved out of my ex-husband's house.

The floor was littered with foil bowls from our Indian takeaway, and I stubbed my toe on one of five empty wine bottles. As I pulled my work clothes out of the wardrobe, I kept giving the crumpled bed-linen surreptitious looks as I remembered things that Max had done to me, and I to him: even the memories made my pulse thud and tiny electric tingles slip up the back of my neck. A cold shower was definitely required.

When I returned from the bathroom, the air in the room seemed heavy with the odour of passion. I wrinkled my nose, threw open the windows to let in the early morning sun, and stripped the bed right down to the mattress before dumping the lot in the laundry basket. It was so full, I had to sit on the lid to close it properly. Maybe Dominique could find me a nice, tame house-slave to wash and iron it all, I thought, as I left the house in a rush with my jacket still undone and my hair pinned up any old way.

Max had left two hours earlier, kissing me hungrily, then dashing home to put on a suit. We had made a date for that night, but I had a feeling that he would call to cancel it, despite the fantastic sex. Max would probably regret the weekend when the wine wore off and he came to his senses. I sat on the train with my bag placed strategically over the ragged hole which I found that the laundry basket had made in the knee of my stocking.

As I watched the greenery shoot past the window I daydreamed about my new alter ego, Dominique, and wondered whether Max would prefer her to me. Maybe I could try to be more like her in real life, but I doubted that. She was exciting and challenging. And I was a dull little mouse, as Eva took great pleasure in reminding me.

I stared at my reflection in the grimy train window and frowned. Who on earth would want to go out with Carrie Horton when they could have a woman like Dominique?

By the time we were approaching Bath Spa station, I had talked myself into cancelling my date with Max before he could do it first. He'd left his number on a piece of paper torn from one of my notebooks, and I had smoothed it lovingly after he had gone, holding it to my nose and trying to catch the last evocation of his smell that clung to the surface.

Shaking my head, I rummaged in the messy depths of my bag, found the scrap of paper and my cell-phone, then keyed in the number. I reached voicemail.

'Hi. This is Max Armstrong. I can't take your call right now, but if you leave your name and a message, I'll call you back as soon as I can.'

Even a recording of his voice, with its tinny overlay, sounded sexy enough to make my pulse throb a little stronger. I shivered a little as I listened, feeling my nipples poke hard against the lace of my bra at the low, melodious tone of Max's voice. More than anything, that voice convinced me to cancel any future contact. Now. Before he did it to me. A man who sounded like that would have crowds of women who were genuinely like Dominique at his beck and call, I reasoned. The only possible reason for dating me would be because he felt sorry for me.

I took a deep breath and, ignoring the disapproving glance of the businessman sitting across the aisle from me, left a message.

Tonight, I would get back online before SamUK forgot who Dominique was.

Chapter Four
hanging on the telephone

*B*y 10 p.m. Monday evening I'd avoided three calls from Max Armstrong, and got a certain amount of pressure from SamUK to send him a picture of myself. We'd chatted for two hours. It was pretty sexy stuff, but even I knew that it probably wouldn't continue if I didn't let him see what I looked like. But unfortunately I didn't look like Dominique.

As I saw it, I had three options:

a. send him a picture of someone else.

b. send him a picture of me with a heavy make-over, or . . .

c. send nothing at all and lose him.

Option c wasn't something I particularly wanted to risk. And option a was just downright dishonest. So Tuesday teatime found me on my knees in my friend Laura's bathroom with my head over the side of the tub and a fluffy blue towel around my neck.

'Wow,' Laura murmured admiringly, aiming the shower at the crown of my head. 'That's really warmed it up.'

'What's it like?' I asked, chin hard to the enamel and hands clenched nervously in my lap.

'Gorgeous, Carrie. You're a brunette goddess. With attitude.'

She was right. By the time she'd done some kind of mascara-blusher wonder treatment, I looked better than I had done for years. The photos came out well and even I didn't think I looked a million miles from the Dominique persona I'd created. Sam would never know.

On Wednesday evening I sent an e-mail with the photo file attached. Sam loved it. I sat at my computer, typing rapidly and squinting at the screen.

Sam was asking me what I thought about pain and submission. Apparently he'd let me do most things to him. Within reason.

Dominique: okay, what do you consider 'within reason'? lol.
SamUK: well, no blood!
Dominique: well, i wouldn't want to hurt you that much anyway, just make you wince!

I grinned at the screen and wriggled a little in my chair. This was so strange: I had talked to Sam for a total of about four hours in all. And here we were on day three of our relationship – if that's what it was – discussing the sort of things that you'd only talk about with a very close friend. Or a very long-term boyfriend. It really was amazing how quickly we'd become intimate.

Dominique: And don't you forget, it's me who deals it out. I'm never going to be yr sub.
SamUK: oh i see but you can inflict pain on me . . .?? how is that fair? lol
Dominique: it's totally fair. Anyway, it won't be that much pain! only nice little butt slap pain, or a tiny flick of a neat little leather whip against yr ass. How does that sound?

35

SamUK: actually, that sounds ok to me, I always wanted to be a sub to some gorgeous girl with high heels . . . so what are you going to do with me oh mistress? (sinking to my knees with head bowed and hands pressed together submissively)

I told him that I was standing over him wearing not much more than a pair of spike-heeled stilettos, flexing a riding crop between black-gloved hands.

SamUK: slipping my fingers across your feet, gliding my hands to the heels and caressing them. oh such high heels mistress, i long to feel them on my back, on my butt, anywhere!

Dominique: oh you'll feel them boy. and don't call me mistress. you may not address me directly at all.

SamUK: ok . . . pressing my lips against your shiny leather toes . . . breathing in and trying to control my excitement . . .

Dominique: flicking a glance down at you from under my lashes . . . mmm, you look so nice, and so turned on.

SamUK: gently cupping your foot and inserting my tongue in between the leather and yr soft foot, exploring your skin.

Dominique: very good, i may reward you later. keep going. I tap your denim-clad bottom with my crop just to remind you who's in charge here.

I was enjoying being in charge for a change. It made me feel powerful. Vital. More alive.

Dominique: stand up!

SamUK: yes, standing up, trying to cover my erection with my hands as its threatening to burst the buttons of my jeans.

Dominique: knocking yr hands aside, i run the tip of the

crop over the impressive bulge behind yr fly. Mmm, I see you have a little something for me, boy.
SamUK: oh yes.
Dominique: maybe I'll find a use for that later. I stare into yr eyes while sliding my fingertips up your shirt front and playing with the buttons.

Was this the kind of pleasure that Patrick had had? He'd certainly been in charge all the way through our marriage. No, I frowned, that was different. Patrick had had a mean streak that he just couldn't control, even when I'd shown that I didn't like it. That had been real violence, real nastiness. What I was doing with Sam was play-acting: pretend pain and pretend dominance between two people who both wanted the same thing.

I sipped some of my wine and tapped at the keypad.

Dominique: kiss me.
SamUK: thought you'd never ask. Kissing you real soft, really gently, showing you that I know who's in charge. You taste really sweet.
SamUK: kissing you deeper . . . pressing my body against you.
Dominique: I can feel your hard cock pressing against my hip . . . nice. like a steel rod.
SamUK: too impatient to release the clasps i pull your bra down and begin massaging your breasts.
Dominique: oh, that feels so good, your hands're so big, and so brown against my pearly skin . . .
SamUK: paying close attention to your hardening nipples. pressing them between my fingers.
Dominique: mmm . . .

Oh dear, I was slipping into sub-mode and letting him call the shots a little too much. I just wasn't used to being in charge.

I tried to focus on who I was pretending to be, what I

was supposed to be doing, and injected a little more Dominique into my words:

Dominique: stop it! Stop it right now, boy, I don't recall saying that you could go this far. On your knees! I said on yr knees (quick flick of the crop across yr shoulders) that's it. down, boy.
SamUK: on my knees, I bow my head and wait for yr next command. I can hardly control myself, I want to touch you so badly.
Dominique: touch me then.

It was so simple, really. Just ask, and you will be given, I thought, smiling wryly as I imagined commanding Sam to do this to me in real life.

SamUK: leaning forward, I slip my fingers softly up the inside of your thigh. Oh your skin is so soft, so warm.
Dominique: (perching on the edge of the table and propping one foot on a stool) lick me, boy, and make it good or you'll get a taste of this (flicking yr butt with my crop)
SamUK: nestling in nice and close between yr legs, holding you open, smelling yr sweet smell and burying my nose in yr pussy.

I could feel a creeping sensuality gradually stroking its way through my limbs as I read my words. And Sam's reply gave me a sudden throb in my ready-juiced sex: almost as if he was actually there in the room and I could smell him, feel him, watch him. I shuddered and sighed. I was actually aching for his touch. I wondered whether he would ever want to meet up in real life. But then remembered that I wasn't Dominique. And that Sam would probably have zero interest in Carrie Horton, new brunette goddess or not.

SamUK: moving my mouth on to you and sucking your hard clit.

Dominique: and slip my hand down to guide you, showing you exactly how to do it.

SamUK: yeah, I like that. show me. teach me.

Dominique: gently slipping back the hood of my clit to show you the neat little bead that you really want to get yr tongue round.

SamUK: making my tongue pointed and looping it round yr clit, and cupping my dick in my other hand cos its gonna burst.

Dominique: nice. real nice sam, lick harder, press a finger into me, boy.

SamUK: oh jeez you turn me on so much. You feel so warm and wet as I ease a finger into you. oh, so tight, baby.

This is turning me on so much, I thought, leaning forward on to the hand that I'd buried down my knickers. I can't keep it up. I need to come. I love this so much. I love reading what he writes. I love the way he does exactly as I say.

Dominique: making you stand up, I lean forward to cup your firm package . . . and squeeze gently. You feel so big through your jeans, so hard. I cant wait to have you inside me.

SamUK: i cant wait to be in you either, but i know i have to wait till you say.

SamUK: see how i obey you, i murmur.

Yes, you do obey me, don't you, Sam, I thought with a smile. I wonder how far we can go with that? I wonder if you'd obey me in real life too? I wonder if you'd like the sound of my voice. I took another sip of wine for courage, and then typed:

Dominique: Sam, are we completely private in here?
SamUK: yes, sure are. why?
Dominique: if I give you my phone number will anyone else read it?
SamUK: shit.
Dominique: sam???
SamUK: you want to do phone sex?
Dominique: if you want to . . .
SamUK: do I want to??? are you kidding???
Dominique: so is it safe to put in my number here?
SamUK: well. probably but don't chance it, you never know. Better to e-mail it to me. Split the code and the number between two e-mails for extra security.
Dominique: ok. Are you going to call me?
SamUK: shit yes.

I told him to give me five minutes to scoot upstairs with the cordless: I wanted to be comfortable for my first taste of phone sex.

In my bedroom, I brushed my hair and stood in front of the mirror for a moment. Props, I thought, I need some props to get me even more turned on. I need to see sexy stuff, however clichéd. I rooted about in the bottom of the messy space I called a wardrobe and came up with a pair of black lace-up ankle boots with pointed heels and toes that I'd meant to throw away when the 80s had ended but never got round to doing – for which I was absurdly thankful now. Then I smoothed a pair of opaque black hold-ups on to my legs.

Hmm, I thought, as I posed in the mirror, very Moulin Rouge, very *fin de siècle*. What next? A smear of amber on my lips followed by a smudge of black on my eyelids made me look suitably sluttish and abandoned.

The last prop, a pale violet dildo in the smoothest eggshell finish, was quickly retrieved from my bedside drawer, and I was ready. When the phone rang I purred a greeting into the mouthpiece in my most sexy, sultry, husky, Dominique voice.

'Hi.' American accent. Deep caramel laid over gravel. It sure as hell wasn't SamUK.

'Max?' Horrified, I sat bolt upright and grabbed a pillow to cover my nakedness as if he could really see me in the flesh.

'Hi, Carrie. I caught you at last.' He gave a low-pitched laugh that made me tingle inside, despite myself. 'You sound pretty darn . . . hot. Want some company?'

'Ah, no. No. I don't think that'd be a good idea, do you?' I stared wide-eyed at my tousled reflection in the wardrobe mirror. 'Um, listen, sorry about leaving you that voicemail. I thought it'd be easier that way. Easier for you I mean. Sorry.'

Dominique had definitely left the building.

'Easier?' He sounded mildly amused. 'Easier for me to do what? Chase you all around town?'

'No!' I was horrified that he thought I was playing a game. 'Oh, goodness no. I don't want you to chase me, Max. I just thought it'd be easier for both of us if I gave you a let-out. You know, we were drunk. I got carried away. I'm sorry.'

'Uhuh.'

'It was just a one-off.'

'Not for me.' His tone was dry. 'Was it for you? A one-off, I mean?'

'No. But I thought . . .'

'Listen, Carrie. Let's not mess around here. I don't like playing mind games.' His voice was firm, very in control. 'I like you. You're sweet and funny and you don't give the big "I am" act like your weird sister-in-law. I had a great weekend with you. I liked what we did.' He paused. 'And I also like to make my own decisions about whether I see people or not, so don't decide for me. I would love to see you again, but you have to want that too; I'm not into forcing people. Think about it. I'll call you in a few days.'

He rang off before I even had time to reply. I stared at the silent handset, my thoughts reeling, and then quietly replaced it. It rang immediately before I'd even had time to consider Max Armstrong and his straight talking.

'Dominique?'

It was Sam. His voice was loaded with about two hundred cheeky grins.

'What are you wearing right now?'

Another straight talker, then. I smiled.

'Not much.' I leaned back against my pillows, watching myself in the mirror. 'Just my long, long, black stockings. Very smooth you know. Very sleek. Like my legs.'

'What else?' He was slightly breathless.

'Boots,' I whispered. 'Black shiny boots. High heels. Lace up the front. Pointed toe. Very sexy.'

'Oh, yeah. Like you. Very sexy.' I could hear a rustle of clothing.

'Are you touching yourself, Sam?'

There was a pause. 'Yes.'

'Did I say you could touch yourself, Sam?'

'No.' Very meekly.

'Well, then don't. It'll be worse for you if you disobey me.'

'OK.' He sighed hard. 'OK. I'm sitting here now, staring at you and wondering what I should do.'

'Good,' I purred. 'Very good. I like that. That's a nice, obedient boy slave. Come here and kiss me.'

'Kissing your soft lips. Oh, you taste so good. I can't hold on: I want to touch you so much.'

'You'll have to wait then, won't you? I say when you can touch me. And I say when you can touch yourself.'

I braced my heels against the thick padding of my duvet and watched in the mirror, admiring the way my knees parted a little and let me see a tiny glimpse of curly pubes and the darker, succulent crescent of my sex below.

'Sam?' I breathed. 'Sam, I'm going to cup my breast in one hand, and I'm going to hold it for you to lick. But you will *not* touch yourself. I'll hear you if you do and I'll punish you. Promise?'

'I promise.'

'We're in a big room. The walls are lined with dark red satin and there are no windows. It's hot in here,' I said, 'very hot. The room's empty except for us. And a big table. A huge carved chair. And a mirror covers most of the wall behind you. I'm cupping my breasts and sitting above you on the chair. You're kneeling between my spread thighs, so your face is just about the height of my tits.' I paused and listened to his breathing, then carried on. 'I let you dart your tongue first over one nipple, then the other, and you feel them pucker and become erect beneath your lips.'

I wedged the phone in the crook of my neck, licked my fingertips, and began to slowly, softly circle my nipples with my fingers. It felt delicious, but it wasn't enough, so I wet my fingers some more and rolled my nipples between finger and thumb, pulling them slightly and making them longer and more pert.

I told Sam what I was doing, reminding him not to even think about touching himself in real life, and heard him groan deeply with suppressed lust. I watched myself in the mirror as I slid one hand down over my stomach and slipped my forefinger through my curling pubes to the lush hot folds of my sticky sex.

'Sam, I'm touching myself now,' I whispered. 'I'm so hot. My pussy's so wet. Oh, it feels gorgeous.'

He groaned again and I shushed him. 'No touching, Sam.'

'I'm not touching; I'm just sitting here on the floor, with my back against my bedroom door, just aching,' he muttered.

43

'Good. I want you to ache. I want you to feel desperate. I want it to almost hurt you before I'm going to let you touch yourself.'

'Oh, Jesus. Where did you learn this stuff?'

'It's no concern of yours.' I couldn't tell him I was learning it on the hoof, so I just went for a little overkill instead. 'I'm spreading my lips now, opening my pussy so that you can see the hot, pink inside, and all the creamy wet that's slipping inside my swollen flesh. I'm so wet,' I breathed, 'soooooo wet. Don't you want to taste me?'

'Y-yes.'

I slid lower in the bed, reaching for the violet dildo and sliding over the soft skin of my thighs. 'I'm rubbing myself,' I whispered. 'Rubbing my hot, wet pussy with a dildo and spreading myself wide with one hand. Then rubbing some more with my fingers. Circling my clit. Oh, I'm so wet. My pussy is swelling and throbbing –'

'– and so's my dick.'

'Shut up. I'm giving you twenty whacks with the riding crop for interrupting, boy.'

'Sorry.'

'Where was I?' I mused, frowning at my debauched reflection and softly massaging my own juices into the skin at the top of my thigh.

'I'm still sucking your nipples. I'm doing as you instruct, Dominique,' prompted Sam.

'Mmm, that feels nice. I think I'll give you a little reward. Imagine you can put your fingers where mine are. Down here. Now. Picture it.'

'Oh, yes.'

'Rub me hard. Feel my swollen clit. I'm jerking my hips, thrusting against your fingers and bringing myself off on your hand.' I paused. 'But you, boy, are not allowed to touch yourself yet. Is that understood?'

'Loud and clear.'

'Two fingers, Sam. Rub me with two fingers.' I was

doing it to myself with the smooth dildo, and the sensation was making my breathing rasp in my throat. It was almost as if he was here with me, in the room. I could hear his rapid breathing so loud down the phone. I could almost feel his hot breath on my skin. I sighed and arched against the soft pillows.

'Oh, harder. I thrust against your fingers. Oh, Sam, I demand that you fuck me with your fingers. Now.'

'Sliding two fingers into you,' he gasped. 'Dipping at first, then easing deeper in. You're so tight. But so wet that I can slip easily in . . .' There was a pause. '. . . I stare up at your beautiful face and ask you if there's anything else I can do for you?'

'There is.' I smiled at my reflection and dipped my thumb against my swollen clit. My pulse rate was knocking at around a hundred and forty, and my body was zinging. I carried on: 'I lean back against the table behind me, the big varnished one with the leather top and the brass studs. I perch up there on the edge, easing the chair away from me a little so that it gives me something good and high to place my foot on. I'm up there in front of you, one foot on the floor, one on the chair. My legs are spread so wide, and I am so wet.' The last part was true: I could see in the mirror the effect that the dildo and the dirty talk were having. 'You can see creamy juices smeared across the pale skin of my thighs as you frig me with your fingers. Hard. Rhythmic. Deep.'

'Shit,' he muttered. His favourite word when aroused, it seemed.

I felt sorry for him. He'd held off really well. 'Take your cock out, Sam,' I whispered. 'Take it out for me and stroke it. But you have to keep the rhythm going in my pussy or I'll beat you. Hard.'

'OK,' he murmured. 'I've got my cock in my hand. It's so hard. I'm stroking it, just like you said.'

I wriggled against the soft cotton of my bed and smiled into the phone.

45

'Good,' I murmured. 'Now imagine that you're here. Imagine that you're standing by the side of that big leather-topped table looking down at me. I'm spread out across it. Can you picture that? In my stockings. And my boots. I'm so wet that you can smell me – all girly and hot. Wouldn't you just love to dive right in, Sam?'

'Jesus. You know I want to.'

'What if I was to say that if you talked sweet enough then you could?'

'Oh. Oh, Dominique,' he whispered. I heard him take a deep breath, almost as if he was steadying himself, then: 'I can just picture you. You're so pretty. Your hair is spread out on the table. And your lips are swollen, all pouting, looking like my cock would just fit in your mouth. I want you so much, Dominique, I'd do anything right now, just to feel you somewhere on my skin. Feel your lips. Or . . .' he paused, then said shyly, '. . . have your pussy clamped round my cock.'

'Hmm, maybe. Maybe we can do that, but you have to be good first.' I wondered how long he'd let me delay him. I could imagine how tight his cock must be, all set to blow at any minute. I dipped the dildo into my own juices.

'Sam, how do you feel?'

'I feel great.' His voice was low, hushed. 'But I need to come real soon.'

Then we were of a like mind. I grinned and twirled the telephone cord around my little finger.

'Well, Sam, I don't want to make you wait any longer than you have to,' I said. 'Because I'm pretty desperate, too.'

'You are? Thank goodness for that. Let's fuck.'

'Sam, I'm moving my hands across your clothes, impatiently unbuttoning and tugging –'

'Jerking my shirt off and dropping it to the floor,' he interrupted. 'And slipping one hand up your honey-soaked thigh –'

46

'Wait!' I cried, half-laughing. 'I'm in charge here.'

'But honey-soaked thigh sounds so good,' he protested. 'And I really, *really* want my hands on you now!'

'But you have to do as I say,' I told him. 'So now I think I'll give you a little punishment for your impatience. I'm slipping your leather belt through the loops of your jeans. Hear the whisper of the leather on denim?' I heard a groan. 'Well, here come your just desserts, boy.'

I told him that I was folding the belt in half, and that I was going to whip his ass, so he'd better bend over. I heard the sibilant hiss of his sharply drawn breath and I knew he liked what I was telling him.

'I'm going to open your flies and hold your cock in one hand, Sam. Then I'm going to push your jeans down a bit. Just a little bit so that I can see your taut little-boy's ass peeking out. I'm going to rub my pussy against you in between sharp licks with the leather belt.' I began to grind a little against the heel of my hand, imagining that it was his behind that I was frotting my sex against. 'Mmm, you can feel soft pussy fur on your butt. Now a nasty little stinging slap with the leather belt.' I paused for a moment. 'Now soft pussy again. Now sharp sting. Oh, Sam, you look good like that. Your bottom is all pink and striped; your skin is blushing. Your ass is so peachy. I'm going to whip you a little harder. A sharp thwack catches you at the top of your thighs. Feel that?'

'Yes. I can feel it. It's just like you're really here . . .'

'I am really here, Sam,' I breathed. 'I'm right here. And I'm all yours. I'm slipping one finger into myself, Sam. I'm making my fingers really juicy and wet. Then I'm rubbing all over my hard little clit while I feel your dick swell in my other hand.' His breathing became a little quicker. 'Your buttocks are so firm and muscular. Your skin's hot against the front of my thighs as I press against you from behind. I'm slipping a finger up the crack of your bottom, seeking and exploring.' I could hear his rapid breathing and the sound made my heart beat faster. 'I love the way your tight little anus flares as I sweep a finger around it. Can you feel my finger, Sam? All slick and wet from where I've been playing with myself. You can feel my juices all damp on your ass. Oh, Sam.' I was feeling really warm by this time, my senses trembling and reeling with the unexpected sweetness of phone sex. 'You feel good, Sam; you make me hot.'

It was true, every word of it. I was as hot as a furnace and in the mirror I could see my cheeks glowing pink and my fingers wrapped tight around the violet dildo. I sighed and murmured again into the phone, 'Sam?'

'Yeah?'

'I want you to strip, and talk to me while you do it.'

'I'm pushing down my jeans,' he replied. 'I'm letting them slip to the floor . . .'

'My fingers move faster on my clit. My eyes are fixed on your cock . . .'

'I'm holding it in one hand. It's so tight, like it's fit to burst. Oh, my cock is so desperate. I want to put it in you, Dominique. I really need to come now,' he begged.

'I want to come, too,' I murmured. 'Remember that table we imagined that I was on?'

'Sure.'

'I'm leaning forward over it, wiggling my tight little ass in the air and giving you the OK to fuck me now, Sam.'

'Jesus.'

'I'm telling you to do it to me, Sam.'

'Shit.' His sigh was laden with regret. 'I wish this was real.'

'So do I, Sam, but it's not.' I was just as regretful as he was but it wouldn't do to let him call the shots, or lose the moment. 'It's not real. But it feels good, doesn't it? So let's just do it, boy. Get in behind me. Fast. Or I'll whip your ass again.'

'OK. Coming up tight behind you, I can feel the silky

skin of your thighs against the front of my legs. You smell so good. You smell gorgeous, like flowers and honey and all stuff that's good to eat. I want to eat you, but I want to come . . .'

I could just hear the quick slick-slick of his fist moving up and down his erection. I pressed the phone to my ear and listened greedily to the sound of skin on skin.

'I want to come inside you. Can I do that, Dominique?'

'Come *on* me,' I said. 'Never in me. I don't allow that.'

I heard a mew of exasperation, and grinned.

'Come on, Sam, you don't have to come in me. Come over me! Imagine how good I'll look with your hot spunk all up my back, or all over my smooth, pale buttocks . . .'

'Oh, yeah. Yessss –'

He was getting close now. And so was I as I slipped my fingers hungrily over my swollen sex. So close. That ultimate goal, brilliant orgasm, trembled through my fingers as I rubbed my clit harder and then slipped the dildo deep inside my hungry pussy. In our heads we were really fucking, and my body was filled with the dildo, all eight inches of it, so it was easy for me to pretend that it was Sam. My senses reeled and I felt as if I was being lifted up and flung towards a spiralling tornado, a twister of lust and desire.

I could hear Sam breathing hard in my ear, and the rapid sound of his hand on his cock was bliss. I told him that I could feel him thrust up inside me as he kicked my legs wider. I told him that he sank straight into me, hilted in one thrust as I opened for him. I said that I was stretched wide, that my cunt was sucking noisily at his cock. Then I heard a deep, guttural groan. He was coming.

'Ah, fu-u-u-ck,' he groaned, his mouth sounding so close to the telephone receiver that it was as if he was kissing it. I pressed it to my ear, desperate to be close to him so that I would hear every last sound he made as he climaxed. Catch every nuance of his breathing. Hear every little flicker of his tongue against his teeth.

The sound of his pleasure was all I needed to tip me over the edge, and I had my own reward. The tornado that had been spiralling just at the edges of my senses suddenly clutched at me, and I felt as if it would tear my senses right out of my body. I grunted with the force of it, feeling it fling me headlong into an all-engulfing, twisting, savage orgasm. A fantastic sensation of tingling electricity raged from my head all the way down my spine to my toes. Knees trembling. Eyes fluttering shut. Throat tight. I was being dismantled piece by piece, nerve ending by nerve ending, and it felt so good.

There was a long silence. I could hear Sam catching his breath and the phone became muffled, then loud again.

'Sorry about that,' he said, sounding almost embarrassed.

'About what?' I asked. 'Sam, never apologise.' I smiled. 'I take it you came?'

'Yup.'

'Me too.'

'You did?' He sounded amazed. I laughed softly: did he think that girls didn't get off on this stuff too?

'Yup.' I mimicked his voice with a smile, and then slid the dildo smoothly out. The smooth surface was sticky and smelled sweetly musky when I held it up to my nose.

Then I made a sudden, irrevocable decision.

'Sam.'

'Yeah?'

'I want us to do this for real.'

There was a silence which seemed to stretch into eternity before he spoke again. My pulse raced and my insides quivered in an agony of second thoughts as I waited to hear his reply.

'I'll wait for you to name the day,' he said simply.

And that was when I knew that Internet sex was simply not enough. And it was also when I realised that Dominique had much more control over my life than I did.

Chapter Five

cubicles at dawn

*T*he following morning I got up at dawn and decided to go for a run before the commuter traffic got going. If I was going to meet up with Sam in real life and have lots of energetic sex, then I'd better start getting fit.

I hadn't done any laundry for days, so my chances of finding a pair of clean knickers after my shower were about the same as the proverbial lottery win/asteroid hit. I'm such a lazy slut around the house, I thought with a smile, as I pulled wide-legged black trousers over a bare bottom.

It was actually quite liberating, feeling the interesting friction of the seam of my trousers directly applied to my sex. And the lack of Visible Pantie Line was something that I had never really thought about before until I admired my own smooth behind in the mirror in our new unisex toilets at Richardson Design Studios. It was so early that I had assumed that none of the other designers were in yet. So I was almost caught out by posh-boy James St John-Brooks, the junior on my team. He banged through the door and stopped short when he saw me.

I managed to save face by pretending to wipe an

invisible chalk mark off my trousers, while he pretended not to admire the curve of my buttocks as he passed en route to the cubicles. I caught his eye with mine and almost winked, but remembered just in time that I was Carrie now, not Dominique. He held my gaze for a fraction too long, bumped into the door, then disappeared into the cubicle with a pink face. I was suddenly struck by the possibility that he found me attractive with my new hair.

James and sex? I thought. How interesting. He had incredibly long fingers – I'd noticed that one day when we'd worked on the Adams pitch together. But I hadn't really thought about him on a conscious level until now. I listened to the sound of his zip as he undid his fly, and watched myself smooth my own bottom one more time in the mirror. No. Surely seducing James would have to wait for another day when I was a little bit more 'Dominique'.

I meant to go back to my desk, I really did. But Dominique obviously didn't like being relegated to the back seat now that she'd had a feel of the steering wheel. She thought she should be driving. All the time.

I listened to the fast, strong jet of James's pee hit the water, then marched to the door of his cubicle and tapped it lightly with my fingernails. I heard him zip up, then the door slowly opened and his blushing face appeared around the edge of it.

'Y-yes?'

'Open the door, James.'

'What?'

'You heard. Open the door.'

'Oh. OK.' He did as he was told and I slid into the cubicle with him. It was cosy and warm, and just enough room for two, so I slid the lock home and turned to face him. He was blushing so much that even his ears had turned red. I almost felt sorry for him. But he was going to be in seventh heaven in less than three minutes, and I bet he didn't feel sorry for himself.

I didn't speak. I didn't want to have a conversation with him: I just wanted to get hot and dirty, so I cupped his package in my hand and weighed it thoughtfully. He sighed and mumbled something so I put my forefinger to my lips in order to silence him. He bit his full bottom lip, and I suddenly had the urge to replace his teeth with my own. I went up on tiptoes, leaned into him, and caught his bottom lip with mine, sucking it in and grazing it lightly with my teeth.

James moaned slightly, his dark-blond eyelashes fluttering, and I watched as he surrendered to me. To Dominique. He was a nice-looking boy, in an expensive and very well-groomed way, with his long lashes, plump rosy cheeks and soft, floppy hair. Fresh out of college – previously educated at some expensive all-boys school no doubt; he talked with a plum in his mouth and annoyed the hell out of everyone at work with his constantly trilling mobile phone – where did he get a social life like that at his age? – and his brand new Alpha Romeo Sport.

But in here, in my hands, he was just a boy like all the rest: shy, unsure, and very, very easy. He was putty in my hands.

He grew and grew against my palm, his erection tenting his fine wool trousers and his balls tucking tight up under him as I slipped my fingers over his tailored fly and stroked him. He was rock-hard in moments. No longer putty but steel and concrete. There was a fascinatingly hard ridge of muscle up the back of his dick that I could feel even through the heavy fabric of his trousers.

I sighed and sucked his lip some more. He tried to kiss me properly, his hands on my hips and his tongue searching for mine between our wet mouths. But I wasn't having that: I didn't want tenderness from someone I barely knew. I pulled back, shaking my head, then I slid quietly to my knees and popped the button on his waistband.

He took a deep, trembling inhalation, and leaned back against the wall of the cubicle, his eyes fluttering closed and his face resigned but happy. I slid down the zip of his trousers, enjoying the tiny, tinny sound in the silence, and slid my fingers inside. He felt so hot: his cotton boxers clung to him and I had to fight a little to get his trousers and white shorts over it and down to his knees. But a careful bit of manhandling soon sorted him out and there he was. All cock and no trousers. Naked. Delicious. Very, very male.

I took a deep breath and enjoyed the smell of him, that masculine muskiness combined with the hint of soap after his recent morning shower. He was clean, and blond, and very hard. His cock trembled a little as I ran one finger up its length and stroked the tip of my nail into the little slit at the end. He was engorged, full to bursting point, and I could hardly wait to get my lips stretched around him.

But I also wanted to make him wait. To make him realise who was in charge here. This was a once in a lifetime event – I wasn't going to make a habit of blowing my colleagues in the unisex toilets – and I wanted it to last long enough that we both remembered it for a long, long time.

James gave a little whimper, and his hands stole to the crown of my head to stroke my soft hair. I knocked him away and shook my head fiercely, relishing the sudden look of hurt surprise in his eyes. There was a long pause, one in which I thought for a horrible moment that he was going to do battle with me. But then he simply nodded, his beautiful face pale in the dim light, and let his head rest back against the wall; his hands went limply to his sides, palms up in a gesture of surrender, and I knew then that he was mine.

I let my tongue play across the skin of his legs first,

enjoying the feel of his muscular, rugby-player's thighs. He tasted of expensive soap. Then I pushed my tongue in a trail of fire and saliva up to the crease where leg becomes groin. He tasted different there, cucumber fresh but somehow sweet. A warmer, more humid taste clung to his skin as I pressed in deeper between the folds of young skin. I could smell his cock, I could feel it graze my cheek, and I could sense the tension in his body although he was being a good boy now and not moving, or making a sound. I dug my fingers into the hard musculature of his thigh and poked my tongue deep under his balls.

He twitched. I sighed. Then I caught one of his neat little testicles with my tongue and rolled it softly around. It was velvety and yet prickly, like a delicious fruit: kumquat, or kiwi, or something else equally juicy and delicious. I played with him, sliding one of my hands up to the other testicle so that it didn't feel lonely, looping my forefinger around and caressing it softly while I drew the first one into my hot, wet mouth. James arched a little, his face turned up towards the saffron-painted ceiling and his hands clasping slightly, then falling open relaxed again.

I softly sucked him, drawing his ball into my mouth, resting it on my tongue as if testing the weight, then giving it an imperceptible suck. I eased the other one in too and widened my mouth to take them both, almost drooling now. He was delicious, salty and yet sweet, and I loved him with my tongue, letting the flat surface of it play over his sac until he was gasping.

My pussy was burning hot. Open and needy and throbbing at the sight of someone else's lovely pleasure. I fumbled with the fastening of my trousers and slid them open, still tonguing James's balls, and slipped a free hand inside. My clit was straining to meet my fingers, all secret and stiff inside its little cocoon of soft pink skin and framing curls. I rubbed a little, stroking lightly and then more firmly as I let James's balls swell in my mouth. A prickle of pleasure stole up my spine and made the hair on the back of my neck stir and lift.

I caught his shaft in my other fist and revelled in the warm, dry heat of its length. I slid my fingers slowly up and down, squeezing slightly as I came to the bulbous end and then relaxing to slip down its impressive length. The ridge at the back stood out hard and proud against my palm, and I suddenly wanted to feel that raised column against my tongue.

I slid my mouth off his bollocks, leaving a trail of warm saliva as I slipped along the underside of his shaft. I tongued that ridge, worshipping it, while above me, posh James trembled and arched against the wall of the cubicle, helpless under the onslaught of my hot tongue.

I used my mouth and my fingers on his warm flesh, and the fingers of my other hand on my own clit, drawing him into my rhythm, wanking him as I slid my tongue up his muscle to the very tip and lingered on the sensitive slit at the end. He tasted gorgeous: a little salty tear wept from the hole. I lapped it up, licking and sucking my way over it until I had the end of his cock held lightly between my lips. Then I slipped all the way down, impaling my face on him, letting his dick surge to the back of my throat while I tightened a circlet of fingers around the base.

He was cuffed like that: my fingers gripped around the base of his cock and my mouth tight on his shaft. I sucked as if I wanted to drain the life out of him. And all the while I slipped and slid my fingers over my own wet hole and felt my heart thud in my chest and in my temples, wallowing in the taste and feel of this deliciously decadent meal that I had suddenly found on my breakfast menu.

I trembled a little against him, my senses suddenly overwhelmed with the reality of the situation. I was closeted in an office toilet – where anyone might walk in, at any moment – with a boy young enough to be my baby brother. I felt a frisson of pleasure that was strangely edged with guilt. Then, with my mouth still stretched around James's erection, I looked up at his face. I saw all my own lustful desire mirrored there, and the guilt peeled away to leave pure, unadulterated pleasure.

What we were doing was fabulous. I could die like this: a hot young cock in my mouth, a fingerful of my own creamy juice dripping down into the gusset of my trousers, and the threat of someone walking in and hearing the loud slick-slick of wet mouth over hard dick. I felt a rush of love for Dominique and all that she seemed to be changing me into.

James feathered his hands across my hair again and stroked my head, his touch tender and full of wonder as his thumbs explored the curves and hollows of my brow, my cheeks, my blissfully closed eyes. I thought about shaking him off, but then didn't.

No, I thought. Let him. If he wants to. Besides, it feels nice.

So I accepted his tender caress as I sucked on his long cock, feeling it harden and become even more solid. I slipped my soft tongue over and under. I got in every-where, tasting all of his skin, all the folds and creases – all the little secret crevices under the collar of pink skin that curled so neatly back from his glans – right down that lovely thick ridge of muscle to his tight, fragrant balls. I snuffled and breathed him in, then slid back up, my fingers kneading and stroking, my chin wet from all the saliva I made as I drooled over his deliciousness. I licked and sucked at him, like a dirty little cat that hadn't been fed for a week.

I heard the hiss of his sharply in-drawn breath and knew he was about to come. I sucked him harder. Ever onward. My mouth tight around him. Suckling and drawing greedily at his cock. A door opened and closed somewhere nearby, and the sudden rush of adrenalin at the possibility of discovery heightened all my senses to fever pitch. I heard the rustle of soft fabric, and knew it was a woman who had come in. She chose the cubicle next to ours and slid the lock home. Whoever it was gave a little sigh, and there was the silvery clinking sound of two bracelets rattling together. James stiffened above me, his cock suddenly jerking in my mouth, his eyes full of terror as he stared down at me.

The woman, oblivious to our presence, settled down in the next cubicle for a nice, long, girly piss. The sound of her pee hitting the water was beautiful, and I swallowed as James let go and filled my mouth with his gorgeous come. He thrust hard against my face, desperately pumping his cock at the back of my throat. A hard white pulse of delight beat beneath my eyelids. I pressed my fingers harder against my swollen clitoris and came seconds after him, sucking and swallowing and shaking along with James as I sank into a dream-like haze of bliss.

That night I cobbled together pasta and pesto, and ate it alone. Max called again and I hedged on seeing him. Despite his talk of not forcing anyone, the man was persistent. Friendly but persistent. Finally I agreed that we'd go and see a film together on Friday night, but as soon as he'd rung off I was unplugging the phone and surfing the chat rooms for SamUK.

He wasn't anywhere, and none of the regulars had seen him. Damn. And I didn't even know his phone number so I couldn't call him. I hung around for a while and sent him what I hoped was a casual-sounding e-mail. But he didn't show, so I went private with a man from Utah called Al who had a rather tantalising way of describing his tongue movements. It was fun. But not as much fun as Sam.

I logged off at around 10 p.m. and mooched around in the kitchen avoiding the washing-up pile. I really had to get some kind of cleaning person to come in and give me a hand. I checked my e-mail again after half an hour, but there was no word from SamUK. I sent another one – how desperate was I? – saying to call me if it was before midnight when he picked up his mail. Then I watched the movie that I'd taped on Wednesday night before falling asleep on the sofa with my head on the pile of ironing that I'd been saving for a rainy day.

I dreamed that I was standing at the end of a large brass bed. Strapped to it with shiny black tape, his limbs spread wide, and glossed with some kind of delicious scented oil, was a young man I'd never seen before. He was lithe and strong, with a hairless chest. I knew it was Sam. He had an erection that flowered out of the tangled knot of pubic hair in his loins. He looked vulnerable, and I liked that.

I stood there for a long time, watching him. Neither of us spoke as I stared, and my scrutiny made him get even more excited. His cock swelled and grew and strained towards his belly button, following the straight line of curling hairs that crinkled up over the centre of his belly. I was dying to lean over and take that loaded cannon in my mouth, but I stood still and simply smiled.

In the dream, there was a movement behind me, and I felt familiar hands smooth up my arms to my shoulders. It was Max: I could smell his masculine scent as he came in close behind me, and the feel of his crisp hairs on the back of my thighs told me that he was naked too. I sighed and watched Sam, who stayed motionless on the bed; his only movement was that of the visible pulse throbbing in the side of his neck, and the slight twitch and sway of his muscular cock.

'Hold me, Max,' I commanded.

He obeyed, grasping me firmly and pulling me back against him. I felt the hard length of his body against my naked back, and sensed his iron-hard erection as it pressed against the swell of my buttocks. His lips sought my ear, my neck, my shoulder. It felt delicious: I tilted my head to one side so that he could lick and kiss the most sensitive parts of my skin.

All the while, Sam watched us, his eyes fixed on mine. He was unable to move from the bed because of the black tape that held him wrist and ankle, but he could writhe and squirm against the pale linen sheets. The muscles in his arms bulged slightly with his futile efforts to loosen the binding. I don't think he actually wanted to escape, or even to stop us. I think he was just so fired up that he wanted a hand free to touch himself while he watched Max and me. But both his hands were right out of the picture – bound tight – and all he could do was twist and tug helplessly with his desire shining from his dark eyes.

Max slipped his hands down over my waist and thrust them through the curly hair into my sex, seeking the juicy warmth of my arousal. My lips swelled to meet his touch, and I heard him inhale sharply as he fingered the creases of my skin and dipped a forefinger lightly into the creamy juice that slicked my insides.

I lifted one foot and placed it on the mattress between two brass struts of the bed end. My movement gave him much better access, and it let Sam see more. They both liked that. I could tell because Max groaned slightly and tucked in closer behind me, one hand cupping a breast and the other delving deep under to my pussy; while Sam sighed and thrust his hips upwards, his cock jerking and straining straight and true from the tangle of dark hair that covered his sex.

Now that I was open, Max cupped my pussy posses-sively for a moment; his hand, sprinkled with black hair, seemed huge between my thighs. He slipped in one finger, then two, stretching me slightly but leaving me desperate for more. I gasped as he introduced a third and fourth finger, feeling myself opened far wider than I had ever been before. Then Max nudged his thumb-pad up to my clit. He lingered there, his fingers blunt and dextrous, rubbing and circling with slow, hypnotic rhythm until I gasped and went taut against him, my body straight and tight as I strained towards the fabulous sensation of his rubbing fingers.

I had the burners on so high I could feel the gush of milky liquid curling away from my insides and slicking Max's knuckles. I could sense that I was lusciously wet, my juice soaking the blunt fingers that were held still for a moment inside my sex: Max was waiting for my tightness to ease. We swayed together, he with his hand up between the milk-white skin of my thighs; me with my head drooping and my hair sticking to the perspiration that beaded my neck. Then he made a little circling motion and I felt him tuck his thumb into his palm.

My cunt seemed to suck at him then. Hungry. Greedy for more of him. I felt my sex swell and bloom to the ripeness of a full-blown flower as I opened wide for him. I rocked against him, moving my hips a little, easing myself down on to his narrowed fist until – with a little slick pop – he was in, buried in my aching flesh right to the wrist.

Sam wriggled a little more on the bed, straining against his bindings, and I got even wetter at the sight of his helplessness and the way his flat belly seemed to tremble with his desire. I caught his gaze with mine and we stayed with our eyes locked like that, while Max slowly arched me forward and began to fist me.

I was stretched to capacity by his hand. His knuckles grazed my tender insides with a delicious burning heat. He probed and pressed, and I eased my thighs wider to accommodate him, gulping at the warm air in the room and sighing as I felt my insides begin to rhythmically ripple against his wrist.

He nudged up high, pumping slightly against the muscular nose of my womb, and I felt myself being caught up in the rush of heat and energy that swept from my toes all the way to my scalp. I was hot for him, my skin fiery and my cunt slipping eagerly wider around his fist. My vision blurred. My eyes flickered closed. I felt my limbs turn to liquid. My orgasm was violent. All-consuming. All-engulfing. The sensations of heat and light rocked my body and threatened to tear me apart as I moaned and bit my lip, revelling in the sudden, hard, clenching, muscular contractions.

Max let me recover. Then gently, tenderly, with little whispers of endearment, disengaged his sticky fist from my honey-pot. He wrapped his arms around my trembling body and held me close, nuzzling my hair and kissing my cheeks, my ears, my shoulders as I steadied my breathing and let the aftermath of orgasm subside.

I smelled Max's male odour strongly as he swayed away from me for a moment: hot and male, almost peppery. Cock-smell. Sex-smell. I wanted him. I wanted him inside me.

'Fuck me from behind, Max,' I said, in a commanding voice which brooked no refusal. 'Fuck me now.'

My knees began to tremble with the surprising strength of my own lust, and I gripped the bars of the bed-end to steady myself while Max spread one large hand on my back.

He pressed me down, his fingers wide and powerful, and I arched until my chin was resting on the brass bar and my buttocks were stuck right out behind me. The ultimate position for deep penetration and full-on fucking. He could hold my hips, or my tits, and really ram into me like that. I shivered with glee and waited for him to get right in behind me and give it to me.

His hot fingers seared my skin as he stroked them down my hips, then under and between my legs, easing my thighs apart and easily slipping into the desperate depths of my newly stretched and hungry sex. He scooped up fingerfuls of my juice, sliding his fingers right in so that I could feel the hard pad of his thumb up tight against my anus, and the length of his fingers deep inside me, his thick knuckles caressing the ruched skin of my insides. Then he slipped out again and I moaned, needing more, used to a wider penetration now that he'd fisted me.

'Do it now!' I commanded. On the bed, Sam writhed and moaned, tortured by the sight of my swaying tits and the lascivious look of abandon on my face.

'OK,' Max said. 'OK, ma'am, I'm gonna fuck you,' he whispered, as he slicked the juice he had collected over the straining head of his hard cock. Then as an after-thought, he murmured a word that I thought I'd misheard.

'What did you call me?' I asked, a thrill of adrenalin pumping through my veins at the sound of the word on his lips.

'Bitch,' he said, his voice hoarse. 'I said, "I'm gonna fuck you, bitch."'

I loved that. It made a thick curl of luscious juice ooze out from my sex and slip down my inner thigh. I was gagging for him to do it to me now. He nestled in close behind me, his thighs tense and legs bent slightly so that he could tuck right in.

I waited. Sam waited. Max waited. The moment seemed to go on for ever.

Then Max entered me with one hard thrust.

There was a collective grunt of pleasure. Then I sighed hard as he slipped into an easy rhythm and I held Sam's gaze again. The hopeless look in his eyes made my whole body feel like it was on fire and I moaned and thrust back against Max.

'Faster,' I murmured. 'Come on, bitch-fucker. Harder!'

Max did as he was told, his cock thrusting and rutting into me, his breathing harsh and violent, hot against the skin of my shoulders. Sam thrust his hips helplessly against the air, his prick straining and desperate, while Max fucked me savagely. I bucked against him. Perspiration beaded my forehead and I felt Max's hand slip up my back with moist ease.

We were both hot. Hot and sweating. Fucking greedily. While on the bed poor Sam watched. He moaned and thrust his solid cock in time to us. Max's hand delved hard between my legs, fingers thrusting and thumb pressing, until I felt my limbs crackle with electrifying sensation and pleasure until I thought I couldn't bear it any more. We pumped against each other, Max's fingers hard against my clit and my ass tipped so high in the air that I could feel his balls slapping loudly against the plump lips of my sex.

Eventually I couldn't bear to see Sam suffer any more, so I stretched over the end of the bed and caught his hard cock in my hand. It felt like steel: taut, hard, throbbing and fit to burst. I wanked him hard but smooth, while behind me Max fucked me with more and more force until I suddenly melted on to him with a shuddering hard torrent of cream. I cried out, overcome by pleasure, and my grip on Sam tightened so that he came too, delicious thrusting little pumps that beat against my fingers as I held him tight in my fist and let his spunk flip across his belly.

Max was last to come.

'Aah, darn it, Carrie,' he groaned. 'Can I screw your sweet little ass? Will you let me? You look so sweet and tight there.'

'Oh God,' I muttered. 'Fuck me anyhow, Max. Don't ask for permission. Just do it.' And I pressed back against him, desperate to have him fill me any way he wanted.

Max slipped his sticky cock out of me, widened my tight little bottom with his forefinger and eased in carefully. It hurt and I cried out.

'Ah, God. Oh! Oh!'

'Quiet,' whispered Max. But I couldn't. With every thrust of his cock he was driving deeper into my ass. I writhed against him, gasping and moaning. His hand clamped suddenly across my mouth, but I knew that I was still making too much noise.

'Ssh!' Max hissed. He pressed his mouth hard against my shoulder and kissed me. 'Ssh. Or I'll have to tape your mouth closed.'

His fingers slackened away from my mouth and his cock rooted deep inside me. I cried out again, louder this time as if daring him to gag me. I wanted him to.

'Don't make so much noise,' Max said. He slapped my buttock, his palm making a resounding crack against my hot skin. Then he reached for the roll of wide black tape that nestled between the mattress and the foot of the bed. It was the same tape that bound Sam's wrists and ankles.

'I warned you.' He tore a piece off with his teeth and taped my mouth closed. I shut my eyes and pressed my body back against his.

I was silent.

Max thrust into me again. I opened myself for him. He pumped harder. Faster. I could feel how tight my ass was for him, and so could he. He came quickly and suddenly, groaning with pleasure as I squeezed on to him. I felt the exploding throb of his hot load deep inside my body. There was a hot wave of bliss and I held him inside me for as long as possible. Then I became vaguely aware that a bell was ringing somewhere.

The ringing got louder and louder and the delicious dream abruptly ended with me shooting out one hand and knocking the telephone off its precarious perch on the arm of the sofa. I caught the receiver and groaned as I put it to my ear.

'Yes?'

'Dominique?'

'Sorry, wrong number,' I mumbled automatically. Then, realising that Dominique was me, I sat bolt upright. I was instantly wide awake with senses reeling and head thumping. 'Shit! Sam!'

I glanced at the clock on the mantelpiece. It had stopped because I had, yet again, forgotten to wind it. 'What time is it?'

He chuckled. 'Were you asleep? You did say call if it was before midnight.'

'Is it before midnight?'

'It's . . .' silence, and I imagined him consulting his watch '. . . eleven-fifteen. What're you doing?'

'Sleeping,' I groaned. 'Dreaming. What a fantastic dream.'

'Oh sorry. Didn't mean to wake you, but when I got your e-mails I thought I'd call.' He yawned. 'I was out tonight. We went to play pool.'

'Oh. Pool.' I almost laughed. I didn't know a single person who played pool. Until now. 'That's the game with the coloured balls, right?'

'Yeah.' He laughed. Then he said suggestively, 'Maybe when we meet up we could have a game with the coloured balls . . .'

'I can think of better things to do when we meet up.'

'So when're we going to do it?'

'When d'you want to do it?'

'Well, I guess it's too late for tonight. But as soon as possible I'd say.'

'Me too.'

The dream was still fresh enough in my mind to feel tantalisingly real.

'So where are you meeting this Sam?' Laura curled her feet up under her and leaned her elbow on the arm of the sofa. We were sitting in her lounge sipping chilled drinks and half-watching our favourite early evening television show. My date with Max was set for 8 p.m., but I'd called in to Laura's because I felt so guilty at having neglected her for my online chat all week.

'Covent Garden, outside a bookshop just down from the tube station,' I said.

'What time?'

'Midday, the time all good assignations should be.' I laughed and took a long slug of wine.

'What if he doesn't look like his picture?' Laura slopped some more wine into my glass. 'What if he's a real nerd?'

I laughed. 'Well, there's not much I can do, is there? Walk away, I guess. Besides, he'd hardly have agreed to meet if he didn't really look like his photo.' I frowned. 'Would he?'

Laura shrugged. 'Who knows?' she said. 'The Internet's full of weirdos, though.'

'No, it's not.' I laughed again. 'It's full of people just like you and me.'

'Correction,' she said. 'It's full of people just like you and Sam.'

'Hopefully.'

'And what about your safety?' Laura frowned and looped a strand of hair behind her ear. 'Have you thought about that?'

'Yes, I have.' I'd spent an hour that morning perusing the personal columns and memorising all the little snippets of information blocked out in bold type in between the ads. 'Tell someone where you're going. Meet in a public place . . .' I counted off all the points with my fingers '. . . don't go anywhere with anyone until you feel comfortable with them, and even then . . .'

My voice trailed off as I become aware of someone standing in the doorway listening. I thought at first that it was Tom, Laura's boyfriend, but he wasn't quite that blond. I twisted my head a little and got a full picture of the angel that stood there, casually propped against the door frame, blond ringlets back-lit from the window in the hall.

I had no idea who he was, or what he was doing there, and the silence of his soft-footed approach made it seem as if he'd just materialised there – like some kind of sacred vision. I glanced at Laura and saw with relief that she'd seen him too. Thank God – that meant he was real, then, so I wasn't gazing at some kind of heavenly mirage.

'Hi!' Laura said to the sacred vision, smiling widely. 'How did you get on?'

'No luck,' he replied. His voice was delicious: milky smooth and slightly musical, like a choir boy. He frowned sulkily as he saw my eyes on his face, and dropped his gaze to study his boots. A tinge of pink flushed his cheeks and his pale lashes trembled and fluttered and made dark shadows on his cheeks. I held my breath as I gazed at him. He was adorable.

I realised that I was staring, and forced myself to slide my eyes sideways in a vain attempt to study the television. The celebrity of the week was being forced to do some hideous crowd-pleasing stunt which normally I would have found eye-poppingly disgusting, but this time was barely aware of.

'Oh well, you've got a couple of weeks,' Laura said. 'You can stay here with me till I move. You know that.'

Laura was moving in with her fiancé Tom at the end of the month. Earlier in the summer Tom had dropped down on one knee beside the fountain in the city centre. Laura said there'd been a violinist busking a few yards away which had made the moment perfect, and she'd said 'yes' without a second thought.

The wedding wouldn't be until February, but they'd decided that they couldn't spend many more nights apart, so Laura had given notice to the landlord with plans to move out at the end of August. But in the meantime, I wondered, who was this angelic vision who brooded in the doorway? And why was he here in Laura's flat?

'Carrie,' Laura said, almost as if she could read my thoughts, 'this is one of my cousins. He's starting Uni at the end of September. He's staying here till he can find some student digs.'

That explained that, then. I nodded and smiled at him. 'Hi.'

'Hi,' he muttered, blushing furiously and twisting his mouth down in a perfect rendition of James Dean's moody scowl.

'I'm Carrie.'

'I'm Gabriel.'

Well, what a gorgeously appropriate name, I thought, and made myself turn back to the television.

When I told Eva that I was planning to go to London, she was predictably unimpressed.

'Good for you,' she murmured, her hard eyes following the line of my fingers as I stroked some soft butter over a piece of bread roll.

Leon had gone down to the cellar to look for some vintage champagne that he said he wanted to show us, and we were alone. Marie-Therese, their stroppy maid, had slammed out of the room and gone to see to the next course. I took a bite from the roll and admired the even, straight line my teeth made in the butter. Eva crumbled the crust of her bread, doing any activity to avoid eating. As usual. Her feline eyes flickered back up to my face and I thought I saw, for a tiny moment, something like concern in their dark depths. 'Take care, though. Won't you?'

I looked at her in surprise. She kept her gaze level with mine and then gave a small smile.

'It can be a mean old world out there,' she said, after a while. 'Don't get hurt, sweetie.'

Her voice held an unusually serious note. She sounded very much as though she was speaking from personal experience, and I was intrigued enough to want her to elaborate. But the door banged and Leon puffed his bulk back into the chair at the head of the table.

'Here . . . it is,' he said, catching his breath. 'Château

70

Falincourt . . . 1966. Cost me . . . nine hundred pounds for the case.'

I smiled politely, and let him drone on as I ate my food and lost myself in a complicated fantasy about Sam and Max and a bathtub full of Château Falincourt.

Chapter Six

tales of the riverbank

Max and I enjoyed the cinema, although his choice of film wasn't quite my taste. We'd tossed a coin when faced with the long list of movies showing at the multiplex. I lost. So we sat through one and a half hours of sweaty action, and all I could remember when we came out was the way Max's thigh had pressed against mine. And the curve of his mouth as he'd come back with ice-cream after the trailers. He had a ready smile: warm, open and so utterly confident in his own abilities. I was going to have a hard time teaching this guy the meaning of the word 'no', I realised.

We went to a nearby restaurant and ate pizza afterwards, sitting side by side in companionable silence, our elbows pressed against each other while we exchanged secretive, loaded grins. It was so easy being with Max. We could talk about everything and anything. And he was highly amused when I told him a little bit about Dominique and my chat-room habit.

'Take care, though, won't you?' he said, topping up my glass of red wine. 'There are probably some really normal people using the net. But you should keep it in your mind that not everyone is who they seem. There are psychos out there, too.'

I nodded and poked a fork at my side salad. 'I know,' I said. 'I've had this lecture before.'

'Well, I usually think that if more than two people are saying the same thing to you, then you should take notice of what they say. Be careful, Carrie. Don't give too much information about yourself to anyone.'

'OK. Thanks.' I smiled at him and stroked his fingers with my own. 'Thanks, Max, for being worried about my safety. I'll be careful.'

I couldn't take Max back to my place, not till I found some kind of cleaner or housekeeper to take care of the piles of mess that kept building up. So we went to the elegant Georgian villa where he was lodging, and crept up the dark stairs, giggling furtively, pretending to be naughty schoolchildren. We fucked like bunnies: up against the door almost before it was closed; off the side of the bed; leaning out on the window sill with Max tucked in behind me and me biting my lips so as not to let the passers-by out on the street below hear my grunts of bliss as his cock drove deep into me.

By the time the dawn light had started to gleam in golden streaks across the palest blue horizon, we had sated our desperate hunger for each other's skin. We had just enough energy left to snatch a kiss and a sip of water from the glass on the bedside cabinet before falling into a deep sleep. I decided that I liked Max. Almost as much as I liked SamUK. And the attention he lavished on me gave me more than enough confidence to feel OK about going to London.

The next week at work, the days flew by in a haze of hastily prepared visuals and client meetings. The studio was very busy and I was beginning to find that my boss, Don Richardson, was not the most pleasant person to work for when the pressure was on. Everything I did he criticised. I was finding it increasingly difficult to bite my tongue on the retorts that welled up inside me.

I'd been at Richardson's for about a year. And in that time they'd only ever known me as the meek and mild Carrie. If I suddenly blasted them with the full force of Dominique's assertiveness, they'd think I'd gone mad. So, I sat at my computer and worked diligently, silently accepting Don's acid-tongued rebukes about designers who were, to quote his favourite saying, 'all trendy typography and no substance'. Meanwhile, Posh James and his constantly bulging trousers seemed to engineer an excuse to drift towards the toilets every time I went in there, but one quick flash of my box of Lil-lets and he was out of there like a scalded cat.

Laura and I ate Chinese take-out at her flat on Friday night. I had wanted Indian but she'd shrieked and said I was mad: SamUK would be blown away by my breath if we ate that. I grinned and conceded defeat, so we had chow mein and lemon chicken in companionable silence while I waited hopefully for the Angel Gabriel to come in.

By ten he hadn't shown, but I didn't want to voice my disappointment to Laura, who would think I was trying to cradle-snatch her cousin. Which I wasn't. No, really, I wasn't, I told myself. I just wanted to have another look at his beautiful Caravaggio-inspired face. At eleven, I thought I ought to push off home, and Laura emptied the bottle of red wine into our glasses as a farewell gesture.

'Here,' she said. 'Finish this. I don't want to stay up drinking on my own. Gabe will think I'm a lush.'

'Where is he?' I enquired, in what I hoped was a nonchalant and disinterested manner.

'Out with some boys.'

'Oh.' I was momentarily nonplussed. 'Is he . . . gay?'

'No!' Laura scoffed. Then paused, frowning. 'I don't think so anyway. Maybe he is.' She drank her wine. 'No,

74

he can't be,' she said, more decisive this time. 'He had a girlfriend back at home. Some pretty little fifteen-year-old who looked just like him.'

'Oh.' I pretended to laugh to cover up any latent and irrational jealousy that I might have had about pretty little fifteen-year-olds. 'Has he found anywhere to live yet?'

Laura shook her head. 'No, I'm a bit worried actually. There's not that much time left and I'm going to start collecting boxes for packing soon. Gabe says he really doesn't want to go into Halls of Res, but he might not have much choice. Apparently good accommodation's really scarce this year.'

'Well,' I joked, 'send him round to Auntie Carrie's.'

Laura looked at me speculatively. 'Are you serious?'

'No!' I gaped. 'Christ, what would I want with some fresher cluttering up my place with his books and files and smelly socks?'

'He's very tidy,' she volunteered.

'No!' I laughed and shook my head. 'Look, I'm going now. Wish me luck for tomorrow, huh?'

Laura put her wine glass down, grabbed me and gave me an enormous hug. 'Good luck, and *be careful*!'

Covent Garden on a hot day in summer is airless and crowded with tourists. I came out of the tube station, breathed in the London pollution appreciatively and took a peek at my watch. Twelve-ten. Good. I was late, it wouldn't do to be early. I smoothed my hair, checked my carefully understated make-up in a shop window and straightened the thin straps of my dress before strolling down towards the bookshop.

I had my little leather rucksack looped over one shoulder, and a pair of narrow-framed sunglasses propped on my nose so that my terrified expression would be hidden from everyone who chose to look at me. I was so nervous, not just about meeting up with someone that I didn't know, but about the impression he'd get of me, too. What if he saw me and didn't like me? He might tell at a glance that, despite the hair and make-up, I wasn't a vibrant brunette with a dominating streak. He might see through the disguise and see that I was actually small Carrie with no personality and no attitude.

I checked my reflection again and swallowed hard. I looked OK. In fact I looked quite good for me. No one would be able to tell that my palms were prickling, my heart hammering, or that my throat felt tight. I wondered whether, when I had to speak, I might instead emit a hideous and high-pitched squeak of fright.

Someone walked past me, so close that they brushed my arm with theirs and I almost jumped out of my skin. Whoever it was walked on without a backward glance and I scanned the crowd, my mind in a spin. What the hell was I doing? Why did I ever think this would be a fun thing to do? And what if SamUK turned out to be some monstrous apparition with greasy hair and sweat rings under his armpits? What if the photo he'd sent me wasn't actually him but one of his better-looking chums?

I began to play a guessing game with myself, one called *Spot SamUK*.

I saw a guy standing a few yards away with his back to me and my heart skipped a beat. Surely not. He was wearing hideous lime green trousers, a nylon shirt, and had an arse the size of an elephant. I swallowed hard and took a deep breath, then exhaled it all in relief as I saw him link arms with an impossibly ugly woman. They strode off together.

This is a really bad idea, I told myself. I should just go home and forget all about SamUK.

'Hi. It's Dominique, right?'

I spun round. I hadn't expected him to come from behind. For some reason I'd thought he would come from the direction of the tube station just like me, not be sauntering casually up the street from the plaza, in his white T-shirt and faded jeans, all sun-kissed nose and wide grin. Oh, thank you, God, I thought. He's so sweet. And his picture really does not do him justice at all. Those honest eyes, that sweep of brown lashes, that strong, smooth jaw.

'Hi,' I breathed. No squeak of fright, thank goodness.

Looking at Sam, I wanted to laugh loudly, then burst into tears of relief and fall on his nicely filled T-shirt. But I didn't. I just stood still, one hand on my hip and the other brushing my fringe out of my eyes, letting my gaze feast on him. He did the same, and we must have stood like that for about five minutes, taking in every curve and sinew of each other's bodies, every freckle and every eyelash lit by the noonday sun, and every little imperfection that made us both human.

'Let's go and get a cold beer,' he said at last. And he took my hand just as if we'd known each other for years and led me down the street to a bar with a terrace and outside tables. He didn't speak again for a while, just went straight to the bar and bought two long glasses full of ice-cold golden beer, sauntered back, slouched into the chair opposite me, and slipped his fingers in between mine on the sun-drenched table top.

We sat for a moment, sipping our drinks and smiling at each other. There was no awkwardness, no uncomfortableness about the silence. I felt totally at home. Completely at ease. As if I'd known him for ever. I was amazed, and knew that it must be a rare thing to get a blind date who seemed so easygoing and who looked this good. That day, I was the luckiest girl in Covent Garden.

We talked for hours, wandering around London and stopping at various hideously themed taverns to quench our thirst with Sam's favourite beers. We ate steaming hotdogs, licked ice-creams, strolled around Trafalgar

Square. Then finally at dusk, we wandered through Westminster to stand on the banks of the Thames and watch the last of the gloriously red-gold sunset. I felt happy and carefree, but frustrated too. Sam had held my hand for most of the day, his palm warm and dry, his fingers strong as they curved around mine – but hand-holding was all he'd done.

At first I thought maybe Dominique didn't live up to his expectations. But several times I caught him looking at me with an expression which spelled out desire, and by the time we were standing by the river, I had decided that he liked me, sure enough, but that he didn't know what to do about it. He was only 23 years old. Maybe he thought it would be rude to exert authority over me. After all, I was Dominique, his phone-sex wet dream and I'd called all the shots then, so maybe he was waiting for me to make a move. Maybe he was a natural submissive and hadn't been acting out a fantasy when he let me take over the reins of power in our phone sex.

I glanced at my watch: it was getting late. I'd have to do it for him, or I was going to find myself using the return ticket I'd bought 'just in case'.

'Where do you live, Sam?' I asked, as we leaned, elbow to elbow, on the wall that overlooked the river and stared down into the murky river water. He shifted his weight from one foot to the other and his denim-clad hip nudged lightly against mine. It felt nice: solid, heavy and reassuring. And carried the promise of some hefty power if I ever got to hold those hips between my thighs.

'Over there.' He pointed south of the river and I followed his finger with my eyes. The opposite embankment was lit up with a line of pale street lights that glowed against the blue of the darkening sky. Behind it was row upon row of shadowy houses and large buildings, some with lit windows, some dark. I tried to imagine Sam's place, what it would look like, who he shared it with. I waited for him to offer to take me there, but he didn't. I sighed and slipped my arm through his.

'Will you show me?'

He turned his face to look at me. He looked nervous, but open to suggestion, so I tried again.

'Take me back to your place, Sam,' I prompted. 'It's hot. My feet ache, and I've seen enough of London. I want to take a shower, lie on your bed, and let you do unspeakable things to me with your bare hands.'

Then I leaned into him and fixed my mouth to his while fastening my hands around the gorgeously tempting butt that had been driving me crazy every time he turned his back to me that afternoon.

His mouth was only slightly open, but it widened under my lips and I snuggled in closer, encouraged, as he tentatively put his tongue out to meet mine. Kissing him was as blissful as I'd imagined it would be: he tasted of beer and the pistachio nuts we'd munched walking around Parliament Square, and I slipped my tongue against his and suckled him on to me.

His hands trembled behind my back, touching my waist lightly, then moving in for a tighter hold on my narrow back as I pressed against him. I wriggled a little, and felt his package spring to life against the front of my thighs; his cock felt almost spring-loaded as it shot up under his fly: long, thick, and tantalisingly hard against my pubis.

I pressed harder, feeling a rush of excitement in my sex that made me wet. I sighed longingly against his mouth. In an instant his hands were tangled in my hair, holding my head, cradling me, pulling me up on to tiptoes as he devoured my mouth with his firm, questing lips. What a kiss. What a fantastic taste. If he can respond like that to a mere kiss, I thought, just think of what he could do if we were naked and alone. I wanted him. Immediately. And I could hardly wait to get to wherever it was that he lived.

I glanced over his shoulder at the dark river and the twinkling lights that were just starting to be switched on in the houses over on the far bank. 'How do we get over there?' I whispered, my hands smoothing down the firm muscles of his back.

His reply was to catch my mouth with his again, thrust his thigh between my legs, and slip one hand up under my dress to the elastic hem of my tiny knickers. Oh my God, I sighed delightedly, I don't think we're going to make it to Sam's place.

I encouraged him with tiny murmurs and little words of endearment as he sat me up on the wall and peeled the thin cotton of my dress up my thighs to reveal my little-girl white knicks. He sighed and closed his eyes briefly, then slid his hands over my brown legs and bent his head to my lap. I gasped with delight, glancing quickly to left and right to make sure that no one else was within staring distance. Then I fluttered my hands over his thick hair and enjoyed the sound of him inhaling deeply as he savoured the scent of my hot pussy.

His jaw felt rough on my skin, his short evening stubble tickling against my thighs as he rubbed his chin lightly against my leg and then buried his face in deeper, his eyes blissfully closed and his face so contented that he looked like a bear that had found its home for the winter. His breath felt wonderfully warm on my sex, his puffed-out exhalations permeating the cotton of my panties, making my pussy swell and blossom. I pressed my knees wide and let him bury his face in my warm nest.

Heat surged through my limbs, and I lifted my head to stare at the passing cars out on the road only yards away, speeding past carrying people who were completely oblivious of what Sam was doing. From where they were, if they chose to look, we might – just – look like lovers entwined on the wall. Maybe, I thought, stifling a giggle, they'd think Sam had lost something and was looking for it in the folds of my dress. Or perhaps that he was feeling faint in the city heat, and had needed to rest his head on my lap.

Sam's hands were on my waist and my long pale dress drifted down at the sides. From a distance it would look as if it hadn't been disturbed, hadn't been pushed up, hadn't been grasped in two powerful brown hands and twisted up to my belly.

I waited to see if Sam would take the initiative now, wondering if he'd be more pro-active now that I'd more or less offered myself on a plate. But he stayed there, his thumbs rubbing tiny circles on my tummy just above the waistband of my knickers, and his breath coming in long sighs into my desperate, cotton-clad pussy. I smoothed his hair back from his forehead and curved forward to whisper in his ear.

'Sam. I'm going to die if you don't do something else. Please. I don't care what you do. Use your mouth, or your fingers, use anything that you want, but you're going to have to do more than breathe on me, boy.'

It was the word 'boy' that seemed to do it. It put us straight back into that dominant woman and her naughty slave boy mode that we'd adopted so easily the night we'd done phone-sex. He grinned up at me, his teeth white and gleaming with health in his tanned face, and his fingers seemed suddenly galvanised into action. He curled his forefinger around the inner leg of my knickers and pulled them out and away from my pussy so that I felt a rush of warm London air caress me. He slipped a finger across my clit in a single light stroke that made me shiver and sigh.

Propping myself back on the wall, my hands wide and gripping the curved surface, I sensed him move in closer. He put his mouth to my breast, catching my nipple through the thin fabric of my dress and teasing it with his teeth. Light licks. Feathering across the surface of my nipple. It sprang to prominence under his warm lips, and my breasts seemed to swell as I arched my back and offered myself to him. An electric tingle started in my tits and made a sudden, critical connection down into my sex that made me juice up against his fingers and wriggle my tush a little to get closer to the edge of the wall and closer to his hands.

Then he stood up straight, wrapping one arm around me and pulling me in close as if we were simply cuddling. I flickered my eyes sideways and saw a couple – arm in arm – walking along the wide pavement. Sam's ears, I thought, must be out on stalks. I was impressed. There was no way we were going to get caught out unawares if he could hear that well. The couple passed us without comment, and then we were alone again, the warm darkness closing around us and the only sound that of the low hum of the traffic and the slow lap-lap of the water behind me.

Sam eased away and stared into my eyes, a smile curving his lips and a playful glint in his eye.

'Are you an exhibitionist, Dominique?'

He grinned, as I shook my head and replied, 'No, I don't think so.'

'Me neither. But it might be fun to get really sticky out here, in full view of anyone who might go past. Then I could take you back to my place and we could do it for real.'

I wasn't about to let him feel that he had to ask twice, so I nodded, slipped an arm around his neck, cupped his dick in my hand and gave it a playful squeeze.

'Mmmm,' I said. 'I love that idea.'

His idea of getting sticky was, in actual fact, to get me really sticky. In the most delicious way possible. He started by running a finger lightly over my cotton knickers and pressing gently on the moist patch that slicked the gusset, then he moved in with his fingers and slipped my panties off completely as I wriggled my bottom to help him. He scrunched up the whiter-than-white fabric in one hand and grinned.

'You'd pass the Daz doorstep challenge.' He laughed. I laughed too, not wanting to tell him that they were brand new, and that the rest of my underwear drawer had that grey-blue tinge of a recent washing machine tragedy.

He slipped my knickers into his hip pocket. I was slightly surprised that he had any room for anything else in there: he was so tightly packed, his thick cock stretching the denim so much. Putting any more stuff in there would surely compromise the blood supply. But he didn't seem to mind, he simply smiled again, kissed the tip of my nose and let his forefingers trail in twin lines of scintillating tingles all the way from my knees to the very edges of my swollen pussy.

He stroked and smoothed my creases, and then curved the hard pad of his thumb over my clit. He slipped and slid in love-juices, fingering and rubbing so that my senses seemed to detach themselves from my brain and make me float. I sighed, relishing the feeling of his firm, dextrous fingers; they were light as a feather one moment, hard as leather the next. My body began to tremble, raw feelings of pleasure and desire radiating out in circles from my sex. I could feel my control gradually slipping until I thought I'd fall off the wall and splash into the dark and odorous Thames below. Sam's fingers were magical: fast then slow. Hard then soft. Warm and nimble and so sweet that I caught my lip between my teeth as he eased a finger into me. Oh God, I thought. This boy is a find.

I widened my legs and let him come in closer so that his hip was pressed against the fleshy pad of my inner thigh and his hand could do its secret magic between the crush of our bodies. What we were doing was a little bit like the furtive adolescent fumblings that I'd experienced on one solitary, disappointing occasion after the school disco. But this time without the guilt and lack of expertise.

This time, in the here and now, I had a boy between my legs who knew exactly what to do with his hands. He pressed and withdrew, making great waves of electricity shudder up my spine into my hairline. He slipped in deeper, his knuckles tight against me, then slid out with a lovely, juicy squelching sound. He used one finger, then two, and when I whispered urgently to him he slipped in a third and frigged me harder, the narrow silver ring on his thumb pressed tight to my clit and his lips glued to mine by the sheer force of suction. We kissed and licked at each other, with his fingers slurping in and out of my wetness, creating delicious sounds and making me giggle with the gorgeous pressure.

He slipped his hand over, turning it palm up, and I felt him make little rocking movements, little circles that started at his wrist and rippled out to the tips of his fingers and against the silken walls of my sex. I sighed as his wrist flexed and circled and his fingers did their magic inside me. I felt like I was sitting on a goldmine. Sitting on a thrusting, circling, swishing golden hand that curved inside me and sent my senses reeling. I wanted it to last all night; I wanted to keep him there with his hand hard against my pussy until dawn broke over the grey London streets. But I also wanted to come. I needed him to fill me, stretch me further, take me to the edge of reason.

I whispered what I wanted in his ear. He widened his eyes – his gaze questioning mine – then he did as all good boys should and obeyed me. He slipped his little finger into the puddle of juice that trickled out over my perineum, lubricated the tip, and slipped it neatly into my tight little butthole. Bliss exploded in my head. All the temptation and frustration of watching him all day – tight jeans, tight T-shirt and gorgeous grin – melted away as I absorbed his hand and drew it up into my body, relishing the feel of his hard tackle penned into his jeans as he pressed it against my groping hands.

I let him fuck me with his fingers, feeling myself getting stickier and stickier just as he'd wanted me to. I gasped against his fragrant, boyish neck as he rubbed my clit hard with his thumb, and then I was suddenly lost, coming hard on to his hand. He pressed up into some unnameable part of my vagina that opened me further and the sensations bloomed into an unbearable rush of ecstasy.

'Oh, God!' I cried, tipping my head back.

His free hand clamped over my mouth and I swallowed my triumphant yell as a lone dog-walker strode past. I thought I heard the man tut as he glanced, horrified, at the movement of Sam's hand between our tight-pressed bodies, but I didn't care. I was in love with London, the river, the sensations, and I could almost imagine I was in love with Sam. I was definitely in love with his fingers, anyway, as they plundered the deepest depths of my hungry, hot, juicy sex and brought me trembling into an orgasm that wrenched my mind apart and made me shake so hard I was almost seeing everything in triplicate.

I licked the palm of Sam's gagging hand, like a grateful little dog, and rested my head on his shoulder. He let my mouth go, smoothed my hair, and gently rearranged my dress. Then he held his fingers up to his nose and inhaled deeply.

'Beautiful,' he murmured. 'You know, when we spoke on the phone I wondered whether you'd be as lovely as you sounded. But you're better, if that's possible. This is fantastic, the best day I've had for a long time.' He rubbed his nose against mine while I melted against him and savoured the stickiness of my thighs as I drew them back together. 'You look gorgeous; you smell fabulous.' He kissed me, his tongue sneaking in between my lips quickly. 'And, Christ, you give me such a hard-on that I think I'm going to burst if we don't fuck soon!'

I didn't have time to do anything except smile, because

he'd lifted me off the wall, stuck his arm in the air, and bundled me into a passing black cab before I could draw breath.

I leaned back against him in the back of the taxi, enjoying the ancient smell of the leather and the millions of cigarettes that had been smoked in there before the no-smoking signs had gone up. I had no idea where I was going, and I didn't care. I was being kidnapped by the Boy Wonder and I couldn't think of a better thing to happen to me.

Chapter Seven
midnight cowboy

*S*am's room was at the very top of a tall London town house. I had somehow imagined, from what he'd told me, that he shared it with several other student-types who all lived in a blokish mess of unwashed plates and general dustiness – somewhere I'd feel at home, given my own housekeeping skills – but not a bit of it. The house was elegant and spotless, with only two other young male lodgers, one of whom disappeared rapidly behind the door of his room when we came in through the front door, never to be seen again.

I looked around me with interest as Sam deposited his keys on a polished oak cabinet and flicked one-handed through a pile of post. The hallway was wide and airy with a cool blue carpet stretching through to the inner regions of the house. Pale creamy walls were hung with abstract prints edged with brushed aluminium frames, and tall palms stood in heavy-bottomed chrome pots either side of each doorway. The doors themselves had been stripped back to bare pine and then waxed to match the banister that led up to the next floor.

Behind me, the outside carriage light filtered through the stained glass window above the front door. Its golden glow made the hall seem warm and friendly despite all the cold silver and blue tones. There was the definite feel of a feminine hand directing all the tasteful, restrained decor.

'Who else lives here?' I asked Sam, glancing up the tall staircase towards the door that had snapped firmly shut as we'd come in.

'That's Laurence, just gone into his room,' he replied. 'I hardly ever see him. There's a bloke called Alexander who lives here too. He works the building sites –' Sam grinned '– but seems to spend most of his time down the pub. He's probably there at the moment. Of course there's me, too. I've been here for nearly a year, now. And there's Mrs Grey, whose house it is. She's a high court judge.' He glanced at me as if he expected me to be impressed so I duly raised my eyebrows. 'I suppose you could call her our landlady, although she's more friendly than that. It's just the four of us.' He laughed. 'She calls us her "boys", a bit like you sometimes call me boy.'

'It's a big house for four.' I tried not to imagine the daunting-sounding Mrs Grey, but found myself wondering whether there was a Mr Grey somewhere, or whether she had her 'boys' to herself.

'There was a fifth. A girl.' Sam looked a little sheepish and I grinned, my fertile imagination instantly making up naughty reasons for his blushing cheeks. 'But it didn't work out. Mrs Grey didn't like her. So she had to go.'

'Oh.' I followed him up to his room and felt a flicker of surprise at its tidiness. 'It's not at all how I imagined the studenty-type of house that you'd live in,' I said. 'Does Mrs Grey keep everything so clean and tidy?'

'No, she hasn't got time for that,' he said. 'We do it. That's part of the arrangement. She charges us minimal rent and we do the housekeeping. Even the cooking. It suits everyone. There's no way I could afford this sort of place otherwise.'

'Oh!' I was surprised, but somehow impressed. Mrs

Grey sounded like a lady who had her priorities sorted. I imagined her as a Cherie Blair look-a-like with a severe frown and exacting standards. Maybe there was something I could learn from her . . .? The essence of an idea for some tame house-boys of my own formed in the back of my mind, so I tucked it away for future reference and took a look around Sam's bedroom.

It was a large room, with lovely wide windows and a huge timber fireplace which had pastel-coloured tiles set either side of the Victorian cast-iron grate. The bed was at the opposite end of the room to the fireplace: high and wide, and very old-fashioned with its wrought iron curlicues and long well-stuffed bolster. Several books were stacked on the night-stand next to the bed, under a small Tiffany lamp.

The floorboards had been beautifully polished and there were shelves of the same pale timber in the alcoves either side of the fireplace. They were positively heaving with more books, as was the desk under one of the windows. Sam's lap-top was at one end of the desk, next to a sheaf of paper covered with his neat script. Apart from the rainbow spines of the books, the main colours in the room were cream and a deep sea-green, so the general effect was that of calm and order. Mrs Grey obviously believed in providing a serene environment for her 'boys'.

On the end of the bed was a black stetson hat. Grinning, I picked it up and perched it on my head.

'Hey,' I said. 'I remember, you told me you wanted to be a cowboy.'

'Yeah.' He grinned sheepishly. 'My dream job, but there isn't much call for them in this country, so I have to make do with studying agriculture.' The way he said it made it sound like he was definitely settling for second best.

'Can you ride a horse?'

'Hell, yes. I grew up in Hereford. There, if you can't

ride a horse, then they chase you out of town.' He laughed. 'I practically grew up in my dad's stables. Cattle and horses, that's my speciality.'

'Did you hunt?' I glanced sideways at him.

'Yeah.' He looked embarrassed. 'But I don't any more.'

'Oh.' I watched him fiddle with the lamp on his desk and fill the room with soft rosy light. He looked so young and so good-looking, I wanted to go over to him and put my arms round him. What are you waiting for then, Carrie? I asked myself. He thinks you're Dominique; he thinks you're in charge. So you can do whatever you like.

So I did. I placed the stetson squarely on his head and wound my arms round his neck. 'Would you be my cowboy for the night?' I asked, my mouth perilously close to his.

He rubbed my nose with his own. 'Why, yes, ma'am. Indeedy ah do.' He laughed, putting on a dreadful Texas accent. And sank his mouth to mine.

We kissed for a while, me with my hips pressed forward on to his so that I could feel the gorgeously tempting bulge of his cock against the fabric of my dress, and he pushed his tongue so far down my throat that I thought I might pass out with pleasure. He was an enthusiastic kisser. His lips slipped and slid across mine, making my heart beat faster and my arms wind tighter around him almost of their own accord.

The rim of the stetson gently pressed against my forehead and I grinned against his mouth: it was like being kissed by someone in *The High Chaparral*. Sam's hands slid to my bottom and he cupped my pert buttocks, squeezing them gently and making tiny circling movements with his thumbs. I groaned against his lips. Tingles of heat and electricity surged through my body, making me feel light-headed, and I slid out of his arms to take a breather. We had all night, after all.

'I'm hot and sticky and tired,' I sighed, stretching my arms above my head and watching his eyes follow the contour of my breasts. 'And my feet are aching.' I perched on the bed and eased my strappy sandals off my feet.

'Oh.' Sam was instantly all concern, dropping to his knees and cradling my feet with both of his big hands. 'Why don't we shower? Then I could cook us something proper to eat. And I could massage your feet, too, if you wanted.'

'Mmm, sounds appealing.' I smiled. 'I like the fact that you want to do the cooking.' I paused as a thought occurred to me. 'Um, Sam? You *can* cook, can't you?'

'Course I can!' He looked almost offended.

'Just so long as you're not planning cowboy beans and sausages over a Primus.' I laughed.

'No, ma'am. Ah'll cook you the best damn thing you've ever eaten.' His mouth twisted in a self-depracatingly grin. 'Probably.'

'What's that then?' I leaned back on my arms, feeling the soft bed squish comfortably under my hands.

'Tiger prawns,' Sam replied. 'In a hot Thai sauce, with saffron rice.'

'Oh, wow. I'm hungry already.' I was practically salivating just at the thought of it. Especially after I'd foregone my favourite Friday night treat of Indian take-out the evening before in honour of his nostrils. Thai food was a good runner-up, and if Sam was as decent a cook as he implied, well, I was just going to let him get on with it.

I wriggled my toes inside the warm curve of his fingers, then pressed my foot down on to the tempting bulge of his package under his denim flies. 'Shower with me?' I asked, arching one eyebrow provocatively.

His eyes sparkled as his gaze met mine and my tummy did a neat little backflip that had nothing to do with hunger and everything to do with desire for something more substantial than Sam's fingers in my pussy on the Embankment. 'Try and stop me,' he said.

He grabbed my hand and we tumbled down the stairs into the bathroom on the next floor. It was almost identical in layout to Sam's room: spacious and pale with a gorgeous fireplace. There was a large Victorian claw-footed bath set in the centre of the room, while a ceiling-mounted shower rose hung from the ornately plastered ceiling and a circular curtain drifted in snowy folds to the floor. The bath was large, almost certainly made for two, and I smiled as I let Sam's fingers wander down the fastening at the back of my dress and slowly, sensuously, unbutton me.

I felt the fabric whisper across my skin as he opened the dress, then his fingers feathered across my ribs and up my spine to the nape of my neck. I shivered with pleasure. Goosebumps trickled like a piece of cold ice along the hairs at the back of my neck. Then I felt Sam's warm lips. He pressed his mouth to my shoulders and then sank downwards, licking all the way down my spine to the crease of my bottom. He stayed there for a moment, both hands cupping the globes of my ass, while his tongue seared my skin as he tasted me.

'Lift your foot,' he whispered, laying his cheek against my bottom so that I could feel the flutter of his eyelashes against my skin. I obeyed, feeling the soft cotton of my dress slip beneath the soles of my feet. 'And the other one.'

He was kneeling behind me and I couldn't see him, but his fingers trailed a warm path up the backs of my calves and lingered for a moment on the tender dip at the backs of my knees. I shivered, feeling my nipples contract and pucker, and my stomach tighten at his caress. His breath felt warm on the backs of my thighs, and I sighed a little as he dipped his head forward and slipped his tongue lightly under the curved underside of my buttock where bottom becomes thigh.

After the lovely fingering he'd given me on the Embankment, I felt totally at home with Sam, totally trusting, as if I'd known him a lot longer than half a day. I murmured this to him, and he carried on gently stroking the curve of my buttocks, punctuating his words with light kisses.

'We've known each other for longer than that, though, haven't we?' he said. He kissed my butt cheek. Then another spine-tingling kiss, a little higher this time, the rim of the stetson pressing lightly a little further up my back. 'Think of all those in-depth chats we've had on the Internet.' Kiss. Smooth warm lips just brushing my spine. 'I know we only met a couple of weeks ago, but the intensity of things in chat rooms means that we know a lot about each other.' He paused, his lips still lightly brushing my skin while his hand followed my hips round to my front so he could run his fingers teasingly down over my belly. 'We've probably told each other things that we haven't told anyone else.' Kiss again, with a little tongue-tip softly touching the curve of one of my ribs. 'Private, deep stuff. The kind of stuff that you talk about when you've known someone for ages. When you're talking through a computer, and you can't see a person, then the communication is much more intense.' His fingertips stole down into my bush, softly probing. 'At least that's what it was like for me,' he finished. His voice was quiet and a little doubtful. Somehow vulnerable.

'It was for me too,' I reassured him, reaching behind and stroking his shoulder. His fingers stole deep into my glossy curls and I shivered and pressed my pubis forward to make it easier for him. I was swollen and wet still from his ministrations by the river: my sex desperate for his touch.

Turning, I let him bury his nose in my curls. He inhaled deeply, and I found that I couldn't see his face because of the rim of his hat, so I had to guess what he was thinking by the sound of his little sighs as he made himself comfortable on his knees and pressed his nose deep into my quim.

His thumbs stroked up my thighs and gently eased me apart. Everything about him was gentle, soft, eager to please. His mission seemed to be to do anything to make me happy: fingering me on the Embankment till I came; massaging my aching feet; kneeling in front of me ready to pleasure me with his tongue.

I sighed and let him do it, thinking how different he was from my ex-husband, whose mission in life had been to make me unhappy. With Patrick, the more I was snivelling and cringing the better. But with Sam, it was as if the more I was sighing and arching my back the better. It made a welcome change. I propped one leg on the curved side of the bath to open myself to Sam's searching mouth, and let him do whatever the hell he wanted.

He kneeled in front of me, all coiled muscles and suppressed power. His fingers slipped over my sex, easing and opening me as if I were a beautiful flower that he just had to see in full bloom. I bit my bottom lip as he paused, then I felt the wash of his flattened tongue as he licked me. Once. Then again. A full, long lick that started right under me and came upwards to linger on my swollen clit.

He lingered there, circling and lightly sucking, tasting me gently and then more deeply until his nose was pressed tight to my mons and I was full of his tongue, his lips pressed wide against my aching flesh and his tongue lapping at me with long, loud, noisy licks that proclaimed how wet I was, how aroused I was. I was creaming his nose and mouth like a fountain, positively gushing milk and honey from the depths of my hungry cunt while Sam nestled in between my legs and carefully slipped his forefinger up inside me.

'Oh yes!' I breathed, tilting my head back and pressing forward to his mouth.

I felt him smile against my pussy, then he delved in deeper, his finger rubbing my insides and rooting deep, seeking all the tenderest bits of me, all the ruched folds and little creases that held untold secrets of feminine pleasure. And all the while his tongue suckled and rubbed against my clit. Up and down. Circling. Round. Round. Eating me like he couldn't get enough.

The sensations that swirled around my body were bliss. I knew that I'd come if he carried on, but I didn't want to climax like that again. Not without him inside me. We'd already done fingers and mouth once, and this time I wanted to have his cock inside me. Feel him thrust. Sense the power that I knew was held in those lean, mean, boyish hips.

I pushed his head away.

'Not yet,' I whispered. 'I want us to come together.'

He stood up and wrapped his arms around me. We kissed deeply, his tongue pressing hungrily between my lips as if he wanted to lick all of the inside of my mouth as thoroughly as he'd just licked my sex. He tasted deliciously of me: sweet honey that had come from deep inside my body, coaxed out by a combination of his tongue and his fingers.

I entwined my arms around his neck and revelled in the feel of his soft hair – pushed down by his hat on to my forearms – and the smell of his hot male body as he pressed it close to mine. I suddenly had an intense desire to exploit that tiny flash of vulnerability I'd heard in his voice earlier. That little bit of doubt that told me he was unsure of himself around girls. I moved my lips away from his and cupped his face in my hands.

'Sam.'

'Yeah.'

'Undress for me. Now. And make it look good, no silly shilly-shallying: I want to see a *Full Monty*-style strip.'

He had the grace to blush – beautifully though – and the sight of his handsome face all pink and flustered made my heart beat a little faster. I grinned and nodded and flashed my eyes at him. 'Come on,' I said. 'I want to watch you take your clothes off.'

I leaned over and turned on the taps of the bath and put the plug in. A generous dollop of what was probably Mrs Grey's favourite Clinique bubble bath went into the gushing water, and I sank into the heat and bubbles. Then I lay back and prepared to watch the show. Sam, however, was still standing in his white T-shirt and jeans with the stetson still on his head. His long bare feet looking charmingly naked and vulnerable on the fluffy white bath mat. I flicked a hand at him and laughed as the droplets darkened the fabric of his faded jeans.

'Come on. I'm waiting, boy,' I said, putting on a mock-stern frown and hard voice. He seemed to like that, his blush deepening to his ears and the bulge in his flies visibly swelling as he slipped a hand round to pop the top button. 'That's better. Move, too. Dance for me.'

'But there's no music,' he protested, laughingly.

'Then play something in your head.' He mockingly rolled his eyes and then stared at me with an expression of half-hearted challenge. I raised an eyebrow and tried to look imperious. 'Go on! Do as I say, boy.'

Sam frowned hard, then acquiesced with a little twist of his lips that I thought was probably a grin. He looked very sweet, very young, and extremely embarrassed, but he still did as I said. He started to do a slow sway, his hips shifting from side to side and his cock pressing hard against the zip of his jeans as if it was planning to escape all on its own.

He jiggled and moved, jokily and suggestively at first, but then with greater concentration as he got into his routine. I watched him slip his unbuttoned jeans down over his hips, and then smiled as he turned neatly on the ball of his foot and stuck his arse out a little for me. He slid the jeans down over the crumpled cotton of his shorts. I watched, mesmerised, as he kicked off the jeans and stood tall and strong. He took the stetson off, dropped it beside the bath, paused for a moment, then ripped the white T-shirt off over his head in one movement.

He looked like a boy-band manager's wet dream: muscular and strong, with lean legs, a narrow, neat little bottom clad in white cotton, and broad shoulders that had been kissed to a pale freckled tan by the English summer. He nearly took my breath away. I wriggled in the warm bath water. Aware that the steam was making my hair kink and curl up at the ends, I slipped a trembling hand over my fringe to cover up my emotions.

I didn't feel as though I deserved this boy. I wasn't beautiful enough. He was too good for mousey Carrie, surely.

Sam turned around slowly and fixed his dark gaze on me. He silently, seriously, watched the tiny, tentative rubbing movement of my free hand over my pussy. His eyes were fixed, full of wonder tinged with desire, and I saw that I was more than good enough for him. I was a dream come true for him. To Sam, I was a thirty-year-old woman with great tits and ass who had come all the way to London to play Cowboys and Indians with him. He stared at me shyly, his chin lowered and his eyes full of emotion. I saw his hands twitch by his sides as if he was itching to come and place them on my body, on my breasts, anywhere.

He cleared his throat. 'Dominique?'

'Yes, boy?'

'You look so beautiful there, all hot and wet in the bath with your little tits poking through the bubbles.' He hooked one hand into the waistband of his shorts. 'Can I come in there too? Would you let me?'

I let him wait for a moment, enjoying the agony of suspense on his face.

'Maybe,' I murmured. 'But you need to be naked, Sam sweetheart, you can't get your shorts all wet.'

He blushed. Then, galvanised into action, tore off his shorts and threw them high in the air so that they flew across the steam-filled room and hooked on to a candle-stick that stood on the mantelpiece. Ever the cowboy, he gave a 'yee-ha!' and I let out a giggle as he took a run at the bath. He landed in on top of me with such a splash that most of the water sloshed over the edge and soaked into Mrs Grey's sumptuous white carpet. I threw back my head and laughed in the now near-empty bath as he fastened his teeth to my nipple, buoyed up by his sheer vigour and youth and zest for fun.

'Oh, God, Sam. You're one crazy cowboy.' I laughed, as he smoothed one hand over my left breast and pressed the other down between our bodies.

Then I forgot about laughing, because he slipped his finger into my creamy hole and I gasped and slid further down in the few remaining inches of warm water. My legs were cramped beneath his so I slid one up and over the edge of the bath and let it hang there, all dripping and silky smooth, while I urged him on with little whispers and endearments as he fingered my hungry sex.

'Oh yes, that feels good . . . Oh, Sam, yes . . . Up a bit, yes. Oh, Sam . . .'

He raised himself up and stared into my eyes. 'Tell me what you want me to do to you, ma'am.'

I thought for a moment.

'I want you to lie underneath me so that I can crouch over you. Queen you. Then you can bury your face in my pussy.'

'Yeah, yeah,' he breathed. 'I'd love you to sit on my face.'

'I want you to lick me until I'm nearly coming. Then I'm going to slide back, and sit down hard on your cock. I'll ride you like you're my rodeo horse.' I laughed lightly. 'Tonight I'm going to be the cowboy.' And I reached over the side of the bath and picked up the stetson. I perched it on the back of my head at a jaunty angle as I kissed Sam. He curved his body around mine and we swapped places. He lay back almost flat on the bottom of the bath, the warm water lapping at his short hair. I smiled down at him and slid forward so that I was squatting over his face, totally open to his mouth.

His tongue felt like silk against my aching clit. He rubbed and licked and smoothed me until I gasped and swore softly above him, my hair all in my face and my shoulders shaking. His hands stole up and caressed my tits, cupping and rubbing and then lightly squeezing at my nipples until they were heavy and full. I joined him, my hands tangling with his to guide him and stroke his fingers as he moulded my swollen breasts to fit into his warm palms.

His mouth felt soft against my sex, then firm, then licking and stroking deliciously so that my nerve-endings started to string out on a voltage-charged wire. I started to feel that familiar heavy, swollen sensation that told me I was going to come soon. But I wanted to feel his cock driving deep inside me when I climaxed, so I slid backwards away from his mouth and sat down hard, just as I'd promised I would, on his rigid, eager dick.

It was surprisingly difficult fucking in the bath. Cramped. But we managed it nicely. I tore the wrapper on a condom that I'd eased from the hip pocket of his jeans, then I wedged my feet either side of his waist. I sat down carefully on his cock, easing it up inside me with slow movements of my thighs. My knees were folded up to my chest, but squatting like that gave me greater purchase on the bottom of the bath-tub, and I could use my hands to get a good rhythm. I moved myself up and down his knob, sliding up so that I could see the shiny, hot tip and then lowering down hard to feel him fill me. He was thick and wide, and felt glorious when he was fully primed inside me.

Sweating slightly in the warmth of the steamy room, I moved faster, watching the shadows play across his face. I really liked the way his sleepy half-closed eyes fixed first on his own cock, then on my wide-open sex as my sheath swallowed his length. He gasped a little, breathing harder and faster as I coaxed him on. The room felt so hot. Taking a bath in mid-summer was probably madness, but the heat somehow added to all the delicious sensations that chased each other through my body.

'Rub me,' I whispered. 'Rub my clit like you did by the river.'

I arched my back and stared up at the ornate ceiling. My clit bulged and lengthened under his fingers, and my cunt felt blissfully good and full, so I rode my bucking rodeo horse harder until I felt the first tremblings of climax shudder down my spine. The high-voltage wire that had begun to string itself along my nerve endings suddenly crackled and flared and I gasped at the sudden electrifying response that I had to Sam's fingers.

'Oh, Sam, I'm coming. Oh yes. Oh please,' I murmured.

He thrust a little harder beneath me, his hips arching in the confines of the bath and thrusting his cock ever-deeper inside me. Strong, rhythmic fingers fretted at my clit, rubbing and pressing, around and around. I could hear gloriously sexy, squelching, fuck-noises that turned me on even more. Hot. Hard. Fiery. I gasped his name as I felt my orgasm rise through my trembling body.

I cried out as I came, my sex shuddering and rippling down the length of his cock. Sam's dick started to swell and throb inside me and I felt the hard, pumping jerk as he came.

'Oh yeah,' he muttered, closing his eyes and letting his head sink back against the pale enamel of the bath. 'Oh, Dominique, you're a born horsewoman.'

It was inevitable that we'd be discovered really. After all, we were in a house where four people came and went at will, and neither of us had bothered to lock the bathroom door.

But it still came as a shock.

Chapter Eight
two birds in the hand

Sitting in the bath, the soapy water lapped against the underside of my tits as Sam tipped a jug of warm water over my hair to rinse off the shampoo that he'd thoughtfully massaged into my scalp. He was kneeling behind me, and I could feel the occasional nudge of his soft penis against the small of my back. It felt nice, familiar and very comfortable sitting up in the bath being tended by my 'boy'.

The door opened and Alexander weaved a slightly drunken path to the toilet. I assumed it must be him because he was wearing a plaid shirt, ripped jeans and filthy boots: the uniform of the building site. He was half-way through pissing before he noticed he had an audience.

Sam cleared his throat lightly. Alex, startled, splashed the polished floorboards, then swore and finished off with a very red face.

'Sorry, man,' he said, buttoning up quickly. 'The door was open, you know.'

'It's OK.' Sam grinned. 'Just make sure you close it on the way out.'

I nudged him in the ribs and sat up a little further so

that my breasts were displayed to a better advantage. I, after all, had had an uninterrupted view of the penis that was now firmly lodged back inside Alex's jeans, and to me it was worth a second look.

'You must be Alexander,' I said, holding out my hand. Alex tore his gaze away from my tits and looked at my dripping fingers. He lurched forward, shook my hand and nodded dumbly. 'I'm Dominique,' I continued.

'Nice to meet you,' he mumbled. He blushed, a dusky pink spreading from inside the neck of his shirt and staining his roughly stubbled cheeks. He was covered in grime and dust. Short and thick-set, Alex had cropped sandy-coloured hair and a big nose which definitely supported the 'big-nose big-dick' theory. I kept a tight grip on his filthy, stubby fingers and pulled him slightly towards me.

'You look like you could do with a wash. Come and join us,' I said. Sam nudged me with his knee but I ignored him.

'Hey,' he whispered in my ear. I turned and speared him with a look.

'I'm in charge,' I pointed out. 'And I'm inviting Alex to join us in the bath.' I glanced at the bulging fly of Alex's jeans and grinned. 'Actually, I think he could use a cold shower, couldn't you, Alex?'

Alex looked at me and grinned back. But he still wasn't committing himself. I could see that I was going to have to tell him what to do. Quite funny, really, I thought. If I'd walked past his building site fully clothed, he'd have wolf-whistled merrily along with the rest of his hod-carrier mates. But give him a naked woman in a bath who's fairly gagging for it, and what does he do?

I beckoned him with a curving forefinger. 'Come here.' He did as he was told. I slid my hand over the bulge in his jeans and then met his gaze with mine. He mumbled something and I sighed with mock impatience. 'Come on, Alex. Anyone would think you were a virgin.'

That got him. He shot me a look and started to unbutton his jeans with hasty fingers. 'Get undressed. Sam'll shift up, won't you, Sam?'

'It doesn't look as though I have much choice,' grumbled my cowboy. I smiled and stood up, then gripped his hand and pulled him to his feet.

'No,' I said simply. 'You don't.'

Alex, despite his being three or four beers ahead of us and slightly unsteady on his feet, made pretty short work of his clothes. He was soon tightly squeezed into the shower in front of me. I pulled the curtain around and turned on the water and the three of us stood under the cool water, letting it smooth our limbs and cool down our hot bodies.

Sam played grumpy at first, declining to touch me if Alex's hand was anywhere near my skin, but I told him not to be so bloody silly and that if he wanted to please me, then he should get on with it. To be honest I think he was quite relieved – seeing as the other option was to get thrown out of the room – so soon I was directing a wonderful three-way stroking session whereby Alex slipped his work-roughened hands over my tits and belly, and Sam concentrated on my ass. I was able to tease Alex's mouth with the tip of my tongue while my fingers slid behind me to comfort Sam's belly and hips.

Warm fingers slipped easily across tender skin, smoothed by the rivulets of warm water that played over our bodies. I shivered, despite the warmth. My nipples were swollen and dark pink, like jelly sweets that just ached to be sucked and stroked. Locking eyes with Alex, I threaded my fingers between his and drew his hand up to my breast.

He was tantalisingly nervous, and so careful. It seemed as if he thought I'd break if he touched me too roughly, but roughly was how I wanted to be handled. So I put my hand over his and squeezed along with him, showing him how I wanted to be held. Eventually, he took over and cupped the mound of pale skin with one hand, tightening his fist until my aching flesh oozed out between his fingers. Then he dropped his mouth to my tit and sucked.

Electricity seemed to flow between my nipple and his mouth. Even when he eased off a little and just rimmed my areola with his tongue it was as if he had connected about a thousand volts to my nip. Sighing, and pressing back against Sam's hard young body, I let my eyes flutter shut and lifted my face to the stream of pure clean water that drenched us from above. Sam's arms wound around my waist, and his fingers burrowed into my wet pelt to find the warm, secret folds of my sex. Pliant and supple, I leaned further back, arching out towards his seeking hand and jutting my breast up to Alex's delicious, hungry, suckling mouth.

After a while, just playing and touching wasn't enough. And it was clear that there wasn't enough room in the shower for anything more than a bit of sucking and stroking. I washed Alex, lathering and soaping his stubby body until he was clean. He wasn't keen when I made Sam join in, and neither was Sam. They both eyed each other warily and only relaxed when they saw how badly I wanted to see them touch each other. But even then, Sam's hands stubbornly stayed confined to the other boy's back; so I made up for it by letting my hands dance across Alex's freckled skin, lingering at his belly, on his tangled knot of pubic hair, and on the strong root that jutted out and looked so tempting.

When Alex was scrubbed and shining we wrapped ourselves up in Mrs Grey's sumptuous white towels and giggled our way up the stairs to Sam's room. The air up there was less humid; the window was open and I could hear the drone of London traffic in the streets below, and smell the fetid scent of the river at low tide. Sam lit a candle and as he tossed the matches back in the drawer,

I saw an unopened box of twelve condoms. Grinning to myself, I rubbed my hair gently with one of the towels.

'So,' I said, glancing at their reflections in the mirror, 'do you two want to do each other while I watch?' Sam's horrified look made me laugh. 'It's OK,' I said. 'Joke. I want to be in the middle of it, anyway.' I kissed the tip of Sam's nose and circled Alex's wrist with one hand, pulling him closer. 'But I wouldn't want to be left out if you two developed a taste for that kind of thing.' I smoothed my tongue quickly over one of Alex's nipples and then looked up at him. 'What d'you want to do?' I asked.

He mumbled. Ever the man of many words. But I caught something about eating me for dinner, and it made my heart jump with excitement. I glanced at Sam. He seemed so turned on by the whole threesome thing that I think he would have said 'yes' to anything that I suggested. So I pushed him down on to the bed and kissed him hard.

'You're underneath for now,' I whispered. 'My naughty little boy.'

Sam kissed me back, his tongue seeking mine and his lips warm and soft and so malleable against my mouth. He tasted delicious, all clean and soapy with the merest hint of my juices still clinging to the soft young stubble that peppered his top lip. I sucked on his tongue and heard Alex sigh behind me.

'Sorry, Alex.' I laughed. 'Didn't mean to leave you out.' I gestured for him to lie down next to Sam. I got them to lie close, shoulder to manly shoulder, and I sat astride both of their waists. Stretching my legs wide, I leaned forward to kiss first one and then the other, swapping saliva, eating their tongues, tasting the difference in their mouths. The two boys were a dream come true: all damp hair and wet skin from the shower, and I could feel my juices swelling, creaming and flowing from deep inside me. A little patch of my milkiness slicked on Alex's hairy

105

stomach. Heat curled up from his body, and I could feel tentative hands slipping and smoothing over my hips, my bottom, my thighs.

We kissed until our mouths ached, and then I slid up Alex's body and turned around so that I could queen him. I was sitting over his face, looking down the gorgeous length of his firm, compact body to his dick, which was proud and hard and probably ready to burst. Grinning, I pulled Sam up so that he was kneeling next to Alex and I could bend forward and do what I'd been longing to do for what seemed like an age: I took his strong penis in my mouth. With my free hand I circled Alex's thick cock and slipped up and down it with a fist, wanking him. Not too hard, not too gentle. Just right.

So there I was, sitting neatly on Alex's face with my mouth full of Sam's cock, and my hand full of Alex's cock. Alex's tongue was a revelation: short and stubby, like his body. But so strong! He pressed his fingers into my creases, unfurling my sex and holding me wide open so that his mouth could dive in and eat me out. He flickered the tip of his tongue round my clit, pushing back my hood so that he could suck at the little nodule until I could hardly concentrate on the blow job I was trying to give Sam. I gasped and then sucked harder at Sam's cock.

Alex wriggled a little below me, his shoulders stretching my thighs so wide that I was nearly flat to his face. For a moment I thought I'd topple over, but Sam's strong hands came up and held me firmly in place. Then Alex started to slide his fingers into me. A little stubby forefinger, coarse from handling bricks and cement, rubbed and frigged at my tender sex. Then Alex plunged a second thick finger inside my sopping sex and I cried out. The sound that came from my mouth was a muffled 'mmff' that didn't sound at all like me, crammed as I was with Sam's finest.

Sam, meanwhile, was thrusting his hips at me. In the

mirror on the back of the door I could see the way his taut buttocks bunched up as he tightened and plunged forward against my face, pressing in hard and then withdrawing so that my lips were just lapping the tight, shiny tip of his shaft. On Sam's face – which I could only really see from the side – was a look of intense, blissful contentment and I redoubled my efforts, sucking harder until he closed his eyes and snapped his head back.

'Oh, Lord!' I heard him say.

The Lord was pretty much on the agenda for that night. Sam called on him several times as he came hard into the back of my throat. I gulped and slurped on my cowboy's sweet-salt come, revelling in the muscular pumping action of his magnificent cock. Then I sat down hard on Alex's face as those short stubby fingers worked their way deeper inside my slick creases. I tried to reciprocate the pleasure I was getting by leaning back a little and rubbing his cock. But I couldn't get the rhythm quite right as I was so intent on the way his tongue and fingers were hogging the limelight underneath me.

Sam, when he'd recovered, surprised me by seeing that my handiwork was being neglected. He quickly nudged my hand aside and palmed Alex's cock – unbeknownst to Alex who was nose deep in my sex – and jerked him off harder, faster, and far more expertly than I had done. I watched, absorbing the finer nuances of his wrist-action. When Alex came it was a hard, sharp thrusting of his spunk. It shot up in great globs of creamy white that pooled on his belly

I smiled at Sam. Our eyes locked. He raised his fingers to his lips and shook his head slightly and I nodded. We were the silent conspirators of Alex's climax. I wondered what the ultra-macho builder-boy would have said if he knew he'd just been tossed off by another man. Probably he'd have punched Sam. But then the narrow horizons of the hetero-male weren't my problem, so I simply swung my leg away over Alex's face and leaned down to press my hungry mouth to his.

'Mmm,' I whispered against his moist lips. 'You taste lovely. Of girl-juice.'

He laughed at that, and I arched like a cat as his work-roughened hands slid down my spine and he cupped my ass. Lifting me slightly, he curved his lips in a smile that seemed to be asking permission for something. I felt the hard rod of his dick against my inner thigh and raised my eyebrows.

'Surely you're not ready again?' I asked, teasing him with my eyes as I reached for the box of twelve rubbers in Sam's bedside table drawer.

'Sure am,' he murmured. 'Ready for you, anyway. A hand job is nothing compared to the feel of your fanny tight around my cock. And that's what I want to feel right now.'

He raised me up and placed me so that the plumpness of my sex-lips were poised over the curving bell of his glans. I sighed, and flexed my legs. Sinking slowly, inch by inch, down on that thick cock was instant bliss. I felt my heart swell and flutter inside my chest and I held my breath until I was all the way down. Sat all the way down on his cock so that my labia unfurled around the curly, stubbly hairs at the base, I could feel his root pressing against my clit.

'That looks so good,' whispered Sam. He was lying on his side next to us, his eyes fixed on my sex while he stroked his soft cock and nudged it back to life.

I controlled the movements for a little while, until my thigh muscles began to tire, then I felt Sam slide up the bed over Alex's legs and press me down so that I was lying on Alex with my toes curled against his ankles and my tight sheath still full of him. Sam stroked me, his warm fingers smoothing and massaging the small of my back, my thighs, my bottom.

I relaxed and rested my cheek on the curve of Alex's

neck, sighing softly as I tightened my muscles on to him. Behind me, Sam parted my buttocks and bent to kiss me, slicking his tongue across my cheeks and then slipping it neatly into my puckered little rose. I tensed for a moment, a little gasp escaping from my lips. But it felt so nice, so good, so right, that I let him lick me and rim me with his long tongue until I was open and desperate for him. Then he held me tight as he laid his warm body on top of me and eased himself gently inside my bottom.

'Oh, please, no,' I whispered, a tiny tear trembling at the corner of my eye. My whole body hurt as he pressed in. My bottom was on fire. I was being pressed wider than I was meant to go. I gasped and shut my eyes in protest: I was already full of cock. I had a pussy full of cock. Surely I couldn't take two?

But it seemed I could: I felt myself opening under the gentle but oh-so-insistent intrusion of Sam's erection. My anus was tense and tight, and it hurt.

'Oooh, oh, Sam,' I moaned, squeezing my eyelids tightly and pressing my face into Alex's comfortable neck. The boys whispered tenderly into my hair sweet nothings about how good it felt, how they wouldn't hurt me, how natural it was to be stretched, how much more pleasure we'd have . . .

Their hands cradled me, one boy above and one boy below, and I melted into the warmth of their gentle caresses as Sam slipped carefully all the way into my ass. I was full of cock.

My cunt swelled and opened and I began to move of my own accord as Alex slipped his hands down and cupped the front curve of my hips. Above me, Sam pushed and retreated. And pushed further in. Then retreated again. His penis curved up inside my bottom so wonderfully, filling me absolutely.

I wondered if Sam could feel Alex's sex through the slender film of skin that separated my cunt from my rectum. It certainly looked as though Alex could feel him.

He was staring up into Sam's face, his eyes wide and full of wonder, while above and behind me, Sam sighed and breathed into my neck and began to move against me with an insistent rhythm.

Mesmerised, I watched the different emotions play across Alex's face as we fucked. He had been taken by surprise by the pleasure he felt: not just the pleasure he was getting from me, but from the feel of Sam, too. Light and dark trembled in the shadows thrown by the candle, making Alex look in turns devilish and then vulnerable as I gazed at him. But then I lost all reason as I felt Sam begin to quiver inside me. His cock swelled and filled me almost too full. I was going to explode. I couldn't take any more. I was coming.

I cried out, shouting with the force of my climax as Sam grasped a handful of my hair and curved me backwards.

'Oh, yeah, Dominique. Come on me, baby. I can feel you. I can feel you so tight And quivering. Oh, Lord, I can't hold it much longer,' he muttered, his mouth tight to my ear. His hips ground hard against my ass as he came deep inside me, his come red-hot and pumping. I was still coming, my orgasm forced into a long, resounding echo that thrilled through my body and rippled the muscles in my pussy.

Alex must have felt it, must have held out for as long as he could against the rhythmic contractions of my tight cunt. But then I think he lost control, because he groaned and moved faster inside my sex, his thick cock swelling and thrusting and his hands suddenly shooting right around both my body and Sam's. He held us tight to him so that the breath was crushed from our bodies and we both groaned.

'Oh, God!' cried Alex. 'Oh fuck me. Oh, yes.'

His eyes fluttered shut and he came hard. An exploding volcano of molten lava that echoed for ever. Endlessly. Right up inside me. I gasped and sobbed against his chin and came again. Short sweet little clenches that rippled through my body down into my box. My nipples went rigid against the short red hairs on his chest and I wept while the boys cradled me in their arms.

Later, when Alex had gone back to his own room, Sam snuck down to the kitchen and came padding barefoot back up the stairs bearing a schoolboy-style midnight feast: slices of toast with honey, and two glasses of cold milk.

We sat cross-legged on the bed and shared the first piece of toast, Sam breaking bits off and feeding me between my mouthfuls of cold milk. With every brush of his forefinger against my lower lip, I could feel myself slowly become aroused again. Hot blood seemed to tingle through my limbs and warm me in most private parts of my body. At last, sated and full of honey toast, I pushed Sam back on the bed and sealed his mouth with my own.

'Close your eyes,' I murmured. 'You have to guess what I'm writing on your skin.' I dipped my finger in the little puddles of honey that glistened on the remaining piece of toast, and swept it across Sam's chest. Tilting my head to one side, I watched his smile widen as I curved and circled and wrote words on his warm skin.

'What does that say?' I asked, my voice soft and low.

'Do it again,' he said.

I used my tongue this time, dipping it to the sweet trail of honey and tracing over the words, licking and pausing in places, then sweeping over his skin. The honey accentuated the tender taste of his flesh. I circled his nipple to dot the 'i' and then sat back on my heels, my fingers curving under his balls and stroking softly as I watched his face.

'It's your name,' he said at last. 'Dominique.'

I smiled and nodded. 'Now you do it to me,' I said.

He pressed me back on to the bed, and cupped his hands softly around my breasts for a moment, nudging

111

my swollen nipples with the tip of his thumb. Then he dipped his fingers into the gleaming golden puddle of honey and touched very lightly by my belly button. I let my eyes flutter closed and concentrated on the soft swirls and light pressure as he slipped his sticky finger over my skin, his touch tantalisingly light and his face so close that I could feel his breath wash across my nipples.

I peeked through my eyelashes and smiled at the look on his face. His tongue was caught between his teeth and a tiny frown of concentration puckered the skin between his eyebrows. He caught me looking and smiled, shaking his head slightly. I closed my eyes again and let myself sink into the heady sensation of his feather-light touch.

'You are so sexy,' I said, laughing at last. Sam grinned.

'Thank you, ma'am,' he quipped.

'No!' I laughed again, feeling warm and comfortable and safe. 'That's what you've written!'

He sank his mouth to mine and kissed me deeply, his tongue riding over my palate and lingering in my mouth as he stroked my nipple with his thumb. His knee slipped between mine and I let my legs fall open, quivering a little as I felt the hardness of his ready erection press against the soft, warm skin of my thigh. 'You are,' he said at last, when he broke off our kiss and came up for air. 'That's what you are, so sexy.'

I curved my legs up around him and his cock slid easily into me. Our skin stuck together in patches with the honey, and Sam tangled his fingers into my hair. He ran his tongue lightly across my throat and whispered against my neck. 'There, we're stuck now. Stuck together.'

I didn't speak, just moved against him as his prick hardened off and lengthened inside me. My hands slipped down over his smooth back and I gripped his buttocks, pulling him into me and beginning to move slowly, sensuously, against him.

When he came, Sam gave a low, sweet groan that

encompassed passion, joy and release in one articulate sound. Then he slid slowly and languorously down my body to circle my clit with honey. He let his fingers curl and curve around, pressing and sliding across the tender little muscle. Then he began to lick the honey off until I came in little tight waves that reverberated through my body. I bit my lips hard to stop myself from crying out.

When we woke at dawn, I found myself curled into the crook of Sam's arm with my nose pressed gently against the sweet-smelling skin of his chest. I smoothed my hand over his stomach and gently stroked his sleeping penis.

'My name's not really Dominique, you know,' I murmured, my lips brushing his nipple.

'Really?' His voice was amused and he raised his head slightly to look at me. I met his gaze and saw laughter shining in his eyes. 'And there was me thinking that you were the real thing. A proper French dominatrix come across the Channel purely for my education in the ways of the flesh.'

I grinned and gave his penis a squeeze. 'Silly,' I said affectionately.

'So what's your real name?'

'Carrie.'

'Carrie.' He rolled it around his tongue, sucking and tasting my name in his mouth as if it was a piece of melting chocolate that made him feel really good. 'Carrie.'

'Yes.'

'I like that name. It suits you.'

I hadn't really thought of my name as suiting me before. It was just a name. Something – just about the only thing, in fact – that my parents had given me before they'd decided to reverse down an exit ramp of the M1 and kill my hopes of a happy-ever-after life. Sam saying such a nice thing made me feel all warm inside and I thought about the sound of my name and smiled. It was a comfortable name. I wondered whether his was really Sam.

He laughed. 'Course it is. Simple Sam, the Internet cowboy.'

'Yeeha! Come here and ride me again,' I said, laughing.

And he smacked my rump playfully, rolled me over, and pressed his body weight down on top of me until the breath was almost crushed from my body and I couldn't laugh any more.

At around 7 a.m., I was ravenously hungry so I bullied Sam into making me an early breakfast. Which was how I finally met Mrs Grey.

She strode into the breakfast room like a woman on a mission and didn't even bat an eyelid when she spotted me over by the window – dressed only in one of Sam's ubiquitous white T-shirts – with a mug of coffee in one hand and a *pain au chocolat* in the other.

I saw immediately why the boys loved living in her house: she was more Catherine Deneuve than Cherie Blair. Beautiful and willowy, with silver-blonde hair styled like a fifties starlet and a figure that presumably cut quite a dash in the courtroom. The boys were instantly at attention although I could have sworn they didn't appear to move a muscle: it was more of an increase of tension in their attitude, a metaphorical stiffening of spines around the sunlit room.

Mrs Grey didn't speak at first. She simply poured herself some tea, and patted Sam on the head as if he were an obedient dog. Then she favoured me with a lovely smile, murmured a few instructions to Alex, and was gone with hardly a backwards glance. After the warmth of that smile, I was almost disappointed when she left the house.

Chapter Nine
treat him like a lady

*A*fter all the real-life sex, I – along with my unused-to-all-the-action vagina – had seen enough friction for a few days. I was, therefore, quite eager to get back to my no-touch Internet buddies. But it was evening before I had a chance: Mondays at work were always hectic.

Don Richardson was on my back almost the minute I walked in through the doors, and I'd forgotten the lustful attentions of James. He somehow imagined that lodging himself at a computer table right next to me and wiggling his bottom at regular intervals was going to make me invite him into the toilets for a quickie.

I stared through him in what I hoped was an off-putting manner, but public schoolboys have notoriously thick skins and he merely grinned and wiggled some more. He was obviously going to hang around for the duration, so I had to forsake my idea of sitting at my computer and getting online at lunchtime.

To escape James, I took my sandwich outside and ate it sitting in the sun on a bench with a few hopeful gulls for company. The seat had a fine view of our car park and the city's municipal rubbish site. We had a very trendy new studio, but the downside of being trendy was that no one else had caught on yet. Also, someone had omitted to tell the council that to make the area more attractive to inward investors, the stinky dumpsters should be moved out of town.

When I got home at about seven, I threw my weekend washing into the machine and shoved a frozen pizza in the oven. I even thought about going for a run, but decided it was too hot, so actually ended up opening a bottle of wine and sitting in front of my computer for an hour. As if I don't do enough staring at the small screen at work, I thought, sipping the revoltingly unchilled Chardonnay and checking my e-mail.

There were two sweet ones from Sam, one from a girl in Nevada I'd got chatting to the previous week, and one from my tiresome brother reminding me of the date when I was next expected at his place for dinner.

Do I really have to go? I asked myself. How the month flies when your social life revolves around a fat banker and his perfect wife.

I dived into the chat site and scanned the names to see if there was anyone I fancied talking to.

Dominique: hey Alley Cat, how you doing?
Alley Cat: hi dominique, ain't seen u around here for a while.
Dominique: got me some real sex, lol, didn't need to come in for a few days!
Alley Cat: OIC!! only need us when ur short of shags?! Dang.
Dominique: you busy?
Alley Cat: Brown Eyes and me r just off to a private room. Shall I ask her if she minds u joining in?
Dominique: no, don't worry Al, I'll just cruise around for a bit.

I jumped from room to room, then saw a private message come up in red.

The Huntsman: want to be Red Riding Hood?
Dominique: do i know you?
The Huntsman: maybe . . .
Dominique: a/s/l?
The Huntsman: 35/m/here and there

I wasn't sure if I wanted to talk to him, but I knew I could always log off if I didn't like him.

Dominique: tell me about the "here and there".
The Huntsman: I move around with my work. I'm in London at the moment.
Dominique: England? I was in London this weekend, too! lol.

Was it only possible to bump into your own country-men here? Surely the rest of the world was Internet-friendly too. I sighed and watched, then cheered up a little when I saw what he typed.

The Huntsman: no, Miss British Empire! there are other countries in the world beside yours! I'm in London, Ontario.
Dominique: oh, lol!

Sassy. I liked that. Miss British Empire, indeed. I wondered what he looked like, but then thought that after Sam anything would be bound to be a disappointment, so I didn't ask him to send a photo.

The Huntsman: so, Little Englander, want to get your red cape on and come into the forest with me?
Dominique: hm, maybe. Only if you promise to leave that great big axe behind.
The Huntsman: can't do that, Miss, might run into some big bad wolves out there . . .

Dominique: well, I don't need protecting, thank you very much!

The Huntsman: sure you do. Even clever girls are at risk from big bad wolves.

Dominique: i'm not afraid of them.

The Huntsman: maybe you should be. Sometimes. The Internet's a dark forest full of wolves, lol. I think you need my protection.

He seemed like a nice guy, with a sense of humour. I let him know we could go private and he named the room 'The Forest'. When we were in there, he didn't waste any time, and I was quickly pressed up against a convenient tree. I soon had my knickers around my ankles, and my red cape flipped back over my shoulders to reveal what he called my 'proud little titties'. I had forgotten how to be the sub, and started to fight back.

The Huntsman: hey, relax, Miss England. I'm not going to hurt you.

Dominique: but you're taking over!

The Huntsman: i don't mean to. Sorry. I'm not used to strident females, lol.

Dominique: I am NOT strident! I just don't want you calling all the shots.

The Huntsman: ok, lol, okay! Have you got red hair to go with that red riding hood by any chance?

Dominique: why?

The Huntsman: just wondered, you're being so feisty, and that usually goes with red hair, doesn't it?

Dominique: hmmmmm, interesting theory.

I stood up for a moment and glanced at my hair in the mirror over the mantelpiece. Had I changed when Laura had put a stronger colour into my hair? Or had it begun earlier than that when I'd first discovered being

Dominique meant that I could take charge a little more? Or was it all just psychological bullshit that gave a reason for my sudden change in behaviour? Who knew?

And who cared? Right now, I had a fight on my hands with the Huntsman, and I wasn't going to let him win.

I started chatting regularly with the Huntsman after that. He hadn't let me win in the forest, but actually I hadn't minded losing all that much. After my weekend with Sam and Alexander, it had been quite fun to let someone else call the shots, and the Huntsman had given me a fabulous time. I'd even masturbated while I read what he wanted to do to me with the smooth, rounded handle of his axe.

We exchanged e-mail addresses – his was a web-based addy which made him a little more anonymous than I would have liked – and soon I was getting a little buzz of adrenalin every time I opened my mailbox and saw that I had mail from him. He was strong, but fair, and he started letting me win a little bit after a few days, and somehow it seemed to mean more to dominate a man who I knew was as strong as I was.

Meanwhile, my little housekeeping problem didn't go away. About three days after I got back from London, I thought a little bit more about the idea that I had got from observing the relationship between Mrs Grey and the London boys.

'Hi, Laura.' I made the call at work, so I had to lean forward in my chair and rest my forehead on my hand so that I didn't have to keep looking at James's hopeful face.

'Carrie, you baggage, why haven't you called me before with the details?'

Laura was miffed that I hadn't regaled her with a suck by blow account of my weekend. I grinned and we made a date for curry and wine, then she moaned for a while about the logistics of moving into Tom's place that weekend. She mentioned that her cousin was still looking for a place to move to, so I dropped my idea casually into the conversation.

'I wondered if Gabriel wanted to come and lodge with me?'

'Oh, Christ, Carrie. You don't want him hanging around the place.'

'Why not?'

'He'd drive you potty.' Her laughter was tinged with audible frustration. 'It's amazing how quickly your opinion of someone can change. You can be very fond of your relatives when you only have to see them three times a year. But when you have to actually live with them, then the so-called "endearing little traits" that your Auntie May refers to with such beaming maternal pride actually drive you up the wall.'

'Oh? What traits d'you mean?'

'He is *sooo* wet under that moody James Dean act. Doesn't say boo to a goose. And so bloody tidy. It's worse than living with my mother.'

I smiled. Gabriel sounded perfect for a tame houseboy.

'Sounds OK to me. Better than having a slob leaving a mess around the place,' I murmured tentatively.

'Hm. Don't you believe it. Living with someone who spends half their time tidying up just irritates me so much that I want to scream. If I see him even glance towards the dustpan and brush it puts me on edge. I can't relax in my own home, Carrie! I'm terrified to even put down a coffee mug before I've finished it in case it mysteriously disappears. And the boy washes up so often I'm terrified that his hands will dissolve –'

Laura was silent for a moment. I could almost hear the cogs whirring as she thought about what she'd just said. 'On second thoughts,' she laughed, 'he would be the ideal lodger for you, Carrie. You can have him.

120

A house-trained teenager that can pick up after you. Superb!'

Max phoned to tell me that he was going away for a while; he had some meetings that Leon had set up for him: one at home in New Mexico and one in Brussels. He wanted to take me out at the weekend, but I put him off. I was so busy with the Huntsman, and my twice-weekly phone-sex with Sam, that I didn't have time for him at the moment. And the weekend was the allotted time for the arrival of the angel Gabriel.

As it was, I could have gone out with Max. I hardly even noticed that Gabe was there the first day: he disappeared into his room and only came out for a clean duster and a sandwich at midday. I went for a run on Sunday and then for a swim at the pool, and by the time I came back late afternoon, he'd been through my house with the zeal of a religious maniac.

I was impressed, but decided not to show it. Instead I stood by the fireplace and ran my fingertip along the surface of the mantel as if expecting to collect dust on it.

'What d'you think you're doing, Gabriel?' I demanded.

He flipped off the television and frowned sulkily at the carpet. His cheeks flushed pink and I bit my lips together to suppress a smile at his obvious discomfort. 'Exactly *why* have you cleaned my house?' I made my voice as stern as possible.

'Mrs Horton. I – I –' He fiddled with the remote control, dropped it, and thrust a hand through his beautiful curls. 'Um – Laura said you might –'

'Laura said?' I barked. 'From now on you do as *I* say, not what Laura says.'

He nodded and met my gaze for the first time since I'd given him his front-door key.

'OK,' he whispered. And I was blown away by the direct simplicity in his ocean-blue eyes. He was positively angelic-looking: all soft, blond ringlets and long lashes.

And by the trembling of his plump, pink bottom lip, he was going to be putty in my hands.

I sat down next to him, took his warm, soft fingers in mine and patted them lightly. He didn't flinch, or move it away, even when I stroked my thumb around the tender creases of his wrist. He simply sat in silence, not moving, not speaking, and let me talk him through the ground rules of his new rent-free status in my house.

'Thank you,' he said, when I'd finished. Then I let him kiss my hand like a good boy should, and he went up to his room with a tent in the front of his loose trousers that showed he was just as happy with our slightly irregular living arrangements as I was. The thought of him jerking off into his pristine white bed linen made me have an early night with my latest sexy novel and my smooth dildo – I didn't dare use the vibrator in case he heard me.

By the following weekend, I thought Gabriel and I had settled down quite nicely together. He appeared to like living with me, even seemed to enjoy keeping the place tidy – and I certainly enjoyed the sight of his taut little bottom sashaying around the house as he mopped and dusted and straightened the cushions.

Things took an interesting turn, though, on the Saturday night.

Gabriel went out with some of his new friends and I surfed a few hard-core porn sites that the Huntsman had told me about. At about eleven, I heard the front door slam and Gabriel came to stand in the centre of the room. I ignored him and carried on clicking and frowning at the computer. He cleared his throat and I lifted my head, pretending to notice him for the first time. He was wearing a dark shirt that emphasised his pallor, and a pair of clean black jeans. His long limbs looked like a pile of pick-up sticks that had been casually propped in my doorway.

'Hello. Had a nice time?' I swivelled around in my seat to get a better look at him. He was frowning moodily at the back of my chair with a look of fierce decisiveness in his eyes. I raised one eyebrow and prompted him. 'Want to share it with me?'

'This isn't going to work out. Me living here, I mean,' he stated. My mouth fell open and I stared at him.

'Why not?' I asked, when I finally found my voice.

'Because . . .'

He shuffled his feet and then twisted his hands together, the picture of youthful awkwardness. Concerned, I stood up and went over to stand in front of him. He stared at the floor, and then fell to his knees in front of me and wrapped his hands around my ankles. I was wearing a new pair of strappy sandals that I was rather pleased with, a red silky skirt and a tiny white vest. He glanced up at me, letting his eyes cover every curve of my body – which had the sudden effect of making me feel so desirable that my nipples stuck out like corks in spite of the heat – and then closed his eyes as if praying.

'Because?' I prompted gently.

His fingers made tiny circling motions on my ankle bones and I shivered. This wasn't part of the plan, surely. I couldn't be seduced by my own houseboy. I waited for a moment and then nudged his long pale fingers gently with my foot.

'It's not going to work out,' he repeated. 'It's too frustrating living with you. I want you to do things to me, Mrs Horton. And you probably wouldn't even consider doing them. You think I'm just a kid. And you think that because I'm just a kid, I'm no good. I'm worthless. Not worthy of you.'

I gaped and then shut my mouth with a click in case he caught me looking like a landed fish again. What on earth was he talking about?

'You've lost me, Gabe,' I said softly, staring down at

the blond crown of his head and the riot of soft ringlets that curled there. It's like having Little Lord Fauntleroy kneeling at my feet, I thought, with a little flutter of pleasure stirring inside my stomach.

He sat back on his heels and frowned up at me. 'When I first met you, at Laura's, I thought you'd take me in hand. You seemed so in control. So . . . mysterious . . . so much older than me. I wanted you to take care of me and sort me out.' He bit his lip and dropped his gaze from mine.

I marvelled. Me? In control? It's amazing how different other people's opinions are of us, isn't it? I thought.

I prompted him some more: 'So what's the problem?'

'Well, I've been here for a week, and all you do is flirt with other blokes in chat rooms and on the phone. You don't even look at me.'

'I'm not supposed to look at you, Gabriel,' I pointed out with a smile. 'You're my lodger.'

'I don't care about that,' he pouted, a sulky look spreading over his pretty features. 'I just want you to talk to me the way I've heard you talk to those other blokes.' His fingers touched the tips of my toes, softly and gently like wind-tossed feathers dipping lightly down to earth. 'I want you to teach me things – make me do things. Like you make them do things.'

I tried to keep my excited breathing steady and regular. Oh, this was beautiful. This was perfect. It was so funny, too: my houseboy not only wanted to wash my dishes, but he wanted me to play with him as well. What was I going to do about it? Because after all, I was the oldest, the one in charge, so I had to run this show. And I wasn't sure whether I could do that yet.

Then an image of Laura's horrified face filtered through my mind and I realised that there was more at stake here than a quick bit of naughty business with Gabriel. I couldn't let this go too far, or I'd lose my best

124

friend. But maybe, if I played it right and pretended to him that I really was as in control as he thought I was, my lodger and I could have some fun and just not tell anyone. Couldn't we? I frowned as I thought for a moment about the way that Dominique would talk if she were real.

'Gabriel,' I said at last, in as stern a voice as I could muster. 'It seems you've been prying into my private life a little bit more than you should be, haven't you?'

'Yes,' he murmured. 'But it's only because . . . because . . . I like you.'

'You like me. How sweet.' I grinned to myself, and then composed my face before he saw me. 'How much do you like me, Gabriel?'

He tipped his head back and gazed at me, the sulky look receding to be replaced by something slightly sunnier. 'A lot, Mrs Horton. You make me feel all knotty inside.'

'Good. Then let's keep it that way. But in the meantime I think you have to pay a forfeit for being so nosy.'

'Like a punishment, you mean?'

'Yes, Gabriel.' I smiled and saw my own smile reflected in his face. 'A punishment.'

He dipped his head down and I felt him kiss my toes. His lips felt soft and warm against my skin and I shivered and wrapped my arms around my chest to stop myself from reaching down and grabbing hold of him. His fingers trailed a delicious line around the heels of my strappy sandals, and I waited breathlessly as he simultaneously mouthed at the rounded tip of my big toe and stroked my neat ankles with his long, lithe fingers. I trembled above him, trying to hold on to my sanity as my pulse ricocheted. I felt sexy and dangerous and slightly out of control of my emotions.

'I'll let you choose your punishment,' I said presently, when I regained my equilibrium a little. 'Perhaps you'd like me to make you do some horrible job around the house? Naked?'

He shook his head.

'No? OK. What about if I spanked your naughty little bottom?'

His tongue worked harder at my feet, trailing a delicious line of warm saliva up over the arch of my foot until he was kissing my ankles.

'Hm,' I said thoughtfully, propping one hand on my hip. 'Maybe I'll save that for a day when you've been a really, *really* bad boy. I think, for now, your punishment should be my gain. I think that you should just continue what you're doing.' He nestled in closer to my feet. 'But don't stop there. Kiss my knees . . .'

He obeyed. I shivered with delight. My skin quivered under his mouth and I could feel a flutter of sexual pleasure in my stomach that promised to grow into something much grander, more turbulent, more all-consuming. I wondered briefly whether Mrs Grey had her houseboys quite as well trained as I had mine and made myself a mental note to quiz Sam about it when he next telephoned. The thought of Sam on his knees before the elegant and very beautiful high court judge made me juice up suddenly. I squeezed the muscles of my sex tightly and shivered again. I realised that I'd just hit on a very satisfactory masturbation fantasy, and I filed it away for future use.

But in the here and now, Gabriel's angelic touch had suddenly hit that tender spot that I love at the back of my knees, and his forefinger was tracing a delicious pattern around the tendons there. I watched him for a moment through drowsily lowered lashes, thinking hard of the possible consequences of what we were doing. Basically, I decided, there were none. We were both adults. We both possessed free will. If we wanted to do this – and judging by the rampant bulge in Gabe's jeans

126

at least one of us was champing at the bit – then we could jolly well do it.

But there had to be ground rules and I had to set them. I reached down and cupped Gabriel's pale face in my hand, forcing him to look at me.

'Gabriel,' I murmured. He widened his eyes and his hands at the back of my knees fluttered still. 'Three points to remember: number one, I am not your girlfriend: we both just happen to share a house and that's all. No ties, OK? This ends when one or other of us wants it to end.' He was silent for a moment, thinking. Then he nodded, so I continued. 'Number two, no penetrative sex. Never. Ever.' He looked as sulky as hell at that one, so I lightened it a little for him. 'That doesn't mean we can't have fun. As much fun as we want. But no penetration. It's not to do with you and me: it's to do with me and Laura.' I smiled. 'She'd kill me. And then you'd be homeless. So it isn't a good idea.'

'No,' he conceded in a soft voice. 'I think you're right.'

'I know I'm right.' I stroked his face. 'And, as far as you're concerned, I'm *always* right.'

I watched the expressions chase themselves across his face, and smiled at him.

'What's number three?' he asked after a while. I frowned thoughtfully.

'I don't know,' I said. 'But when I do, I'll let you know. It's always a good idea to have something in reserve, don't you think?'

Gabriel made a comical face, turning the edges of his lips down in an exaggerated sad-clown fashion. 'OK,' he said. 'You make the rules around here. What I think doesn't come into it.'

'And you love that, don't you?' I raised an eyebrow and ran my fingers from the corner of his silky blond brow down the side of his face to the open collar of his soft cotton shirt. He shivered, nodded, and I felt him tentatively finger the hem of my skirt. He didn't speak, though, and I was impressed, he certainly knew how to ask without words.

'Right, back to your punishment, Gabriel,' I said. 'And your education, too.'

'Yes, Mrs Horton.'

'I'm going to teach you how to make a girl happy. And the punishment part of it will be the amount of time you spend on your knees,' I said with a grin. 'Because sometimes making girls happy takes a very, very long time.'

'Show me,' he said softly, his eyes wide and innocent. 'Show me. Punish me. For as long as you want.'

So I did. I taught him how to slide my skirt up over my hips and how to finger the gusset of my knickers to one side. I taught him how to lick, gently as a little cat, at the tiny peeking clitoris that nestled in the soft folds of my skin. I showed him how to ease back the pink hood that covered the ridge of my clit and lick it all around, firmer and firmer. I guided him as he learned how to slip one long forefinger inside my wetness. Then two. Then a third when I was really hot and ready.

I murmured encouragement as he crept closer in between my thighs and ate my pussy with long, hard licks and little suckling, gobbling noises. He moved his fingers rhythmically, first slow, then faster, faster in time to my excited breathing. The sensation I got from peeking through my lashes at his blond head buried between my thighs was one that sent me ever closer to my climax. My thighs trembled. My hips shook. My fingers feathered over the back of his head. I rubbed my own nipples, circling and pinching and stirring myself up until I arched up towards Gabriel's mouth. And finally I sighed with pleasure and let my body succumb as he slipped his whole, narrow hand inside my wide-stretched juicy sex and brought me off in a gasping, whirling, sopping shout of joy.

It was the best night I'd had since he'd come to live under my roof, and when I sent him to his room at 3 a.m., I curled up in my bed and slept a deep, dreamless sleep. Who says there's no rest for the wicked?

Chapter Ten
something for the weekend

*A*fter that, I was so busy that my feet hardly touched the ground. At work we were busy on some hideously complicated project for a big aerospace company. This involved James and I working at close quarters, which unfortunately he took rather literally. He ended up moving his desk so close to mine that he was almost sitting in my lap every day.

At home I had the angel Gabriel hanging on my every word and licking me to orgasm whenever I felt the need. And on the net I had Sam sending me sexy e-mails while the Huntsman put in the occasional appearance in our chat room. My life seemed complete.

After we'd been chatting for a while and we'd begun to trust each other, I asked the Huntsman where he'd learned some of the stuff he dreamed up when we had Internet sex. What he told me sent a shiver of excitement up my spine. Apparently he had a group of friends who used the Internet solely to link up for sex. They regularly met in unusual places to satisfy their hunger for the unusual and often downright bizarre. Sometimes they had fetish parties. Sometimes they split up into smaller groups. Sometimes they just hired a nightclub and danced all night. I was intrigued: it sounded like total freedom to be who you wanted to be with a lot of other people who enjoyed the same thing.

When September came and the temperature cooled off a little, I decided that I really needed a break. A weekend away. It was becoming increasingly difficult to behave like the old mousey Carrie at Richardson's. So when the Huntsman suggested meeting up with some of his friends, I jumped at the chance.

But not too eagerly.

Dominique: well, I don't know. I hardly know you.
The Huntsman: I'm not asking you to meet up with ME. I'm asking if you fancied a drink with some of my friends.
Dominique: how do i know they're aren't weirdos?
The Huntsman: well, I'm not, am I? so why should they be?
Dominique: well, i don't know. I don't know you at all, really. Its one thing to chat here, but meeting up in RL . . .
The Huntsman: you can bring someone if it makes you feel easier.
Dominique: I haven't even decided whether i want to come at all yet, so don't you go inviting my friends.
The Huntsman: . . . just trying to make it more comfortable for you. You said you needed a break. why not have a weekend away? No commitments. If you meet with some people and you don't like them, then you can just walk away. And if you're with a friend it makes leaving easier.
Dominique: I'll think about it. Anyway, have to go now.
The Huntsman: ok. well, mail me. I'll be out of town for a day or two but you can leave mail. I'll reply as soon as I'm back. Bye.

He was gone before I could even say OK. And that was when I really realised that I knew nothing whatsoever about this guy. What he did. Where he worked. Even where he really lived, because after all, you can tell people what you like on the net; and he might have never even laid eyes on London, Ontario, much less lived there.

The morning after our chat, I rode into work on the train, deep in thought, and nearly missed my stop.

At lunchtime I rang Eva – after all she was the one who got me into this – and asked her to meet me for food and a drink. The food would be for me, obviously, since she never ate anything unless it was crisp and green with virtually zero calories. She made noises about it not being convenient and 'couldn't we just leave it until our Friday dinner', but I insisted. I didn't want Leon hearing one word of what I wanted to talk to Eva about.

Eventually, she relented and chose a swanky new place in the centre of Bath that served fresh sushi and little else. I poured from a huge jug of chilled wine spritzer and smiled at her across the table.

'So, where are you meeting?' she asked.

'I haven't said that I will, yet.' I took a bite of something wrapped in seaweed and chewed thoughtfully. 'It's just an idea.'

'Well,' she shrugged her narrow shoulders, 'you did OK with that Sam guy, didn't you?'

I nodded. 'Yes, but this is *two* guys. I wonder if it's something a bit weird.'

'Carrie.' She leaned forward and I dragged my gaze away from her notchy sternum that supported two of the firmest – and most publicly on view – tits. 'You won't know until you've tried. And anyway –' she sipped her wine and left a mulberry lipstick stain on the glass '– you might like weird. There's nothing wrong with weird, believe me.'

That night, I spent my first evening alone in the house since Gabriel had moved in. There was a £1-a-pint promotion at the student union bar so Gabe and his mates

132

had jumped at the chance to get legless on a tenner. I was doing my stretches after a punishing run when the phone rang.

'Carrie, it's Max.'

My heart gave an involuntary little flutter at the sound of his deep, rich voice and I grinned into the phone.

'Hi, Max. God, it's been ages. Where've you been?'

'I had to go back to the States for a few meetings. And then your brother got me all tied up with a darn conference in Brussels, so I haven't been around much over the past ten days. I'm sorry if you think I'm neglecting you.'

'No!' I laughed. 'Why on earth would I think that? It's not like we're an item, Max. We both have busy lives.'

'Yeah, especially you.' He chuckled. 'Your phone's always engaged. You still doing that crazy chat-room thing?'

'Sometimes.' I was guarded. I really had no desire to blur the lines between the two lives that I was developing.

'Well, have you got a window in your hectic schedule for me?' I could almost hear him grinning. 'You know I'm not going to hang up the phone until I've persuaded you to say yes.'

I let him stew for a bit as he tried to wangle a date out of me. I listened to him telling me how small the leg room was on trans-Atlantic flights, how boring financiers were, and how the thing that he most wanted at the moment was to take me out for a meal.

I was tempted, but somehow real-life dates seemed dull when I had the Huntsman intriguing me at every turn, and Gabriel quivering in his boots whenever I brushed past him in my skimpy summer dresses. Eventually I saw a compromise, a way that Max could fulfil his wish of seeing me, and I could make more palatable an evening that held less and less charm the nearer it got.

'Come with me to Leon and Eva's on Friday,' I suggested. 'I've got to go anyway, and with you there it might actually be a pleasurable experience.'

I laughed happily as he grudgingly said yes, and then rang off.

I like Max, I thought, smiling to myself as I unplugged the phone and checked my e-mail.

Girl in a red hood,
Re: what you said about meeting up with some of my friends. Well, I've been thinking. Personally I think it'd all be too much for you, you probably aren't up to it yet . . .
regards, H.

Aren't up to it yet? Damn cheek of the man! I frowned through the rest of my mail and then went back to the one from the Huntsman. I clicked on reply and penned something to send back.

Dearest man with an axe to grind,
ha ha ha re: me not being up to it. I think you said that on purpose as you KNOW I can't resist a challenge. Name the place and time.
Dominique xxxxxxxxxx

I sent it, and then surfed the chat rooms for a bit. There was mail for me again within ten minutes:

Red,
I love it when you act all tough. Inside I just know you are quivering with desire and softness. Submit to me while there's still a chance.
regards, H.
PS: name a city/town.

I shot back with:

You tell me a city/town. Where do they usually meet?

He left me dangling till the next day, but when I accessed my mail at work I found something from Sam, too.

Carrie. Cowboy needs to meet up in RL. Can you ride? Sam xxxxx

I laughed and sent him something placatory, then opened the Huntsman's mail.

Girl in a Red Hood,
I've heard Bournemouth is nice at this time of year. Shoemaker will measure you for new boots and Virgin will lead you into temptation.
regards, H

My pulse ricocheted around in my wrists as I stared at the e-mail and read the date, time and the name of the bar where I'd meet these strangers. This was what I wanted, wasn't it? But now that it was a definite date, I was torn between elation and fear.

Damn, I thought desperately, what do I do now? Do I go? Are they weirdos? What if I'm kidnapped and never seen again? Then again, what if I have such a great time that I don't want to come home? Frowning, I closed my mailbox and tried to get on with my work.

My brain was buzzing, and little quivers of adrenalin kept thudding in the pit of my stomach every time I thought about the last e-mail from the Huntsman. The Bournemouth invitation niggled and nagged at me, getting in the way of my work, until I decided that the best thing to do would be to do exactly as the Huntsman had suggested: take someone with me.

Dear Sam,
Hi. Sorry I left you hanging for a bit, its been a hectic

week. How would you like a weekend in Bournemouth?
Tick yes or no.
Carrie xxxxxx

He'd replied by the time I got home and plugged in
that evening. I smiled at his short but sweetly simple
affirmative and started to make plans for a late summer
weekend in a seaside town.

Friday came far too soon. Max arrived to pick me up and
I experienced a hot rush of pleasure when I opened the
door and saw his dark, unruly hair and the friendly grey
of his eyes.

'Hi.' He grinned.

'Hi yourself.' I mentally kicked myself – was I destined
to be forever the Queen of the Inane Reply? 'You look
nice. All dressed up.'

He'd put on dark, smooth-fronted trousers and a pale
cotton shirt that enhanced his eyes. A jacket was slung
casually over one shoulder and the stretched-up arm that
had hooked it there with a single finger was strong and
powerful, his biceps bulging against the fine stitching of
his shirt sleeve.

'So are you.' He smiled, his eyes running appreciatively up and down the green silk dress and short, trendy
coat that I'd put on. I raised an eyebrow and stopped
myself from doing a little twirl. I grinned, grabbed my
little velvet bag and slammed the door behind me.

Leon was just mixing drinks when we arrived and I
chose a Bacardi and coke while Max declined alcohol
because he was driving. This led us into a debate – or
rather a lecture from Leon – about the uselessness of taxi
companies to get you where you wanted on time so that
you could drink until you fell down.

I sat in my chair, idly twisting the glass in my hand,
not really listening. Eva was nowhere to be seen and the
house was strangely silent apart from the muted strains

of Wagner that Leon had turned down as we entered the sitting room.

By the time dinner was served by their maid Marie-Therese – a beautiful teenager who wore a severe black dress and an irritated expression – I was beginning to think that Eva had done a bunk. But she swept into the room just as Leon was urging us to start our soup.

'Sorry,' she breathed. 'Just couldn't get my hair right.'

It was a lame excuse. And an obvious lie because her hair was as immaculate as ever. Smooth, sleek and looking much like it had been painted on to her head with ebony gloss.

She flicked a look at me and I caught the expression in her eyes: alert, excited, and somehow terrifying. She also looked a lot like someone who'd just been fucked in an extremely satisfactory way by a person who knew very much what they were doing. A quick glance at Leon's bland and pudgy countenance told me that he wasn't the person in question.

Ten minutes later, when we'd finished the soup and the bad-tempered Marie-Therese was clattering fresh plates down in front of us, I heard the front door being quietly closed. It seemed that no one else did, or if they did they chose to play deaf. The only hint that anyone else was aware that an unknown person, or persons plural, had left the house was the slight pink flush that stained Eva's cheeks.

Leon was impassive and completely immobile, his gaze fixed on Marie-Therese's shapely bottom, while Max simply leaned back in his chair and watched as the garlic roast chicken steamed gently in the middle of the vast table.

The food was delicious, and the wine flowed smoothly as it always did at Leon's, but I was glad when I was sitting outside the house in Max's rented Mercedes. He'd parked it on the gravel sweep that curved around the house. I took a deep breath and slid the window open to blow the heavy scent of Eva's perfume from my nostrils. Hooking my hair behind my ears, I glanced sideways at Max. He was watching me, his face interested and open.

'Why do you keep coming here, Carrie?' he asked, propping a cigarette in the corner of his mouth but not lighting it. 'These visits are obviously hell for you. Why do you put yourself through it?'

'I don't know really.' I picked at the hem of my dress. 'Habit, I suppose. And Leon's the only family I have now.'

'But you don't have to do it,' murmured Max, his fingers smoothing the curved metal edges of his Zippo. 'A lot of people choose to make new families. Families that they like being with, instead of ones that it's torture to stay with.'

I looked across at him, tracing the line of his strong straight nose with my eyes.

'Make a new family?' I asked. 'How can you do that? Who with?'

'Friends. People you meet who you know are like you,' he said. 'Kindred spirits, although that sounds darn corny. You know –' he flipped the lighter open and the smell of petrol filled the close air of the car, intense and somehow comforting '– when you meet someone. And things just click. You can choose your friends, any time, and they'll always be there for you. But family.' He lit his cigarette and drew a long drag of smoke down into his lungs. 'Family. Who needs them?'

'You sound like me on a really bad day,' I laughed softly in the dim light that glowed from the tip of the cigarette. 'What happened to your family to make you so disillusioned?'

'Religion happened,' he said simply. 'And I don't mean the real stuff. I mean cult stuff that eats your brains and empties your darn bank accounts. I stood it for most of my childhood, but when I turned sixteen I ran away and never went back.' He drew again on the cigarette. 'Never

ever went back. Made friends. Made close friends that are like family. Put myself through college. Now I have a whole lot of people who are there for me when I want them to be, and who stand back if I don't want them to be. And that's just how I like it.'

'Is there anyone special in this family?' I knew I sounded like a moron, but it was suddenly very important to me. Big strong Max had suddenly revealed a vulnerable streak and I realised that I wanted to see more. To get in closer.

His eyes sought mine. Then he grinned.

'Sometimes,' he said with a nod. 'But the situation's vacant right now. Want to apply for the job?'

'Maybe.' I twisted in my seat and avoided his eye. 'I'm not sure.'

'Well,' he said. 'I can wait. For a while.' He flipped the half-smoked cigarette out of the open window on to the smooth gravel, then glanced over at Leon's house. 'You know,' he said, 'I know it ain't any of my darn business, but you don't ever have to come back here again if you don't want to. You know that, don't you, Carrie?'

'Yes.' I glanced up and watched as one of the lighted windows was partly obscured by Leon's bulk. My brother reached out as someone else came into view. The other person took his hand and held it to her jutting breast. It was Marie-Therese, the maid.

Holding my breath, I watched as she slipped her free hand into the waistband of Leon's trousers and massaged his groin. Then she dropped down to her knees and buried her face there. Glancing at Max, I saw that he was transfixed too, a strange look on his face. I looked back at the window and saw that, while I had been looking at Max, Eva had come to stand next to Leon and was kissing him deeply while her narrow hands smoothed Marie-Therese's hair. The scene was oddly tender and I was touched, in spite of my antipathy towards my brother.

'Let's go,' murmured Max, and started up the car. The

threesome in the window didn't pause when the engine roared to life only yards away from them.

As we drove away I wondered idly whether they had thought we'd already gone. Or whether they'd actually put on the little show for our benefit. That question plagued my thoughts for the next few days, and I was still wondering the following weekend when I took the train to Bournemouth.

Chapter Eleven
having the whip hand

*I*f you don't possess a car – and I don't – getting from Bath to Bournemouth is devilish. Old-fashioned routes take you to the crowded, Kiss-Me-Quick delights of Weymouth, where a slow change at an end-of-the-line station sets you up for a journey across Hardy's Dorset heath to Bournemouth.

I had no idea what the place was like, because the nearest I'd ever been to the south coast before was a day-trip to Salisbury with Leon. But the brochure I'd picked up in the travel agent's showed long pale beaches and pretty hotels that offered gym facilities and excellent room service. I'd chosen one near the gardens because it had rooms with balconies, and I had an idea about what I fancied doing on a balcony with Sam.

I packed a bag and left right after work at five-thirty on Friday. We'd had a busy week at Richardson's. I was looking forward to a break from the routine of getting up, going to work, having my work criticised and then going home again. The tedium of the train journey south was relieved momentarily by an incident which set my pulse into a feverish spin.

About an hour after we drew out of Bath Spa, I made

my way slowly along to the buffet car to get a cup of coffee.

At the far end of the corridor from me, neatly blocking the doorway between the first-class compartment and the buffet car, was an elegant suitcase made of expensive leather. Long, slender and entirely white, it had the initials SQ tooled in navy blue on one surface.

Standing next to it was the most arresting woman I had ever seen. She looked like an Arab princess. Not beautiful by any means: her nose was rather too big, her flashing amber eyes slightly too wide, her lush mouth on the generous side of voluptuous. But arresting all the same. The sort of woman that commanded attention wherever she went.

She was wearing an outfit made from the same leather as her baggage. Supple white leather – contrasting so exquisitely with the polished mahogany of her dark skin – covered almost every inch of her body like a fitted glove made of soft, touchable, pliant kid-skin. Narrow shoulders. Tiny waist. She was expensively clad in a long flowing skirted leather coat that was buttoned simply at the waist.

From where I stood, slanting my eyes eastwards to drink her in, I could see that her swelling, abundant cleavage was kept in place by a boned white leather top that enhanced her breasts and pushed them skywards. Her long legs were encased in boots that disappeared under the coat and probably stopped somewhere near mid-thigh. One elegantly gloved hand clasped a folded newspaper while the other slid up to hook her smooth waterfall of silken ebony hair behind a delicate ear. Her nostrils flared a little as she read, and a frown creased her otherwise smooth forehead.

She was delicious, positively oozing sex appeal, and the entire male content of the first-class carriage behind her seemed to have screwed around in their seats to get a good look at her. I think they thought that a fabulous supermodel or movie star had somehow contrived to get standing room on their rural train ride along the coast.

'Yes?' The steward was frowning impatiently at me. I dragged my gaze from the girl to him and forced a smile.

'Coffee please. Black. No sugar.'

He grunted and got to it while I rocked back on my heels and snuck another secret glance at her. But when I looked up, my sensation of fear and excitement took my breath away. She was staring right at me.

Catching my breath to find those wide, slanting eyes burning on my face, I felt my skin blush a deep pink. I leaned my elbows nonchalantly back on the counter, trying to appear as if I hadn't actually been trying to study her at all. But she wasn't going to let me get away with it. She folded up her newspaper, neatly stepped over her case with a flash of naked thigh, and strode down the corridor towards me.

I swallowed hard, and tried not to be impressed as the men that were queueing up behind me were thrust aside, scattered in her wake. She nestled right up to me, rested her elbows on the counter in a parody of my pose, and summoned the steward with a haughty toss of her lovely head.

'Coffee,' she demanded in an authoritative tone. 'White. *Very* white. With plenty of nice sweet sugar.'

Then she turned to me, fixed me with those flashing amber eyes, and stared into me as if she could read my thoughts. Her eyes didn't leave my face as she received the coffee in one gloved hand and took a long, silent sip. Then she held my gaze as her tiny pointed tongue flicked out and licked the creamy residue off her top lip. I stared, fascinated, aware of a sudden tightening in my warm sex and a thrill that fizzed through my veins like hundreds of tiny effervescent bubbles.

'I like mine white. It tastes better on my tongue,' she whispered, her voice steel cloaked with satin. She leaned back and away from me, twisting slightly so that I

143

couldn't resist glancing down at the swell of her cleavage. Her eyes swept my body from toe to tit. Then she turned on her heels and stalked away.

I paid the steward, took my black coffee and went back to my seat with a deep frown carving my forehead. Had that been a come-on? Had it been anything at all? Who was she?

I kept my eyes peeled for the rest of the journey, but didn't see her until we got to Bournemouth. She got off ahead of me, as the first-class passengers always do, but I was just behind her as we went out of the doors to the taxi bay. I watched as a whey-faced girl in a smart grey suit climbed out of a white Rolls-Royce and took SQ's white suitcase to stow it in the boot. She touched her peaked chauffeurine's cap deferentially and handed SQ into the back of the Roller.

I was impressed: an Arab princess with a uniformed chauffeurine. Bournemouth, with its echoing Victorian station buildings and ultra-modern station car park, suddenly seemed rather more glamorous than it had when I'd first seen it from the dirty windows of the train.

When they drove away, I thought that I would never see them again.

The taxi driver took me as near to Bournemouth Pier as he could and I told him to wait while I found Sam. Crossing the busy road, I could see the bay sparkling just beyond the pier, and the sea breeze was fresh and crisp with a hint of the coming autumnal chill. The sun had dropped low in the sky, even though it was only four-thirty, and I felt a touch of late-summer blues swill through my guts.

I wasn't keen on this time of year. The smell in the air and the slight drop in temperature always brought back powerful memories of being back at school after a long summer holiday of freedom. Melancholy sensations and nostalgic regret clutched at me and I blinked the feelings

144

away as I reached the other side of the road and walked across the sand-swept tarmac to our rendezvous point.

This time it was me who was late, and Sam who had been waiting. He was staring out to sea, his elbows on the wall that separated the promenade from the slope of stone that led down to the golden sand. There was a battered canvas rucksack at his feet. He was wearing a short leather jacket and clean blue jeans that hugged his neat bottom so tight that I wondered how he'd managed to get into them. His trademark stetson was firmly in place, and I could see a hint of tempting five-o'clock shadow around his jaw.

He turned, as if he could sense me approaching, even though there was no way he could have heard me over the booming surf that hit the beach and echoed under the pier. His face shone with a happy grin that showed off his even white teeth and his eyes crinkled at the corners good-naturedly. I found myself grinning in return. Then I stepped up my pace and almost ran at him as he widened his arms. We hugged. Close. Muscular chest to soft bosom. And I felt his steely, more private welcome pressing against my pubic bone.

I had almost convinced myself, on the journey, that London was a one-off; that when Sam and I got together again there would be some kind of awkwardness or tension. But no. Easygoing Sam wasn't like that. He wasn't like my ex-husband Patrick with his weird moods and his hidden agendas. Sam was just a nice, straight-forward, uncomplicated guy with a hard-on.

I dragged him back to the taxi and we checked in at the hotel, raided the drinks in the well-stocked fridge in our room, and lay companionably side by side on the bed with our shoes off sipping drinks. Me with a Bacardi and Coke. Sam sipping a cold beer straight from the bottle.

'Wow, this is great,' he murmured, wriggling his toes

inside fluffy sports socks. 'This hotel is really nice. Much better than I thought it'd be.'

'What did you expect?'

'I dunno. Something more kind of seedy. You know, like they have in old movies of Graham Greene books. The hero has to hire a private dick to photograph him doing the deed so's he can get a divorce from the nasty wife who only married him for his money.'

'Private dick, huh?' I smiled and set my glass on the bedside cabinet. 'I like the sound of that. What deed are we talking about specifically?'

'I don't know.' Sam grinned, expressively spreading his hands and shrugging against the soft pillows. 'I think in those days they just had to stay one night in the hotel and get photographed coming out the next day.'

'Well, I'm afraid there's no camera around here,' I said. 'But there is a dick.' My hand curved over the growing bulge in his jeans. 'And I want to see what deeds it's capable of.'

'You do?' He leaned over the edge of the bed to put his beer on the floor, then pressed me back against the pillow, rubbing the tip of his nose against mine. 'Well, it's pretty anxious to show you. It wants to do a private investigation all of its own.'

'Sam,' I breathed against his searching mouth, 'Sam. Just don't make me wait too long. Do it now.'

I took his hand and guided it up under my skirt. I'd worn a short twill number with over-the-knee socks and little lace-up boots. My knickers were an itsy-bitsy slip of silk that I'd bought especially for the weekend because when I'd seen them I could think of nothing but Sam's teeth gripping the gusset and tearing it away.

His hand felt firm and strong on my aching skin as he let me guide his fingers up over the top of the long socks to the bare skin of my thigh. Then I let him continue on his own as the pad of his finger met the soft damp resistance of silk-covered quim. He locked his eyes on to mine and held me there, unable and unwilling to move, as he put a little pressure on my sweetly creamy slit.

'Oh,' I breathed.

My pulse thudded heavily in my veins and I tipped my head back, breaking my gaze with Sam so that I could flutter my eyes closed. He pressed a little more, and then curled his finger around and under the sodden silk. My eyes flashed open and I stared up at the dove-white ceiling as he slipped one finger across my clitoris and brought it instantly to life.

'God, Carrie,' he murmured. 'You're so wet. You smell so good. So ripe. I want to eat you.'

'Later,' I muttered. I gazed into his eyes and found myself almost drowning in the liquid brown of his irises. 'Do that later. Right now I just want you to fuck me. Fuck me now. Fast. We can do the tender stuff later.'

I reached up and ripped at the front of his T-shirt, dragging it off in one sweep. Then I yanked at the buttons of his jeans and growled at him to get them off. He stripped so fast that I was nearly left behind. I got down to my over-knee socks and hesitated. They looked quite cute. Kind of like a Victorian housemaid, so I left them on.

Kneeling in front of him on the bed, I pulled a couple of plump pillows and tucked them behind me in the small of my back, then watched Sam's face. He paused in the tearing of a condom wrapper, and just stared as I curved backwards with my legs still folded under me. I felt like a fantastic flower, a blooming lotus, all open and gaping. No legs. No arms. Just a cunt and tits swelling up to reach the fit young man who was going to fuck me quick and hard with absolutely no foreplay whatsoever.

Sam, kicking his discarded denims across the room impatiently, gaped when he saw my sex widen, split and open for him. I was so wet just from anticipation, I could feel my own juices running free and glistening on my thighs and the curve of my buttocks. Widening my knees

147

a little, I reached up and encircled Sam's wrist with my fingers.

'Come on,' I said with relish. 'Just do it. Now.'

He didn't hang around for a second invitation. He kneeled between my outstretched knees and gripped my waist in his big hands. Glancing at my face briefly, he flipped his hips towards me and slipped in with lubricated ease, sighing and tensing his buttocks as he thrust all the way home.

I bit my lip and swallowed hard. I'd forgotten how wide he was. He stretched me, especially in the position that I was in with my feet folded back either side of my hips and my pelvis thrust up almost to his face. Deep penetration is not the word for it. I was plumbed to the depths of my very soul. And when I urged him to move, he took me into orbit.

Squeezing my hips, I pulsated against him and we got into a rhythm. Hard fucking. In and out. Fast fucking. Thrusting deep. Fingers bulging against my clit. I could hear my own ragged breathing as I urged him on with little sighs and whispers. Sam's thumbs were everywhere, rubbing and pinching. His forefingers made little circling and pressing movements on that sweet wet spot, while his thick rod thrust deep and filled me so that I thought I'd never stretch far enough for him.

I was coming. Shuddering hard against Sam, I gripped his strong shoulders with both hands and cried out as my orgasm rippled through me. It was a blessed relief. A release of all the built-up tension since I'd last done it with him. Negating everything that had gone before. Sweeping my mind clean of Gabe. Of Max. Of Eva and her power-play with my loathsome brother. I let myself go and spiralled down into the dark bliss of climax.

As the sun sank down into a golden sunset streaked with cloud, we had all the time in the world for tender kisses and playfulness. Sam slid down between my legs. and licked me until I was alive again, my whole body crying out for his touch. His tongue drove me wild: long slow strokes that covered every inch of hungry skin and dipped into every slick fold of my sex. When he slid his fingers inside me and made a spiralling, twisting movement, I felt a line of firecrackers light up and blow their fuses all along the length of my spine. He really knew what to do with his hands and tongue. Licking. Rubbing. Circling. I was happy to lie back and take it with just the occasional murmur of encouragement, or a little repositioning of his hand if his fingers slipped wide of the mark.

When I'd come again – a sweet, long, tension-releasing climax that swept all the hair on the back of my neck into waves of pulsing pleasure – I decided that it was Sam's turn. So I unpacked my bag and laid out a little selection of interesting toys I'd bought with me to pass the time until we went to meet the others in the bar.

Honey-coloured suede cuffs, lined with creamy soft velvet, and a matching collar. A pair of elbow-length leather gloves with a neatly tailored zip that went all the way up the underside of the wearer's arm, from the curve of the wrist to the inner cubit of the elbow. Next out of the bag was a gorgeous new vibrator that was a muted shade of powder blue. Multi-speed and almost totally silent.

The vibrator was one of my favourite new purchases. Laura and I had spent hours in a ladies sex emporium in London, totally amazed by the lovely items there. I hadn't intended making a purchase at all, but the pale blue vibrator had caught my eye. It wasn't one of those embarrassing Big Boy things made in surgical appliance-grade salmon-coloured plastic that most manufacturers seem to think is a real turn-on. No, this was something far better. Something more discreet. Something more arousing. Something that any girl would be proud to carry in her handbag for those little orgasmic emergencies.

Sam picked it up and weighed it in his hand, a little smile quirking the corner of his lips.

'Nice,' he murmured. 'Aren't you going to be needing me, then?'

'It's to supplement you. Not replace you,' I said, snuggling my body in behind his on the bed and peeking over his shoulder. The vibrator looked slender, small, and somehow very erotic in his big hand. 'And it might even be *for* you. You never know.'

He twisted a little and stared into my eyes, then he grinned.

'You're kidding, right?'

'No, why should I be?'

There was a long pause. Then he laid the vibrator down next to the other toys, turned on to his back and pulled me on top of him. His mouth sought mine and we kissed for a long time, tongues curling warmly and lips slipping. Then he broke off and cupped my face in his hands.

'I'm yours,' he whispered. 'Do anything you want. I trust you, Carrie. I've never met anyone like you before. You're in charge and I really love that.'

I rubbed my cheek against the stubble on his jaw and smiled to myself.

Me? In charge? If he only knew that it wasn't me who was in charge, but Dominique. But while he believed that it was me I may as well capitalise on the pleasure I was getting. I reached out and caressed the suede collar in my hands, revelling in its softness, then I buckled it round his neck and sat back on my heels to admire the effect.

He looked like a lovely slave-boy, or a handsome dog. My dog. Our eyes met, mine full of wonder and his full of trust and anticipation. I grinned and kissed him full on his generous mouth, my tongue playing over his smooth teeth before delving deep against his palate as he sucked me in for a delicious moment.

150

Next, I reached around and took his wrists in my hands, looped the suede cuffs round and buckled them up. They had neat little gold buckles which complemented the honey-coloured suede beautifully. Once they were done up, I slipped a long, plaited length of cord through the gold D rings on them and applied a little pressure.

'Come on,' I said, pulling him slightly. 'Up. On your feet, boy.'

I led him over to the French windows which went out on to the secluded little balcony beyond. Our hotel was higher than most of the buildings around it, and across the road was the tree-lined privacy of the Leisure Gardens, so we wouldn't be, couldn't be, overlooked. Stretching Sam up, I looped the cord around the cross bar that separated the open French windows from the ajar casement above.

I pulled a little. He was almost suspended but not quite, his weight taken by the balls of his feet and the sturdy, white-painted bar of wood above him. I tied him fast and then stood back to admire the view as I slipped into the long, soft gloves and zipped them up.

Lean and naked, with a lovely contrast between the honey-coloured skin of his back and the whiteness of buttocks that hadn't seen the sun all summer, Sam looked like St Sebastian without the arrows. His arms stretched up either side of his head and his biceps bulged and tautened. His tapering waist, and the neatness of his hips, was accentuated by the way his leg muscles bulged and moved as he tried to find a purchase on the shiny floor with his toes and the front part of his feet, only just getting the balance right. His manhood, heavy with lust but not even nearly erect, hung like a delicious ripe fruit, slightly darker than the pale skin of his groin, and surrounded by the lush tangle of his pubes.

He trusted me. I could do whatever I wanted with him.

Unable to resist touching him for a moment longer, I stepped in close to Sam's body and rubbed my gloved hands over his stretched flanks. His skin rippled lightly under my fingers like a horse's does when it's given an especially vigorous grooming by an experienced stable-hand. I kissed his shoulder, and then his throat, darting my tongue out and tasting the prickle of stubble that grew there. He tasted of soap and delicate sweat, and there was a hint of leather from where the collar of his jacket had rested there all the way down from London and imprinted his skin with its sex-ritual smell.

My hands drifted downwards and cupped his neat package. His cock swung suddenly in my hands, jerking to half-mast as he groaned a little. A cool breeze from the outside caressed his hot skin and I felt him goose-bump under my fingertips. Kissing his ear, I suckled for a moment on his lobe, then gave his lengthening cock a gentle squeeze.

'You look good like that,' I said. 'Like a sacrificial lamb.'

'And you're the goddess that I'm sacrificed to,' he said, quick as a flash, his eyes probing mine. I smiled and nodded and kissed him again.

'Then let's begin the rituals,' I said with a smile, as I turned back into the room and picked up the slender sapling cane that was still curled around the base of my bag.

Sam liked it when I patted his bottom with the sapling. He bit his lower lip and then asked me to do it a little bit harder. I obliged, curious to find out the level of his co-operation as well as the extent of my own domination with the whip. The sapling made light pink streaks across his skin and I handled it carefully, anxious not to actually hurt him, weighing its weight loosely in my fingers and whipping him with the gentlest of strokes.

One. Two. Three. Sam sighed and jerked a little against the soft restraints that kept him bound to the horizontal beam above his head. I smiled as I admired him: his skin glowed pale in the dusky light of early evening. I let the sapling stick rest idle for a moment, and then caught him a neat little zing under his buttock, making him gasp. From where I was standing, I could see the sudden jerk and throb of his erection. The hard ridge of muscle darkened and jerked skywards. My pussy swelled and juiced at the sight of him.

I tried that again. A little stinging lash that marked his skin just a little bit more than the last. He closed his eyes and groaned as his cock jerked again and a little salty tear glistened at the slit on its top. I swallowed, feeling a tense pleasure in the depths of my stomach that tingled down through my sex. This whipping game was exciting, much more so than I had imagined it would be. And Sam, by the ecstatic look of mild suffering and immense pleasure on his handsome face, was loving it too.

I flashed the sapling whip against his skin again, striping him with pink. A droplet of clear fluid trickled from his glans over the plump muscular head of his cock. It trembled for a moment before the surface pressure became too great and it dropped like a salty tear on to the shining wooden floor beneath his feet. Another immediately welled up to take its place. I had only just enough self-control to prevent myself from kneeling down, sliding my tongue into the slick slit at the head of his shaft and drinking him dry.

I closed my eyes briefly and then streaked his buttock again with the sapling. Tender this time, hardly touching his skin. Just a little tap to remind him that I was there. Then I reached for the elegant, powder-blue vibrator and flipped it to 'on'. A low buzz thrummed through my hands and I pressed it briefly against my tongue, enjoying the tingles that flooded through my mouth from the battery-powered body. Then I held it lightly against my naked nipple and smiled as the pleasure coursed through me; I saw my nipple tweak to an instant cone of raspberry pink tautness against the pulsing blue.

When he heard the barely audible hum, Sam arched and curved to see what I was doing, so I treated his bottom to a quick lick from the sapling that must have stung like hell because he gave a tiny whimper and swung a little on his bindings. I walked past him, caressing his prick with one curved hand as I passed, and went to stand against the waist-height wall of the balcony. There were long shadows cast by the wall and the chairs, but I knew that Sam could still see every move I made.

Bracing myself, I placed my feet wide and hitched one elbow on the top of the wall while I ran the vibrator down from my breast, over the little mound of my tummy, past my lush bush and into the tangle of hairs that covered my sex. I found my clit, my eyes fixed on Sam's, and let the vibrator play over it for a moment until I could feel it swelling and bulging.

Sam, desperate to drop his eyes and watch, seemed to be begging for permission, but I held his gaze and slowly shook my head. I turned up the speed a little and felt my own legs buck a little with elation. The nose of the vibrator was slender and slightly pointed, wonderfully suitable for seek-and-destroy missions to the most intimate parts of my anatomy.

Lifting one leg, I rested my foot on one of the low chairs that stood on the balcony. That gave me fabulous access and I slipped the vibrator slowly across the juicy wet slit of my sex, making the rounded head of the device creamy and wet. Then I purred it home over my clit again. Warm sensations of delicious energy hummed through my limbs, while Sam's liquid-brown, puppy-dog eyes hungered and begged for me to let him look down. His dick was enormous, springing out from the tangle of hair at his loins, wide and thick and dancing a jig to the sweet, near-silent music of the vibrator.

At last I nodded and he dropped his gaze to the ripe

fruit of my cooch. His eyes widened and his cock bulged some more, so swollen that I thought he might just come without me even having to touch him. Spreading my sex wide with the fingers of one hand, I played the vibrator hard over my clit, seeking and then finding the little spot that I knew from past experience would send me over the edge. Sweet sensations coursed through me and my heartbeat seemed to slow down for one long, agonising minute, then it powered up to a double pace and stayed there as I pulled the hood of my clit back with my forefinger and pressed the vibrator hard.

I was almost lost, then, when I looked into Sam's face. His expression was one of blessed torture and he was sighing heavily, his face flushed and his chest heaving. His hands, still bound high up in the cuffs, twitched a little as if he wanted nothing better than to wrestle them out of there and grab his cock. To wank himself to overload and spray come all over me. I leaned harder against the wall, slid the vibrator up inside me to give my grasping, hungry sex something to look forward to, then played it back over my clit again, my finger pressing and pushing the controls up to 'maximum'.

That was it. I was gone. The honeyed waves of bitter-sweet orgasm crushed over me, prickling my scalp and making me bite back a sob as my knees trembled and my hips bucked up to seek fulfilment. My other hand didn't need to hold back the hood of my sweet clit any more because the little muscle was poking out so long that it must have looked like a tongue. I let my hand leave my clit and slipped it around and under me. I thrust two fingers in. All the way in. Plumbing into my grasping, clenching cunt and pressing up hard.

The vibrator was still humming in my hand, sending tremors of release all up through my wrists and into my brain as I sagged against the wall and watched as Sam groaned and wept another little salt tear from his engorged dick. His neat balls were tucked tight up under him and his thighs were flexed, every muscle defined and gleaming as he held on for dear life, swinging slightly but held deliciously immobile by the cords that bound him. My orgasm was so powerful that my eyes flickered closed and I surrendered myself.

When I had recovered enough to step away from the safety of the wall, I strode over to Sam, wafted the vibrator under his nose so that he could smell the stickiness of my female musk, and then turned it to 'off'. With the shaft of it held tight in one hand, I let him watch as I slid the thing back and forth between my legs, coating it with sweet lubrication from deep inside me, then I shimmied around behind him.

'You know what I'm going to do, don't you?' I murmured.

He hung his head and I nudged it against his pink-striped, beautifully whipped buttock. 'Don't you?' I repeated. 'Remember when we were in your room? You liked the feel of Alex's cock in your hand when you jerked him off, didn't you? You liked the fact that he didn't know it was you,' I continued. 'Imagine it's him here now. Imagine I'm watching as he sneaks up behind you and snuggles in close.'

I pressed my body close to his warm back, relishing the feel of his crisply hairy thighs on the soft skin of my own legs. 'Imagine his dick is naked against you. You can feel it pressing against the skin of your bottom. Mmm . . . Alex's lovely cock. You're wondering if he's going to butt-fuck you. You can feel him swaying slightly, and shifting against you. He's getting hard as he senses how turned on you are. And you are turned on, Sam.' He shook his head dumbly. 'All steamed up by another guy. By Alex.'

Sam groaned and shook his head. 'No.'

'What did you say?' I whispered, standing on tiptoe so that my lips caressed the curve of his ear. 'Did you say no?'

'Yes.'

'Yes? Hmm. So no means yes, does it?' I smiled against his neck, letting my nose rest on the hard pulse that thudded there.

'I mean . . . no, I'm not turned on by that,' he said. His voice had a pleading quality to it that should have made me want to stop. But perversely it made me just want to carry on. To make him beg. Or to make him admit that the idea of another guy turned him on more than he cared to admit.

'I think you are,' I whispered hoarsely. 'I think you'd love it if Alex licked his hand, wet his dick and tried to spit-fuck you.'

'W-what?'

'Spit-fuck,' I breathed. 'To use your spit to lubricate a person. Especially the ass.'

I felt him quiver against me as I spoke and it made me smile. I felt so powerful: Sam's pleasure was in my hands. I pressed closer against him.

Slipping the sticky nose of the humming vibrator between the muscular cheeks of his ass, I told him to pretend Alex was there. To picture Alex easing himself gently between Sam's manly butt cheeks. To imagine that Alex was spreading Sam's legs wider with his workman's boots and putting a finger in his own mouth. Wetting his finger. Making it slippery and lubricated with saliva. Slipping it down and then easing it in. Opening the gateway to Sam's soul.

I made the exact movements that I told him Alex was making. I wet him, moistened him, lubricated him so that he could take the nose of the vibrator without any discomfort. Then I eased it in, inch by enlightening inch. Sam gasped and tried to writhe away. But when I paused, he pushed back against me, arching his back a little with a telling little whimper that made me smile and push it home a bit more. The vibrator was sheathed.

Or rather Alex was sheathed. All the way up inside his friend. Then I turned the vibrator on.

He came in moments. Sweet, murmuring moments that I spent whispering in his ear and stroking his straining cock with my free hand. My right hand held the vibrator in his arse, all the way to the ridged control ring. My left hand tightly gripped his shaft, slipping up and down the rigid, steely length. I felt powerful and bold and utterly in control.

When he came I felt as though I had created a wonderful piece of art. A work of sublime living sculpture that was entirely my own making. He sprayed and jetted his thin-slick load and I heard it patter on the polished wood floor in soft little splutters that sounded like late summer rain. Sam's head drooped and his body became soft. Every muscle had surrendered to sensation.

When I'd untied him and we lay down on the bed in each other's arms, I glanced over at the open French windows and saw that the September rain had started. It slowly washed away the silky globs of his come and left the wooden floor slippery and gleaming.

We spent the rest of that evening in bed, and the next day we wandered around Bournemouth enjoying the sun that occasionally rayed out from behind gathering clouds. We walked on the beach and let the sand crunch up between our bare toes. We window-shopped hand in hand. We ate steaming fish and salty chips with our fingers from paper bundles bought from a chip-shop up near the Triangle. Then towards six we went back to the hotel and made sweet, languorous love on the soft carpet at the foot of the bed for no other reason than that we felt like it.

Afterwards, curled into the crook of Sam's arm, I dozed for an hour, then we showered and dressed and set out to meet the Virgin and the Shoemaker.

Chapter Twelve

the virgin and the shoemaker

'*H*i, you must be Dominique.'

The Virgin was not at all what I had expected. For him to be a virgin I had stupidly assumed that he must be either too young to be legal, or an ugly guy who couldn't get a girlfriend.

I was wrong on both counts.

The Virgin was dark, lean, and slightly shorter than me. Heavy-lidded, sensual eyes, a riot of black gypsy curls, and wiry arms that threatened to split the sleeve seams of his tight linen shirt. His nose was well defined, aristocratic-looking and slightly flared at the nostrils. If he'd worn a yarmulke, I'd have sworn he was a good Jewish boy. Maybe he was. Or maybe he was a bad Jewish boy, I thought with a wry grin as I returned his curious stare.

His intense dark eyes swept me up and down. There was a pause while he assessed me closely, then he held out one hand. I shook it nervously and smiled as he gave me a friendly grin.

'Hey, Dominique,' he said. 'Don't look so scared. The

emphasis here is on pleasure ... No one's going to bite your head off, you know.'

I took a sip of my drink and tried to relax my tense shoulders.

'Don't worry.' He rested his elbows on the bar and pressed against me, his voice low, warm and conspiratorial. 'Everyone's nervous at first. But I'm sure you'll be fascinated. And if you're not ... well –' he shrugged expressively '– if you don't like us then you don't have to see us ever again, do you?'

'And what if you don't like me?'

'The same applies.' He grinned. 'We'll be gone.'

'Oh!' I glanced sideways at Sam who was lounging in a huge leather chesterfield sofa that he'd bagged as his own the minute we'd walked into the bar. He smiled, raised his glass and then took a long sip of beer.

I turned back to the Virgin, aware of the heat that emanated from his body as he leaned on the bar next to me. He smelled gorgeous: all soapy and fresh with the merest hint of woody aftershave; which was obviously just for show as he didn't look as though he'd shaved since the morning.

'So, what do we do now?' I asked.

'Just have a drink, get to know each other,' he said. 'The Shoemaker's late, as usual. He'll be along soon.'

We sauntered over to Sam and curled up on the sofa. Being in the bar made me think we'd been transported into the set of *Friends* with all the comfy seating and low tables. The windows were wide and sparkling clean, and outside the evening trade out on the square was brisk: street-sellers, buskers, and people taking advantage of the late summer warmth to promenade around Bournemouth. I curled against Sam's warm comforting arm and sipped my mineral water, listening to the Virgin's deep voice talk affectionately about the Huntsman and the Shoemaker.

'Do they have real names?' I asked. 'These fairytale things are a bit of a mouthful.'

The Virgin grinned. 'Yes,' he said. 'But it's more fun this way, don't you think? What we do when we're here is just nothing to do with real life. So having names lends even more distance. And it gives what we do a fairytale quality, creates a fantasy in which we can all be whoever we want, not the people we are in our humdrum lives.' He smiled and ran his fingers through his curly dark hair. 'Very few people are completely happy in their everyday world.' His eyes met mine. 'Are you? I don't think your real name is Dominique, but I wouldn't want to know what your real name is. For me, Dominique serves well.' He smiled and let his forefinger rest lightly on my wrist. 'It doesn't matter what your name is. It's who you are that counts.'

Sam shifted next to me, and I tried not to focus on the way his arm felt beneath the curve of my waist. He was my rock. My solid foundation that was going to make all this OK. But next to me was a man who met up with a group of other people for the whole purpose of sexual pleasure.

I glanced at him from under my lashes. The effect his touch had on me, the way his fingers seemed to tingle against the skin of my wrist, had surprised me. He was very attractive. And what he said was so interesting, and somehow liberating. It was actually OK to want sexual pleasure simply for the sake of sexual pleasure. It was actually OK to have it outside of some kind of socially acceptable relationship. With the Virgin and the Huntsman and their friends, I could have what I'd never actually dreamed about before. Guilt free. No strings. Pure pleasure.

The thought sent a funny little erotic frisson of electricity up my spine, and I spent the rest of the time until the Shoemaker arrived in a dreamily relaxed state, listening to Sam and the Virgin make easygoing small talk.

Around nine-thirty, the four of us walked through the town centre. Sam and I weren't going to join in the fun, the Virgin said, because the group didn't allow that until they'd got to know newcomers better. But we were going to go to a party and meet some people, just to get a taste of what they did.

Outside, there was a light, sea-salt breeze which blew my hair around my face and cooled my warm cheeks. The evening sky was a bruised blue-black – almost stormy-looking, despite the rain of earlier – with a fat creamy yellow moon sitting low on the horizon. In the trees strings of brightly coloured glass lights cast slanting rainbow rays that lit the lovely buildings. Bournemouth was beautiful at night, and the Shoemaker – an elderly toe-queen who'd shown an inordinate but on reflection probably predictable interest in my long shiny boots – pointed out interesting little details to us as if he was a tour guide.

We made our way through the crowded streets, revelling in the carnival atmosphere of the town at night. The Virgin led us along Westover Road, then past some expensive hotels and up a well-maintained walkway to a huge white house set high on a rocky cliff. The road up there overlooked the wide bay, the beach and the funicular railway. We stopped for a while and I took great lungfuls of sea air, feeling strangely at peace and no longer nervous. As long as I had Sam with me, I was happy.

The house seemed huge. Painted a pearly white with sea-green duckboards and a marble front step. The sweeping front drive was neatly gravelled and parked up with cars. A couple of European car plates showed that people had come from quite a long way to make it to the party. Music and light spilled out of open windows, while the sound of laughter and merriment was blown across the grass as we crossed the lawns towards the wide front porch. The door stood wide open and two beefy, shaven-headed men in tuxedos stood on the top step to welcome people.

Ahead of us, I saw a tall, elegant woman and an elderly man alight from their car and approach the door. They were dressed expensively as if for a cocktail party, and I was suddenly aware that Sam and I had not made the right kind of effort with our clothes. Sam was casually dressed in a pair of clean black jeans and a white T-shirt, while I'd put on a pair of knee-high boots, a short black suede skirt and a red cotton shirt that was tied just above my waist. We looked nice, but not as nice as Mr and Mrs Cocktail-Gown.

'We're too scruffy, surely,' I whispered to the Virgin.

'Don't worry.' He smiled. 'When you get inside, you'll feel fine.'

He gave my hand a squeeze and I was grateful for the warmth that emanated from his wide palm. Taking a deep breath, I let him lead me across the crunchy gravel and on to the porch.

'Good evening, sir.' One of the men in tuxedos welcomed us and watched carefully as the Virgin signed in with his security code. They were obviously taking no chances with gatecrashers. Inside the house, brimming flutes of Mimosa were pressed into our hands and the music grew louder. I glanced back at Sam and saw that he was frowning and negotiating with the statuesque drinks-bearer, but even his friendly grin couldn't elicit a beer. I gave his arm a squeeze.

'Try it,' I whispered. 'You might like it.'

'What's Mimosa?' He peered circumspectly into his tall glass.

'Champagne and orange juice.' The Shoemaker laughed. 'The English call it Buck's Fizz. There's nothing more guaranteed to wake you up and make you feel good.'

Sam sipped, frowned, nodded, and then gave me a rueful grin.

'Jeez,' he said. 'Guess I could get used to this.'

* * *

163

Two Mimosas later, I lost Sam in the crowd. One minute he was there leaning against the wall with a bemused expression on his face, the next he was nodding and smiling at a petite brunette in a leather dress. Then he was gone. I felt a wave of panic, but the Virgin's warm hand on the small of my back comforted me.

'Don't worry,' he said, steering me towards a wide archway that led into another set of rooms. The first room had been cleared for dancing, and was filled almost to capacity by warm bodies which twisted and writhed against each other. As we drew closer the noise level picked up and I found myself tapping my fingers against my thigh to a trance classic that thrummed from the speakers. The Virgin grinned at me.

'See? Sam's not far away,' he said.

He wasn't. I could see him dancing with the brunette on the edges of the crowded room. He had a huge grin on his face and his glass dangled empty from the thumb and forefinger of one hand. Smiling tolerantly, and trying to ignore a tiny and very unexpected flutter of jealousy, I turned to the Virgin.

'Can we dance?'

'Thought you'd never ask.' He laughed, rolling his eyes and slipping his palm further around my waist. His touch gave me a genuine thrill, and as I turned and plunged into the gyrating crowd, I felt suddenly bereft as his hand lost contact with my skin.

I pushed through to the middle of the bouncing dance-floor, out of the way of Sam and his girl – I didn't want to cramp his style by looking like some kind of official girlfriend – and twisted and turned to the music, letting it beat through my body and mimic my heartbeat. Faster. Faster. I sighed and rocked my hips against the Virgin, flicking my hair back from my face and smiling widely at him.

We turned and moved, mirroring each other's movements. Usually I hated dancing, especially with someone new. I normally felt as if everyone else was judging me, as if Patrick was still around to sneer at my clumsiness. But tonight dancing felt right. Everything just felt so free and fluid. My arms curved and swayed, my hips swung, and my dance partner seemed to think that I was wonderful. I tipped back my head and laughed with the sheer joy of being at the party, with the pleasure of being somewhere where no one knew me, and with the thrill of being Dominique.

'I can't keep calling you the Virgin!' I yelled over the top of the din. 'Can't I call you something else?'

He grinned and shrugged, but didn't answer, simply hooked his forefinger into the waistband of my skirt and pulled me closer so that I could feel the rod of his warm cock pressing my hipbone. I swallowed hard. And ground myself against him. He pressed back at me, one hand slipping around the soft suede of my skirt to cup my ass. He rolled his hips to the music, tantalisingly close to me. It made me feel tingly and hot. I glanced at his face and he held my curious stare, then rolled his hips some more. For a virgin, he knew some moves.

'I'm going to have to call you Virge,' I said. 'I can't stand it otherwise.'

He nodded, still silent, his wide mouth pressed firmly closed. I studied his impassive face and then, shocking myself with my boldness, I leaned forward and stuffed my hand down between our bodies to cradle his package through his trousers. When I fastened my lips to his, his mouth parted under mine and I tasted his tongue.

'Don't,' he whispered at last, reluctantly breaking away from me and stroking my hair. 'You're not supposed to be indulging. You're just here to get a feel of things. And to party.'

'I want to party with you,' I murmured suggestively, slipping my fingers around the tempting shape his bag of tricks made inside his soft trousers.

He gazed at me for a long time, his eyes intense and

dark, his expression almost unreadable. I was aware of the beat that the loud music made through my veins, and the proximity of the bodies crushed on to the dance floor.

There was no sign of Sam and the girl. And no sign either of some of the other guests, like Mr and Mrs Cocktail-Gown, who had been early arrivals with us. But there were still a lot of people crushed into one small space, and the heat and noise and the scent of sweat was making me horny, something probably helped along by the champagne I'd consumed and the feel of Virge's package that was growing to hardness under my playing fingers.

I slipped my hands behind him and gripped his butt, pulling him in to me and grinding against him. My nipples, free of a bra tonight, poked eagerly through the red cotton of my shirt and I swept them against his shirt front, hoping to entice him in any way I could. But the man was not for turning. He simply twisted me around and curved in behind me, his cheek pressed to my shoulder and his cock nudging the crease of my suede-covered bottom. But if he thought that was going to deter me, he was wrong, because I wasn't in the mood to take no for an answer.

Rubbing back against his front, I danced and slid an arm back around his neck, pulling him in close and twisting my head to seek his mouth. He took some persuading at first. I had to twist my tongue around his and coax it out to play. But at last I got him interested, and the feel of his cock hardening to steely rigidity against my bum made me juicy and slick.

Even though Sam and I had made love in the hotel room earlier, I wanted more. I wanted someone else. I wanted Virge. Or whoever. Scanning the room, I began to make a contingency plan. If Virge was going to play reticent virgins, then maybe the Shoemaker would do. I could learn to like older men, and the Shoemaker's silver-haired elegance and his long fingers had intrigued me in the bar earlier. I thoughtfully slid my forefinger over the gold coin in my shirt breast pocket. It contained three condoms, and I would be happy if I just got to use one of them.

I scanned the crowd for the Shoemaker, but when I saw him, I knew that he was going to be a hard nut for a girl to crack. He was dancing about three couples away, his limbs entwined with snake-like simplicity around a lean boy with cropped hair and a lime-coloured T-shirt. The Shoemaker caught me staring, and winked. I grinned back and closed my eyes, leaning back against Virge and sighing deeply.

It was going to have to be the bird in the hand, I thought, with a wry grin. Virgin or not.

Eventually he gave in, as I hoped he would. He took my hand and led me out of the dance room and through a series of inter-connected chambers all decorated with lush fabrics and rich colours. Open windows showed a wonderful view of the moonlit sky and the sparkling sea, while the sound, once we were free of the dull boom of the music, was of whispers and low laughter and soft wavelets rushing up the sand on the beach far below.

At the far end of the house, a curving stairway led up to the rooms above and I glanced curiously up at the three women who leaned over the balustrade and watched us with lascivious smiles from under heavily made-up lazily drooping eyelids. But we weren't going up. Virge and I were going down.

The basement reminded me of scenes that I'd seen in films of ancient Roman baths. Curving, pale, cavernous rooms with myriad gold-lit tunnels leading to further mysterious delights. The air was heady with the lingering scent of ylang ylang. There was a pool – dark, deep and steaming, with a mosaicked floor and a low domed ceiling; alcoves all around containing padded loungers and daybeds, most made partly invisible by long, diaphanous

167

pieces of muslin which hung from the ceilings; ghostly steam rooms lined with glistening white tiles; and lastly, a whirlpool set down into a fragrant womb-like space that had blue candles burning in little niches cut into the walls.

As we walked, hand in hand, I saw bare skin – some pale, some gold, some darkest brown – just flashes of it, gently covered by exploring hands. I saw glistening pink lips softly parted. I saw, in the dimness, curving mounds which could have been knees. Or shoulders. Or buttocks. Or the underside of a breast.

We stopped by the whirlpool and dropped our clothes, not speaking, not touching. I stepped into the water first and let the heat tingle through my limbs as I found the curving seat and lounged back, letting the warm, frothy bubbles play under my chin. And when I lay back in the warm water I almost swooned with heady, sensual lust, fed by images of other people's pleasure, other women's desire, other men's submission.

Sitting opposite, his dark eyes fixed on mine, sat Virge, his shoulders just visible above the water. His hands on my thighs felt strong, yet tentative. He nudged my knees apart with his toes and slipped a foot between. He smoothed a passage with his toes and found the wet slit that opened so readily to his probing. He slipped and slid, his eyes fixed on mine. His toe fluttered against my pouting skin. Playing and touching.

I smiled. His big toe pressed on my clit felt good. But I wanted more, so much more. I didn't want gentling and coaxing as if I was a silly frightened female vessel that needed to be charmed before it blossomed fully open. I wanted it hard and rough. I wanted him to take me.

Suddenly I longed for Max; he'd know what I wanted instantly and instinctively. In two seconds flat he'd have had me on my back with his cock plunging hard inside me. He'd make me so wet, so slick, so stretched. I closed my eyes and gasped lightly as Virge's toe swept across my clit. Then I gripped his foot – hard – and pulled it up, half-submerging him in the process.

I made a pouting *moue* with my lips, and slid my mouth down over his toe. Virge's eyes widened with surprise, then flickered closed. He groaned, sighed, and let his head tip back to rest on the side of the whirlpool. His neatly circumcised dick, strong and dark and elegantly long, broke the waves and I was tempted to replace his toe with it. But then I changed my mind. He looked so relaxed, so lustfully submissive. Wasn't there something else that his cock could do for me apart from being a lollipop?

I surged through the water and straddled him, wrapping my arms around his head and pressing my breasts to his chin.

He's a virgin, I thought. What if he stops me? What if he wants to stay a virgin?

But he didn't stop me. He let me sit over him, with the warm water swirling around our bodies. I slid my hand down, revelling for a moment in the warm silkiness of my own inner thigh, then I grasped his penis and held the skin tight. I slid it back with finger and thumb and held it at the root of his cock, making his already exposed glans even more sensitive. I kept it stretched there as I positioned myself above him and then slipped down on to the lean length of his dick.

He filled me. My pussy ached around him, widened and slightly stretched by his throbbing rod. The water washed and shushed around my vulva, caressing and stroking, and then I reached down with my other hand and mimicked the water with my fingers. I stroked his root and my lips. My fingers slipped and slid around, through the wet tangle of my curls and around his balls.

Virge held my gaze and let me move above him. Up. Sliding right up till I was almost off him, then down and plunging hard so that he knocked the neck of my womb and made me gasp a little. His cock seemed to rear up at that, at that little frown of pain that creased my forehead. I sat back a little, getting him further in, arching my back and widening my knees so that I could run my fingers over my clit and play with myself in the water.

'Oh, that's good,' whispered Virge, his hands spread wide on my hips as he steadied me. 'Get down harder. Deeper.'

I moved some more, making the bulbous head of his straining cock bounce hard inside me and penetrate so deep that it almost hurt. He thrust a little against me, filling me, and I felt him swell inside me a bit more. I was so full. I gasped. He wasn't wide, but he was long. The nose of his dick felt as though it had taken up every inch of my insides. He slid down in the seat a little more and then let his finger smooth up the crack of my ass while I played with my clit.

I was breathing faster by this time, my eyes closing intermittently and my senses on red alert. I could feel the tingling around my neck and hair that made me shiver and rub harder with my fingers. Virge moved under me, helping me as my thighs flexed and strained. We moved faster and harder, fucking each other in the hot swirling water. I could feel a hot pulse beating in my veins, a reedy drubbing beat that made me sigh and arch my back, straining up so that my hard clit got even more of my fingers. Virge sucked my tits noisily, slurping and drawing with his full lips, then letting his teeth play to the tips until they were hard and red and sore.

He seemed to like to see me wince a little, not give me pain exactly but just to add a little bit of zest to what could have been an everyday fuck. Then I ceased to care as his thick thumb pressed abruptly into my tight arse-hole and I gaped and whispered and tried to widen myself for him.

When I was full – full of cock, full of thumb and most of all full of need – I began to move harder and faster. I rubbed and fretted at my clit with my fingers, chasing the heady sensations that seemed so close and yet so far away. Virge bit hard on my nips, making me squeal as the tips turned scarlet. But it was exactly what I needed: a little bit of nastiness.

I gasped and groaned as that tiny essence of pain thrust me into orgasm and I came hard on to his thrusting cock. My clit pulsed beneath my fingers, like a giant pulse with a beat all of its own. I subsided and moaned against Virge's shoulder, my teeth bared and ready to bite. God, it felt great. I was warm and relaxed and sleepy afterwards, and Virge smiled as he pushed my hair out of my eyes.

'You're not really a damn virgin, are you?' I challenged, spreading my fingers wide on his chest.

'Nah.' He grinned. 'It's just a name I had that's kind of stuck.'

'I knew that. I did.' I grinned back, trying to convince myself. But there was a twist of disappointment in me too. I did quite fancy deflowering a real virgin. Maybe one day, I promised myself, as we wrapped ourself in oversized towelling robes and padded hand in hand over to where we'd left our clothes.

It was only on the way out that I noticed the tiny CCTV cameras that panned every inch of the whirlpool and surrounding alcoves. I stood still and watched as the eerie black eye stared back unblinking from its socket near the top of the domed ceiling.

Chapter Thirteen
storm clouds

*V*irge glanced up and then smiled.

'It's OK,' he said. 'No one gets to see the footage except the Huntsman. It's just done for security. Protection, if you like. No one wants strangers to see what we do, but equally no one wants anyone getting hurt. He's big on protecting people.'

'So where is he?' I asked, buttoning my skirt. 'Where does he watch from? And whose army does he send down if anyone gets out of order?'

'He's here somewhere,' Virge said. 'I don't know where. And as for armies, they're never needed.' He waved to the unblinking eye. 'This is just a safety net.'

As he turned to leave, I tilted my face up to the camera and smiled sweetly just for the Huntsman. Then I followed Virge out through the curving tunnels and back up to the party.

I found Sam an hour later. He was arm in arm with the brunette from earlier – and with a new girl. She was a supercilious-looking blonde who annoyed the hell out of me for no obvious reason. Around us, the party seemed to be winding up. Either that or everyone had melted into the shadows, or down to the basement baths, or up the curving staircase to the bedrooms.

The Shoemaker was nowhere to be seen, but Virge stood out on the porch and grinned a farewell to us as we left. The couple in the cocktail outfits were just leaving too, and Sam and I stood to one side of the driveway and watched their gleaming German car pass with its low, restrained hum.

We walked home along the cliff road in silence, the skies overhead heavy with the storm that had been threatening all evening. Rain hadn't started, but it was up there, waiting. The air was heavy and oppressive, and I became grumpier and grumpier as we walked. It felt as if somehow the weather was having an effect on my mood.

I realised as I listened to Sam's chat that I was jealous of the blonde that had been glued to Sam's side when I'd found him. I didn't want to be jealous; it disturbed me. Sam and I had no real thing going: we were just friends on a sex odyssey, weren't we?

So why did I feel all chewed up when he told me that the girls had led him to a room upstairs? Why did I feel knotted inside when he described how they'd placed their warm, soft lips to his groin and proceeded to suck his cock in a hundred different and imaginative ways without once letting him come? He gave me all the details as we took a short cut through the well-lit Leisure Gardens. I folded my arms across my chest as I walked, trying not to concentrate too hard on the finer points of his deep-throat descriptions.

'Just shut up about it, will you?' I snapped at him as I jammed the keycard into the slot and let us into the hotel room. Outside, a low rumble of thunder reverberated around the skies. I stalked over to the balcony doors and slammed the casement shut just as the rain started lashing against the glass.

'About what?' Sam's ever-reasonable tone of voice suddenly irritated me.

'About how wonderful those girls were. Anyone would think that *I* never gave you a decent cock-suck.'

He was silent, standing with his back to the door and a frown on his face.

'Oh,' I said after a moment, deliberately misunderstanding his silence. 'So you're saying I don't blow as well as them, are you?'

'Carrie!' He laughed and spread his hands out in a slightly pleading way. 'What do you mean? Of course you do. Better! You give me the best head I've ever had.'

'So why were those two so bloody newsworthy then? Anyone would think you'd fucked them.'

'So what if I had?' he asked quietly, a tiny puzzled frown creasing the usually smooth skin between his eyebrows.

'So what nothing. I suppose you did and you just forgot to tell me.'

I turned and jerked the curtains closed, then unbuttoned my shirt and threw it on the floor before reaching for the oversized T-shirt I planned to sleep in. Sam stepped up close behind me and put his arms around me, cupping my breasts and nuzzling against my hair. I could smell the champagne and orange juice on his breath, and a darker, unfamiliar scent. Something erotically female and musky washed across my cheek as he exhaled. Pussy.

'Don't fight with me,' he murmured. I bit my lip impatiently and tried not to imagine him with his mouth pressed against the blonde girl's cunt.

I wondered why he suddenly irritated me so much. Sam was just so nice. So reasonable. Most of the time, I loved the way he was, and fighting with anyone was just another reminder of the bad old days with Patrick. But tonight, I felt edgy and irritable. It could have been the stormy weather that had settled in. Or it could have been

174

that I was getting a little tired of being in charge all the time. Being the leader was OK, but it did get a little wearing after a while. Maybe I wanted someone else to take the lead for a change. Or maybe it was just the green-eyed monster rearing up her ugly head at the thought of being unfavourably compared with a girl who had long, glossy blonde hair, perfect lips and a bosom that heaved and swelled out of the top of her tight silk dress.

I elbowed Sam off and stomped into the bathroom to clean my teeth.

'Anyone would think that you were jealous. *Are* you jealous?' he asked, frowning and coming to stand in the doorway, one arm reaching above his head to grip the top of the doorframe.

The muscles in his arm threw long dark shadows down the inner curve of his bicep and his white T-shirt was pulled taut across his chest. I was reminded of his similar stance when I'd tied him and suspended him in the balcony doorway, but now the memory didn't arouse me: it just irritated. Why did he have to be so sub all the time? Such a peacemaker? I dried my mouth, pushed past him and sat on the bed.

'Carrie –'

'Shut up, Sam,' I snapped. 'I don't want to talk about it. I don't want to think about it.' I lay down and pulled the duvet up over my head so that I wouldn't have to look at his puzzled face any more. 'And by the way, I fucked Virge in the whirlpool.'

There was a long pause before he spoke. When he did, his voice was as reasonable as it always was. 'So what?' he asked. 'Am I supposed to go into a towering rage and ban you from having any other blokes?'

'You might at least act like you care.'

'I do care. I care that you had a nice time. I care that he treated you right and didn't hurt you. Unless, of course, you wanted to be hurt.' He sighed deeply. 'I care

175

that you seem to making such a ding dong about me getting a blowjob when you went the whole shebang with this guy. But basically I care that you are ruining a brilliant evening by being weird and moody.' He went round to the other side of the bed. I felt the mattress give under his weight. 'Unless I've missed something here, we're not an exclusive item. I thought we were free to do whatever we wanted, with whoever we wanted.' His voice dropped to a soft, coaxing pitch. 'But if you want to change that, I'm willing to talk about it.'

I didn't say anything. I couldn't. He was so nice and I was being such a bitch. Was I turning into Patrick? Did being the dominant one in a relationship mean that you had to be nasty? I swallowed a lump that had swelled in my throat and silently prayed that I wouldn't cry.

After a while, my silence got to Sam.

'Carrie, talk to me.'

I turned over in bed and buried my face in the pillow.

'God, PMT or what?' he said mildly, getting up and going into the bathroom. When he came out, I pretended to be asleep, and in the morning we hardly spoke.

It was hard to concentrate on work once I got back from my weekend. The aerospace job wasn't going that well, and we'd lost a pitch for another client to a rival consultancy. Max didn't seem to be around, and I was determined not to call Sam for a while, although he mailed me a couple of times and left a tentative message on my answerphone when I didn't e-mail him back.

Tentative was one word. Submissive was another, I thought, as I pressed my finger on the *play* button of the answering machine and listened. Even Sam's voice irritated me now, and I deleted the messages without listening to them again. I needed some space and time to think about him, and about what it was that I wanted. And also about what it was that had irritated me so much about him at the end of the weekend. It had been such a good couple of days. Exciting, fun and tantalisingly erotic. Until I'd spoilt it.

My mind kept re-creating little scenes from the Bournemouth party, and I was constantly checking my e-mail, waiting for a word from the Huntsman. But when I got something on the Wednesday, it wasn't exactly what I'd expected:

Dearest Dominique,
When I said come to Bournemouth, I didn't actually mean come. You were supposed to make friends with the boys, not screw one of them, LOL.
You look beautiful when you're fucking. I love the way your eyelids flutter when you come, and with that wet hair you looked like a mermaid. Maybe you're ready for more? A girl after my own heart . . .
Regards, H.

He must have been glued to the CCTV, I thought, smiling as I rested my chin on my hand and reread his e-mail. *You look beautiful when you're fucking*, he'd said, I thought with a frown. Someone else had said that to me recently, as well. But I couldn't remember who it had been.

Hoping to intrigue him, I didn't bother to reply for a few days, and spent my evenings teasing Gabriel – who seemed to have acquired a girlfriend during my weekend away – and playing silly flirting games in chat rooms with people I didn't know. It passed the time, and helped me avoid picking up the phone and calling Sam. I was determined that I wasn't going to ring him. I was a free agent. And I wanted to stay that way.

Really I did.

But the next e-mail came from the Huntsman on a bleak Thursday at the very end of September. I was frustrated at work, bored at home, and I hadn't been for a run for over a week. I was also half a bottle of Chardonnay down when I checked my mail.

Dominique,
Haven't heard from you for a while. Can't be bothered to play mind games. But if you want to come out to play again, let me know. Its next weekend. Cambridge. The ball's very much in your court so either pick it up and run with it or throw it back my way.
Regards, H.

Because of the wine I'd consumed, I dialled Sam's number without even thinking about it. Mrs Grey's cool, well-modulated tones echoed out from the answerphone. I didn't feel like leaving a message, so I cut the connection and decided to go to Cambridge alone.

Chapter Fourteen
the snow queen

*A*ctually, I didn't actually get to see much of Cambridge. I spent the evening at a restaurant playing footsie with Virge while the Shoemaker went on at length about a particularly lovely pair of horse-hoof boots which he thought would suit me, but which I thought sounded truly inelegant. He grinned at my curling lip and raised an eyebrow.

'Come on,' he coaxed. 'Haven't you ever thought about being a horse? Imagine shaking that ass with a little swishing horse's tail hanging there. Imagine cantering around with the ring of metal striking out from the tarmac as your newly smithed hooves clink on the ground. You'd love it!'

'I'd feel like a complete idiot!' I protested, laughing. 'But if you want to get yourself all dressed up and be my pony, then carry on.'

He swept his pale eyes over my form and shook his head with a smile. 'No, sorry, dear. You girls just don't do it for me. But *her* . . .' he indicated the slim waiter with the narrow moustache and trendy goatee '. . . oh, mama, open the door and let me in.'

We both watched as the waiter sashayed over to the

next table and I admired the neat bulge of his buttocks under his black trousers. Then I grinned across the table at the Shoemaker.

'He's mine,' I said.

'Oh no, sweetie.' He shook his head and widened his eyes in a good-natured challenge. 'She's mine!'

We exchanged conspiratorial looks and I giggled. Virge gave a huge sigh, then leaned forward and ran a finger across the back of my hand.

'Why don't you two stop vying for supremacy and eat your food?' he said. 'It's obvious neither of you would win this particular competition.'

'Oh yeah?' we chorused. 'Why's that?'

'Cos I'd win hands down. And I don't even like boys.'

'Then why would you even *want* to win?' I asked.

'Because I don't like to narrow my horizons,' said Virge, grinning. 'Now eat up and let's go. We'll be late. It's party time, Dominique.'

This time the party was in a stately home on the outskirts of Cambridge. Heaven knows how they persuaded the local heritage people to let them party in the building, but they did. Maybe one of the heritage people was at the party, who knows. I saw some of the same faces from the Bournemouth weekend, and a few new ones too.

The party was fun, although I was still a spectator. I didn't see anyone who might be the Huntsman, although his identity was now something which occupied a lot of my thoughts. I really wanted to know who he was, what he looked like. I danced with Virge and a few others, and drank tequila-and-lime until 3 a.m.

The next morning I woke up alone in my hotel room. I had a thumping headache and my make-up was still smeared under my eyes where I'd forgotten to take it off before falling into bed.

The weekend was over too soon. Home seemed drab and dull, and the weather started closing in so that it seemed as if we'd missed autumn altogether and launched straight into winter. I still kept the silence up with Sam, and after a while his e-mails dried up. It didn't stop me checking my mailbox eagerly every day, though. I knew I was being stupid. He was a nice, uncomplicated guy and I was losing a good thing, but I wanted to keep my distance. The experiences I was having with the other people I'd met on the Internet were making me into a new person, and until I found out exactly who I was I didn't want a relationship cluttering things up.

I found myself going out more with Max. He'd been back to the States for a few weeks, but Leon needed him again, so back he came and took me out when he had time. He was so different to Sam, and so much more what I felt I had needed that night in Bournemouth: someone to kick against, to spark off of. Someone who was the least submissive man I knew apart from my ex-husband, but in a far, far better way.

The time I spent with Max was fun and we had great sex, but I was distracted. I found myself thinking about the group all the time. I gleaned a lot of information over the next few weeks from my chat with the Huntsman. There seemed to be a select inner core, almost a family, that consisted of Virge, the Shoemaker, a gorgeous male flamenco dancer called the Marquis of Carrabas, the Twins who were girls who had eyes mostly for each other but who apparently experimented with boys when they had nothing better to do, and several others that Virge had mentioned but that I'd not yet met.

I was still an outsider, not a real member of the family, but by Hallowe'en I'd been to three more weekends. I fancied Virge, but I also fancied the Marquis. And when we all dressed for Hallowe'en and went to a fetish party at a nightclub in Bristol, I fell head over heels in lust with someone else in the group.

I recognised her the instant I saw her, even though it was weeks since she'd stepped off the train at

Bournemouth with her expensive leather suitcase. Tall, slender and clad in her trademark white leather coat, SQ had her chauffeurine in tow and led another girl on a leash, like a dog.

Virge had taken me to see the Grope Box up on the first floor of the club. This was a wide horizontal box that a person could lie down in if they wanted. Along all the sides and in the top were oval holes that had been fitted with inverted gloves made of smooth ebony rubber. The person inside couldn't see who was feeling them, but just had to lie in the dark and enjoy the sensations as anonymous gloved hands slipped between their legs, over their chest, along their arms. It was the ultimate in submission: let yourself lie back and be plundered.

SQ – the Snow Queen – put her dog-girl in the box and spent a playful half hour smoothing her hands all over the girl along with a few other individuals who had intense expressions of desire on their faces. SQ, in contrast, looked utterly unconnected with her actions; she stared into the middle distance and pressed her fingers into the dog-girl's tight little ass, whispering occasionally to make the girl change position or open up further.

Finally the girl came, trembling and sighing. SQ, with a look of boredom on her lovely face, swept her hair over one shoulder and simply walked off, leaving the chauffeurine to get the poor dog-girl out of the box. I was outraged at SQ's callousness and followed her, leaving Virge to be a gentleman with the dog-girl, who he seemed to have a particular interest in.

SQ stalked around the club, ignoring most people despite their obvious interest in her. She paused for a while by a rubber-seated swing that was suspended on a short length of gleaming silver chain from the ceiling. We both watched as a pretty little black girl sat on the seat, and then hooked her bare feet into shortened stirrups. The stirrups were positioned so that her heels were pressed tight to her bottom and her knees were spread wide up by her shoulders.

The girl's companion was a man of about forty with a tattoo that snaked from under the waistband of his leather chaps up to his left shoulder. He stepped forward and gave the girl a deep kiss. I watched, a rush of heat warming my body, as he tenderly pushed up her skirt, unpopped the fastening on the gusset of her knickers. The girl was totally open, pink and glistening. The man stood still – buttocks tensed and cock at full erection – and pushed the swing gently, and waited for it to arc the girl's cunt on to his ready cock. There was no need for either of them to move, they simply let the swing rock back and forth. The girl sighed and leaned back, letting her weight swing the seat a little faster, thrusting her cunt forward harder on to her satyr-like boyfriend.

SQ watched for a while, her face inscrutable, then she strode towards the bar. She knocked back a double vodka, straight up, then ran quickly and lightly up the wrought-iron stairs that led to another floor. I was a few paces behind, but she didn't see me. I was pretty anonymous in my tight, buckle-bound, PVC mini-skirt and matching bra-and-collar ensemble, blending in with the crowd who all looked like extras from a photo-shoot for the *Fetish Times*.

There was a chill-out area upstairs. If I perched on a sofa and sipped water, I looked just like all the other clubbers who lounged around with their zips and straps and rubbery outfits. But from where I sat I could see into a little office room that SQ had entered.

The desk light was on, and behind it sat a young woman in a tight crimson rubber vest top and a short black rubber skirt that gleamed in the soft light. The rubber had been lovingly polished until it looked almost wet and slick, and just looking at it turned me on in an oblique way. The woman had a shining collar around her neck and a pair of earrings that looked like lethally pointed spikes.

When SQ entered, the woman glanced up, her short bleached hair glistening in points around her head and her eager eyes darkly rimmed with kohl. She was punky and raw and exciting-looking. She also looked like she should be the one who was in charge. But she wasn't. She obviously got a kick out of SQ being in charge.

I watched, almost forgetting that I wasn't alone, as SQ strode over to a small refrigerator that was set on a desk in the far corner of the office. There was no talk, no preamble. She just did it. I was impressed, and a shiver of anticipation zinged up my spine. SQ extracted what looked like a dildo from the freezer department and turned to look speculatively at the woman, her hand clenched around one end while the thumb and forefinger of the other hand circled it and swept up its length as if it were a dick that she was jerking off.

I realised, as I saw what looked like steam rise in curls from the dildo and a few wet pearls of moisture form on it in the heat of the club office, that it was made of solid ice. A perfectly cylindrical ten inches of arctic steel. The thing looked huge in her hand and I wondered how anyone was going to get that inside their pussy.

I was aware that a couple beside me on the sofa had started quietly making out. There was the wet swish of tongues kissing, and a hissed inhalation of pleasure as the girl massaged the boy's leather-clad crotch and finally freed his slender, veiny cock. They were sitting so close that I could smell the girl's perfume and sense the masculine odour of the boy's sex. The girl's elbow brushed mine and she murmured an apology which hardly disturbed the beat of her hand as she slid her fingers up and down the length of the boy's dick. I smiled. Such a public display of affection didn't seem to matter. In this club, as I was learning, anything seemed to go.

The woman in the office walked slowly around the desk and sat on the edge of it, then peeled her rubber skirt up to show her neatly trimmed bush. Her crimson-glossed mouth moved as she spoke to SQ, but I couldn't hear what she said because the beat of the drum and bass, even up here in the chill-out area, was still loud enough to drown out most sounds except those that were very close.

SQ moved closer to the girl, spreading her hand wide on the girl's rubber-clad chest. Her mere touch made the girl's nipples contract and poke through the fabric like hard little pellets of candle wax. She coaxed her, kissing and licking at the girl's mouth, until the girl turned and positioned herself on all fours on the desk, her surprisingly white, plump bottom peeping out from under the ebony rubber of the skirt, and her sex glistening with arousal. Her wide ass was facing the door: anyone could have walked in; anyone could have seen her through the gap between the doorframe and the handle. But maybe that thought turned her on even more. I had a fine and uninterrupted view. I was tempted to slip a finger up under my own skirt and rub myself, but I held the desire in check for the present.

SQ gripped the fleshy rump that had been offered to her, one hand wide and steadying. She dipped her nose to the girl's sex and inhaled, an expression of pure pleasure lightening her face. It made her look more human and more involved than she had before. The boredom she exhibited earlier seemed to have gone completely, and she looked relaxed and happy. In her element, I supposed, as I watched her move in and lick the dark, fruity lips of the girl's sex. Her tongue was long and she held it stiffly, like a miniature penis, as she dipped and licked, making the girl's flesh gleam with saliva. A gush of cream loosened from deep inside her pussy as the girl became more and more aroused.

The Snow Queen spent a long time there. Her movements

were leisurely and tender, her amber eyes dreamily half-closed and her fingers playing lightly over the ice dildo that she still held in her right hand. It had begun to melt, and a little puddle of freezing water darkened the carpet near her booted foot, but then she decided to bring it into play. Sliding it in a path of cool, melted water up the back of the girl's thigh, she smoothed it around the girl's buttocks and swollen sex-lips, making the girl jut her bottom out. I heard the girl's voice then.

'Oh, please,' she said. 'Please, darling. Don't make me beg.'

The Snow Queen smiled and shook her head lightly.

'I don't have to *make* you beg, do I?' she murmured. 'You're going to do that anyway. Aren't you?' And she slid the dildo away from the girl's pussy.

'Oh, please.'

'Let me hear you say it, Christine.'

'Please.' Her words sounded almost wheedling. I wondered why she didn't just say it, but then, seeing her shiver as the ice dildo slid across the back of her thigh, I realised that she liked the delay. It was, in a subtle way, making her feel more in control. If she said the right words then the dildo would be pushed inside her; but not saying the words until she, and she alone, wanted to say them gave her the power.

SQ slipped and slid the icy cock up her other thigh, touched it lightly on her anus, and then sent it on a glistening path along Christine's spine. The girl shivered and I saw her pale skin pucker into goosebumps.

'Say it, my love.'

'No. No. Just do it,' murmured the girl.

There was a break in the music which gave me a ringing sensation in my ears. Little whispers of pleasure emanated from the couple next to me and I sighed with envy. I didn't dare look, but I knew they were having a good time. I could hear the slicking sound of lips across hard muscle and, in the office, I could see more than

enough to keep me at a fever pitch of anticipation and
desire. Fiery fingers touched through my hair and made
my scalp tingle, while my pulse seemed to have slowed
right down to a thumping beat that echoed along my
veins. Moisture creamed my inner thighs and I squirmed
a little against the soft, ancient leather of the sofa, wishing
that I'd seen fit to swallow my pride and ask Sam on this
trip. Or that Virge would come and find me. But all I had
was my own company, and my own fingers which had
snuck under the hem of my tight little PVC skirt and
were doing a private dance across my warm, pouting
sex.

I was glad that I followed SQ. Watching her taught me
things that I needed to know if I was going to carry on
being Dominique. And watching her was also pure
pleasure. At that moment, I was infatuated with her. It
was like having a crush on one of the older girls at
school: you want to be just like them in every way. And
in your fantasies you are.

I stared through the gap in the door. Christine was at
boiling point now, her juicy ass pressed out as far as she
could get it, her shoulders on the surface of the desk and
her cheek crushed down on to the timber. Her back was
curved in a dynamic arch, and her eyes were closed, her
expression blissful. As the beat of a new music track
thumped through the air, I saw her lips move and knew
she'd consented to say the begging words that SQ
wanted to hear.

The Snow Queen licked the end of the dildo, as if to
warm it, and pushed it slowly between Christine's bulging cunt-lips, rotating and pressing it in until it was
almost all swallowed by the girl's hungry sex. I wondered how it felt. Was it freezing cold? Or did it feel
almost hot against her feverish skin, the way your icy
fingers do in the winter when you put them under
running water? I stared at her, trying to imagine how she
was feeling, aware only of the picture that she made, and

of my own lust swelling up inside me so that my pulse sped along at a cracking pace and my own hungry sex swelled and bloomed against the leather of the sofa.

SQ twisted the dildo, sliding it out, and then slipping it easily back in. It was beginning to melt, both with the heat of the atmosphere and with the body heat from the burning Christine. Great drips of freezing water slid down her thighs, making gleaming wet rivulets that pooled at the little dip at the back of her knees, and then trickled on down to the table top.

I could see her panting, see her shoulders shivering with her pleasure. I rubbed a little harder at my own sweetly moist slit and let a shiver of pleasure run through my being. This was such a turn-on. I watched as the Snow Queen worked hard on Christine, diving in every now and then with her gloved fingers to rub and tweak at Christine's clit while her other hand frigged and fucked with the ice dildo. It was melting copiously, a gush of water and creamy juices running down the girl's legs. Her hips bucked and rocked, and even above the music I could hear her groans of pleasure. Great sighs and moans.

She was totally absorbed, and so was SQ. The look of boredom I had seen earlier was completely eradicated and replaced with one of enjoyment. She was wonderful. This was wonderful. I was entranced. Relaxed and absorbed, I slid down on the couch, letting the back of my neck hook against the comfortably squishy sofa-back. I widened my knees and got stuck in with my hand.

The sounds, the warmth and the pleasure that surrounded me had made me hotter than I had realised. I was soaking wet. My sex was all swollen against my own fingers, while a tingling rocket of firecrackers zipped suddenly up my spine. The couple next to me were totally abandoned. They'd manoeuvred themselves into a neat little 69 and were licking and sucking their way to oblivion.

In the office SQ was down on her knees with her face buried against Christine, licking hard and furiously at her clit while she buried the melting dildo deep inside the girl. The fingers of her free hand slipped and slid over the wet skin, then she impaled the girl's ass on her forefinger, delving in deep. Her hand twisted and rolled, both her wrists supple as she fucked the girl's pussy with the dildo, and her butt with her finger.

I, despite my usually private nature, slid suddenly into a tight little climax that made my eyelashes flicker and my sex swell up and throb against my fingers. It was delightful, delicious, and I gazed with longing as Christine came too, bucking against SQ's hands and giving a loud, guttural cry of ecstasy. As I lay back with my head trembling against the high leather back of the sofa, I watched SQ stand up and begin to unbutton her long coat. I realised that the show was far from over.

Unfortunately, the couple next to me chose that moment to move suddenly. Their motion caught the periphery of SQ's vision. She looked up, directly into my eyes. I stayed still, frozen, and her eyes widened a little as if in shocked recognition. Then she strolled slowly towards me. I thought she was going to speak – hoped for one irrational and exciting moment that she was going to invite me in to join them. But no such luck. She merely gave me an imperious look and kicked the door firmly shut.

I was left with Mr and Mrs Oral, and a very sticky left hand. But I didn't mind. I'd seen enough to give me quite a few good ideas for the future.

Just over a week later, Laura and I strolled down the high street, peering in windows that had been tackily decorated with fake fireworks and orange flames. Remember, remember the fifth of November. That had been and gone a couple of days previously, but our local

189

shopkeepers hadn't quite got round to taking down the frillies.

'Aagh! Look at that monstrosity!' Laura was browsing for a wedding dress that might at a pinch be suitable for a chilly February wedding. But so far all we'd seen were off-the-shoulder puffball numbers that would leave her frozen solid in no time. The ivory dress in the window of a shop which called itself Gloriana – subtitled Shoes and Wedding Belles I noticed with a suppressed giggle of disbelief – was huge. A creation of pale chiffon layers and an exaggeratedly scooped neck which would have the vicar reaching for his bi-focals.

'God, no,' I murmured. 'Don't any of these designers know the meaning of "less is more"?'

'All these dresses look the same,' moaned Laura. 'It's either bodices and big skirts, or bodices and Empire-line skirts. Where's the originality? I don't want to look like everyone else!'

'You won't,' I reassured her. 'You'll look like you and no one else. What about having something made?'

'Too expensive.'

'What if *we* made something?'

She cast a sceptical eye in my direction. 'You are joking. I hope.'

I shrugged and turned away so that I would no longer have the glare of Gloriana's glory in sight. There was a young couple coming up behind us and for one heart-stopping moment I thought it was Sam. With another girl. I felt incredibly sick and empty as I watched them approach. I couldn't take my eyes off of them. She was gazing up at him with a look of total trust and adoration.

But as they stopped, she with hands thrust in the big pockets of her coat, he with his arm around her shoulders, I saw that it wasn't Sam at all. Just someone who looked a bit like him. But even so, it made my heart thud painfully and my insides twist with regret.

Why had I let him go, I wondered. No, I hadn't let him

go. I'd positively chased him off. All because I was afraid of getting involved. And because he wasn't quite perfect enough for me. I shoved my hands down hard into my coat pockets and swallowing the tearful lump that had swelled in my throat.

'Come on,' Laura said, linking arms with me and giving me an odd look. 'I'm freezing. Let's do coffee.'

We stayed at the coffee house for too long, but as soon as I got home I sent a tentative e-mail to Sam. He didn't reply. His continued silence made his submissiveness seem like a distant, and maybe not very accurate, memory.

Chapter Fifteen
fire and ice

*T*he next weekend that the Huntsman arranged was a week later. A hotel in the Norfolk Broads. In case I still wasn't to be included in the sex games, I took along a few toys, including a little ice-bag containing a couple of ice dildos that I'd been perfecting in the evenings when Gabriel was out.

I had hardly begun to unpack my clothes when there was a tap at the door.

Outside, lounging casually against the door frame, was the Snow Queen.

She didn't speak at first, simply pushed the door wide with one hand, stepped inside, closed it firmly behind her and raised an enquiring eyebrow.

'So,' she said. 'We meet again, Miss Dominique.'

I swallowed hard and tried to look brave.

'Indeed we do, Snow Queen.'

'I've been thinking,' she murmured, trailing one pale-gloved forefinger along the timber surface of the vanity unit as if checking for dust. 'And I've reached an interesting conclusion.'

'Yes?'

'I think you need to be tutored in dominance.' She

smiled, a tiny, cat-like curving of her lips that didn't quite reach her amber, slanting, beautifully made-up eyes. 'Let's face it, you're not actually very good at it. Are you?'

I was astounded at the cheek of the woman. We'd seen each other twice before. Briefly. Very briefly. And even then she'd done her level best to take absolutely no notice of me whatsoever. And now here she was, wearing her best leathers and telling me I needed to be tutored. I folded my arms and tried to stare her down but she simply laughed.

'Dominique, my sweet.' She reached for me and circled my wrist with her white-gloved fingers. 'Don't be offended. I only want to help you along. I've seen you in action, you see. The Huntsman showed me the footage of you in Bournemouth.' She smiled. 'Beautiful. But hardly inspiring, my dear.' Her fingers tightened on my wrist.

Her touch – although separated from skin to skin contact by the white leather of her gloves – made my hand zing as though there was molten lava in her fingers. I tried to jerk away, feeling as if she'd stung me, but she simply tightened her grip and moved in towards me.

I was aware of a sudden clenching sensation of desire in my stomach as I caught a whiff of her sultry perfume. She was so near that I could see the tiny flare of her exquisitely shaped nostrils, hear the slight rasp of her breath in her throat. She stared into my eyes, her gaze so much braver and more direct than mine felt, and smiled.

'I'm not going to hurt you,' she whispered. 'Dominance isn't about pain –' her lips curved in a tiny smile '– or at least not always. It's about who's in control and who's not. And I think you need to be shown how a woman can be in control. Then when you go back to your young Sam, you'll be the woman he always dreamed of.'

Sam? My heart gave a little twist of sadness, but I was

determined not to give her the satisfaction of telling her that he wasn't 'my' young Sam any more.

'How do you know I'm not already the woman he always dreamed of?' I challenged.

'I can tell you won't be able to keep him. Do you know, I saw the look in his eyes at that party in Bournemouth.' She laughed and shook back her long black hair. 'He stared at you with such longing. Such love –'

'Love!' I spluttered.

'Oh, yes. He probably imagines he's in love with you.' She paused. 'But that won't last if you can't effectively show him who's in charge.'

I realised that her fingers had been working their way down my forearm, slipping and smoothing a passage of fire to my elbow. She pushed back my wide sleeve with her thumb and began to rub – so delicately that I could hardly bear it – on the tender skin there.

'What you do is not enough.' Her voice had dropped to a whisper.

I felt a flare of anger that she made such assumptions about me, and about other people's relationships. She had no right. No knowledge on which to base her suppositions. I felt my lips set into a stubborn, hard line and wrenched my arm from her grip. 'Stop it.'

'Oh. So you do have a little fire in your veins. The Huntsman said as much. He likes you, you know.' There was a shadow of something which could have been envy in her voice. 'He likes you a lot. I've never seen him as protective as this about anyone else before.'

She gazed at me speculatively and then reached forward suddenly and grasped my left breast in her hand, squeezing quickly and firmly. I gasped at her audacity and knocked her arm down with the back of my hand.

'How dare you,' I said. 'You don't know me. You don't know anything about me. And neither does the Huntsman.'

'But you're wrong. We can read you like a book,' she said, giving a little half-laugh.

I meant to push past her and get out of there. She made me so angry. How dare she follow me in here and start lecturing me?

But somehow my hands – instead of unlocking the door – flew to the fastenings on her long leather coat. I wrenched it partly open and jerked the sleeves down, trapping her arms by her side and feeling a small thrill of satisfaction at the flicker of surprise in her eyes. I pushed her back against the door, pressed my body to hers and fastened both my hands on her ample breasts.

'If you can read me so well, how come you couldn't tell I'd do this?' I asked, and kissed her. Hard.

She twisted her head and tried to push me off but the coat was so tightly fitted around her arms that she could scarcely move. I insinuated one knee between hers and roughly parted her legs. She fought me, her eyes angry at having the upper hand so rudely snatched away from her. Her breasts heaved beneath my hands. She felt delicious, all muscular and toned but with these lovely, soft, ripe breasts that I could feel swelling under my fingers.

I dropped my mouth to the heaving mound of her cleavage and sucked lightly at her skin, enjoying the surprisingly sweet taste of her. I slipped my fingers into the top of her bra and hooked out a nipple: hard and pink, like a coffee-flavoured sweet, it was possibly the most tempting thing I'd ever seen on a woman.

I bent my head and placed my lips to it, remembering what I'd seen her do to Christine. I drew hard on her teat, feeling it lengthen over my tongue. It was like a hard bullet in my mouth and I had to restrain myself from biting it. I sucked and circled it with my tongue, glancing up to see that her eyes were fixed on my face and her cheeks were flushed. There was a little crease between her dark eyebrows, as if she was frowning hard.

195

She probably was: she had seemed good at frowning when I'd seen her in action.

With my mouth still suckled on to her tit, I let my hands wander down her body and smoothed the skirts of her coat open so that her bare toffee-dark legs were uncovered. She shivered slightly at my caress and I smiled against her breast, gratification warming me as I smoothed her soft thighs with my fingertips. Her flesh goosebumped under my hands and I knew I had her then: I knew she was aroused, as aroused as I was, and it made me let my own feelings surge through my body: beating heart, thudding pulse, tingling palms and feet, a sick knot in my belly that would need release either with my hand or hers.

I sucked my way off her nipple and studied its swollen length. It was dark and delicious, and elongated to about an inch. I kissed it and slid my tongue from there up over her rounded breast to the little hollow at the base of her throat. My hands gripped her narrow hips and I jerked her pubis against mine.

She stopped wriggling and let her head tip back against the door but I didn't let up the pressure of my body on hers just in case she was faking.

I kept my thigh locked between hers, my leg tense and hard against her soft inner flesh, while my hands probed and smoothed the dusky orbs that swelled so enticingly from her white bra. She seemed to be wearing nothing under her coat except the bra and a pair of lacy, smooth French knickers that peeped out from the under the fastening of the coat. The silky slip of her tiny gusset did little to conceal the warmth and juiciness of her neat little sex that pressed involuntarily down on to my leg.

Trembling against her, I felt delighted with my dominant role in the sudden turn of events. I loved seeing her helpless and bound against the door with my hands on her tits. She looked like a gorgeous slut: red lips, flashing eyes, one bared breast, and a great mane of hair that flowed down over her semi-naked shoulders like a cloak.

I had only ever seen her in command before, in control, the Snow Queen, making them all squeal and squirm with her long, ice dildos and her skilled fingers that seemed to flicker and make girls come just by the lightest touch. But now here she was. At bay. Caught and bound. Just by little old me.

The feeling I had was one of triumph and victory and I shoved my leg up a little harder to press against her moist sex. She gasped, bit her swollen bottom lip and glared into my eyes. I raised one eyebrow – remembering that that was exactly what she'd done when she'd first followed me in here – and then I did the last thing that she expected: I smiled warmly.

'What are you doing?' she hissed.

'Exactly what you told me I needed to do.'

'Oh, yeah? What's that?' She was almost belligerent.

'Taking control of the situation.'

'This is my show.'

'Well, I've just stolen it from you.' I smoothed back her hair with one hand and cupped her cheek against my palm. 'Now don't say another word unless it's something nice. All I've heard from you is sniping and bitching and telling people how useless they are. Say something pleasant, or don't speak at all.'

I kissed her again and felt her lips go soft and pliable under mine. She seemed determined not to kiss me back, not to give me any acknowledgement that she might be enjoying the feel of my mouth on hers. But I knew better because the soft slick of cream that wet my thigh was evidence enough that she didn't want me to stop.

I slipped a hand under her buttock and lifted her slightly, making her sit up on the vanity unit. She wriggled and locked eyes with me, challenging me, waiting to see what I was going to do. I spread her knees with just the lightest pressure of my fingers and then swept

197

one hand up between her legs to cup her sex. She felt humid and sticky, positively glowing against my palm.

'Nice,' I murmured. 'So warm. I wonder if you need cooling down?'

She didn't reply. So I left her there, sauntered over to the little refrigerator and retrieved some of the frozen dildos that I'd stowed in the ice compartment. The Snow Queen stared, and then gave a small, low laugh.

'You should pay me royalties,' she said. 'Let me see.' Her fingers ran deftly over the surface. 'Hmm, pretty good. But you need more practice.' Her eyes flickered up to meet mine and she gave a rueful little smile. 'But not bad for a beginner. Have you tried them yet?'

'Not yet.' I encircled the long ice dick with thumb and forefinger and rubbed it slightly. 'I thought I'd do that now.'

There was a long pause. Her eyes were fixed on the length of the thick cock in my hand and I could swear that she licked her lips, like a little cat. She nodded slowly. 'OK. But let my hands free first. I need to hold on to something, brace myself on my arms.'

'OK.' I trusted her enough to know that the pleasure on her face was genuine and that she wasn't about to do a runner. I placed the ice dildo on the table and undid her coat. She massaged her wrists gently and frowned with that adorable little crease between her brows showing up again.

'Thanks.'

And that was it. She unhooked her bra and tossed it over on to the bed, then slipped out of her wispy little French knickers. I pressed her shoulders back against the mirror and she hooked her high heels up on the edge of the timber surface. I sighed as she did that: she looked so open, so available. It was as if her body consisted of just a jutting, perfectly topiaried pussy and nothing else. Her limbs were folded and her arms disappeared behind her to brace herself. She shook her abundant hair down her back and tipped her chin at me.

'Fuck me, then,' she said. 'Show me how good it can be to get fucked by a girl with an ice dildo.'

I slid one hand down the folded length of her leg and gripped her, took a firm footing on the floor, and then placed the nose of it gently against her juicy slit. She gasped at the cold and shivered and I stared – fascinated – at her tits as her nipples sprang erect. I wondered if I ever looked as good as that, as beautiful and ripe, but then I ceased to care what I looked like as I became absorbed in her pleasure, her shivers, her sighs. She was beautiful, and she only ever fucked girls. Only ever did it to other girls, never got other girls to fuck her. And here she was, in my room, on my vanity unit with her legs held wide and her hole opening like a dark flower for the thick penetration of the ice dildo that I'd made.

I began to move it a little quicker, listening to the delicious sucking noise she made as I withdrew the length of it and then thrust it home again. It began to melt slightly in my hot hands, cold water dripping down and darkening the carpet, leaving cool rivulets on my wrist as I smoothed it in. Out. In. Deliciously out. I found myself kissing her, our lips soft together and lightly scented with lipstick. It was so different kissing her to kissing Sam, Gabriel or Max. But in this foreign country I felt totally at home.

She started to make wonderful little sighing noises and I dropped to my knees in between her legs and kept up the smooth, icy slip and slide of the dildo as I kissed her bulging clit and began to circle it with my tongue. She groaned, and I sat back on my heels to admire her briefly. Then, when I saw the tiny flare of her rosebud anus, I couldn't resist. I licked my third finger and slipped it in. She bucked a moment, and then began to writhe, her breath coming in great gasps as she pumped her arse against my hand and seemed to swallow up the ice dildo.

199

'Oh, please,' she gasped. 'Lick me again. Mouth. Please!'

Well, it would have been rude to refuse, and she was such a delicious dish. I pressed my mouth against her clit again and imagined how lovely the warmth would feel combined with the ice in her honeypot and the soft strength of my finger in her bottom, and then she was coming. Great moans and rhythmic clenching of her sex on the dildo. Her clit poked against my tongue and she gripped the back of my head and directed me in even closer so that I was thrust against her muff and working hard. Working my tongue. Working the dildo. Filling her.

'Oh, fuck yes!' she yelled. I almost came myself with the sound of her pleasure.

She took a while to recover, her forehead beaded with sweat as she slumped against the mirror. The last of the ice melted between her lush legs and I massaged the cool water into her hot flesh. Her muscles flickered and jerked under my hand, and then she smiled at me from between sleepy lashes.

'Dominique, I was wrong about you,' she murmured affectionately. 'You're OK. If you work at Sam like that then he'll be eating out of your hand for the rest of his life.'

I smiled quietly and didn't enlighten her. The fact that Sam wasn't part of my life any more was none of her business.

As winter began to set in, Richardson's became inundated with work. I went in on the last Monday in November and was immediately landed with a new account for an independent financial consultancy, plus the aerospace stuff that seemed to be an on-going project. But it seemed that either I'd lost my flair or I wasn't giving enough to the job, because Don Richardson frowned at everything I did. Apparently my recent work was 'bereft of any ideas, poorly presented and super-ficial', according to my shoot-from-the-hip boss.

'What the hell is this?' he queried just before lunch, his voice ominously quiet. Opposite me, James did the sensible thing and ducked his head down behind his computer screen, rendering himself invisible and out of the firing line. I watched as Don flipped a dummy box I'd spent all morning making from one hand to the other.

'It's the dummy for the product launch pack,' I said patiently.

'No, it's not,' he said with a little lilting sneer. 'It's something that a college leaver would have chucked out as being too flimsy, too amateurish and too –' he searched for a suitable descriptive word but came up with one of his usual eloquent ones as he pulled the box apart at the seams '– crap.'

I felt my face burn and stared at him. 'Oh,' I said, when I found my voice. 'Sorry.'

'Don't just stand there wasting time and apologising,' he said, his voice rising slightly. 'Just get on and do it again. Properly. Or I'll have to damn well do it myself.'

Wondering why it was that I didn't have the guts to do a Dominique on Don Richardson, I turned away, bit my tongue hard, and resignedly pulled another sheet of box board towards me.

On Saturday night Gabriel was out with his girlfriend, Clara. She was doing Sociology and Psychology at the same university as him. They'd hooked up the weekend that I had been in Bournemouth, and been pretty much inseparable ever since.

Since the advent of Clara, Gabriel and I had toned down our mistress/houseboy game and become more like flirty friends. He'd even made a few noises about getting a flat with Clara next term. I knew I'd miss him, and I couldn't help half-hoping that they'd go off each other soon, because I wanted to keep him for myself.

Finding someone to fill his Marigold gloves would be a problem.

Gabriel stooped to peck me on the cheek as he left and I grinned and waved him off, feeling more like his mother than his landlady. When he'd gone, I curled into the sofa and ate half a tube of Pringles while I watched TV. The Internet didn't hot up till around ten when the Americans came online, so it was late when I finally logged on, without much enthusiasm, and peeked into a few chat rooms. But then I found I couldn't settle to chatting with anyone.

Surfing the adult rooms suddenly all seemed so pointless. So dull. What had begun as an exciting foray into cyberspace had become, essentially, a chore. Everyone was looking for the same thing: some dirty talk to get them off. That was fine. That was exciting for them. But for me, once I'd done it for a few months, it had become as dull as a muddy ditch in the deepest countryside. The real people I'd met through the net, and the parties I'd gone to, were the whole point for me now. Meaningless chit-chat with someone who could be anyone seemed to have lost its savour.

I idly chatted to someone who claimed to work for the FBI – yeah, right, like he'd be on the web bragging about it – and then a horny little number in New Jersey who was leaping all over the place like an energetic monkey. He was desperate for phone sex, but I no longer had the energy or the inclination. I logged off and checked my mail.

Nothing.

Something had to be done.

I clicked on 'new message'.

Sam,
I miss you and I'm sorry.
Carrie xxxxxxxx

There was no reply that night. At work next day I checked my mail at lunchtime and smiled at a dumb joke Max sent me, but there was nothing from Sam. Then when I got home my heart jumped as a message flipped into my mailbox:

Carrie,
That's not really going to do it for me.
Sam

I tapped a reply asking whether we could be friends again. He must have been online because I got a message back almost straight away.

Carrie,
I don't know if I want to be friends again. You really hurt me.
Sam

I frowned and sighed. The thought of Sam being hurt by me was almost more than I could bear. Why had I been so nasty? I hadn't meant it. I really liked him. *Really* liked him. I tapped quickly on the keypad.

Dearest, darling Sam,
Can I kiss it better?
Love love love
Carrie

But he'd logged off. Either that or he didn't want to reply. I went to bed that night with a heavy heart and woke up in the morning feeling sick and headachey. It was the beginning of a monster flu bug that laid me low for almost a week.

I had a raging temperature and a throat that felt like I'd swallowed a football. If I'd been on my own I think I would have given up hope of ever feeling human again.

But Gabriel really looked after me. I had hot toddies at night and a bath run for me each morning, and while I soaked in steaming, fragrantly mentholyptus water, he changed my pillow cases and fluffed up the duvet before trotting off to classes. It was a bit like having a wife, I thought, grinning to myself as I settled down to drool over the Christmas spreads in the colour supplements. I promised myself I'd say thank you to him in the nicest possible way when I was better.

After three days off sick, I was well enough to go back to work, and checked my mail over a breakfast coffee in my dining room. There was still nothing. Sam was making me pay. Not so submissive as I'd assumed, then, I thought wryly. Maybe I'd been wrong about him.

The commuter train was delayed, so I got home from work angry, tired and desperate for the comfort of my bed. Three days off sick should have been fine, but in my absence they'd given the product launch for GymTech to posh James to oversee and he'd lashed it up. Which was – according to my increasingly irrational boss – my fault.

I'd spent most of the morning on the phone trying to calm the understandably irritated client, and the afternoon making amendments on the text. Don Richardson had severely criticised my handling of the problem. During the long journey home I stared out of the grimy carriage window, barely seeing the rain-streaked fields and hedges as I fantasised about looking for another job. Richardson Design Consultants were getting heavily on my nerves.

I quietly let myself in the front door, and went up the stairs slowly, my legs heavy and my body tired. I wasn't in the happiest of moods. When I got to the angle of the landing where I could see into my bedroom I stopped abruptly in my tracks. Gabriel was in my room. And he wasn't on his own.

Chapter Sixteen
my naughty angel

I could hardly believe the cheek of it. The angel Gabriel in my bedroom was one thing. After all, when I'd been languishing in bed all week I'd got used to him doing the rounds with a duster and a can of polish. But the angel Gabriel and his friend Clara? In my bed? With my toys?

I leaned against the doorframe and took a deep calming breath. The little traitor.

I peeked again and watched him steer the vibrator down the inside of her slender leg. She seemed to like it; she was writhing, and I could hear her breaths even above the regular, buzzing, electrical drone.

God, I thought. What the hell am I going to do?

The old Carrie would have sneaked down the stairs, closed the front door with an ostentatious bang and called, 'Hi! I'm home!' before going into the kitchen to give them enough time to come downstairs fully clothed and their faces set in expressions of innocence. But the new Carrie, with fully installed Dominique software, took a deep breath, shrugged, and decided to roll with it. I flipped open the top button of my shirt and strode into the bedroom.

'Hey, kids.'

Their faces were almost funny: I had to bite the inside of my mouth to prevent myself laughing. Clara nearly fainted and sat bolt upright with the duvet clutched to her bee-sting breasts. I raised a stern eyebrow and she went pale. Gabriel, true to form, went bright red and dropped to his knees beside the bed.

'I'm so sorry. I'm so sorry.' He began to wring his hands. 'I'm so sorry.'

'Change the record, Gabe.' I strode forward and jerked the duvet out of Clara's weak hands and threw it on to the floor. 'So,' I said, 'not only are you not working, you are also entertaining your little girlfriend here. In my bed. How dare you?'

'I'm so sorry.'

'I think you should be punished for that, Gabe.'

His eyes gleamed and a tiny worm of suspicion niggled at me. Had Gabe engineered this just so that I'd find them? I glanced across at Clara, but by the look of intense horror on her face, she'd obviously not been in on it if he had. I smiled at her.

'It's OK. You can go. I'm not going to punish *you*.'

She made a dash for her clothes and I watched with interest as she shrugged into a little black T-shirt. Her nose ring caught on something and she winced and then wiggled it with her forefinger. I wondered what it was that she saw in Gabe. He was so slight, and angelic, and she was so naughty-looking with her crimson-dyed hair and her rebellious piercing.

She caught me staring at her and eyed me back, as if daring me to say something. I knew that she was probably at a disadvantage – standing there in her t-shirt and nothing else, with all her tangle of black pubes on show which demonstrated just how natural her hair wasn't – so I decided to press home my superiority.

'Clara.'

'Yes?' She looked surprised that I knew her name.

'Next time, ask me first, OK?'

'OK.'

And she was gone. The only thing left of her presence was the lingering scent of her light perfume and the merest hint of musky pussy. I sniffed the air and then turned to glare at Gabe, hands on my hips. I knew I looked terrifying today: James had quailed when I'd taken the same stance with him. The fact that I was wearing a mannish-cut trouser suit with a tailored shirt, while Gabriel's longer hair made him look like a girl, made it all the more surreal.

'So,' I said, towering over him, 'what happened to the good little boy I used to share a house with, huh? Did he leave home? I think he must have. Because the only thing I can see in front of me here is a bad boy who needs a thorough punishment.'

'Sorry,' he whispered again.

But I knew that he wasn't because his eyes shone and a tiny smile hovered at the corner of his mouth. I strode over and hooked his chin with the palm of my hand. Tilting his face up, I felt a tingle of delight flare through my veins. Gabe was just so pretty, it was almost unnatural. He'd have been much better off as a girl, really. I bit my lip, watching the emotions play across his face, then an idea occurred to me that made me smile.

'Get up,' I commanded. 'Stand up, come on, look lively. I'm going to give you a make-over.'

So I sat him down in front of my dressing table and fiddled around with pots of lip shine and glossy kohl pencils until he looked like a rather naughty and slightly subversive girl-doll. Then I tapped my fingers against my trousered thigh.

'What next, I wonder?' After sliding open the drawer to his left, I ran my fingers lightly over the silkiness of its contents. Lingerie spilled out across Gabe's trembling knee. Satin, lace, and the occasional piece of wispy cotton. The colours contrasted beautifully with his pale skin:

ruby reds, emeralds, gold and the dark mystery of matt black silk. Gabriel shuddered slightly as I held up a pair of Directoire knickers. I looked into his eyes and smiled, feeling devilish.

'Get dressed,' I said softly. 'I'll find you something to put on over them.'

The something that I found was a long, elegant dress that Patrick had bought me not long before I'd finally summoned up the guts to walk out. I'd hated the dress, but he'd made me wear it to one of his corporate dinners. I'd sat, cowed and miserable with goosebumps all up my arms, in the scarlet beaded evening gown at a table where the little black dress was obviously the height of understated elegance. The other wives had all looked marvellous: smooth sleek coiffures and careful make-up. I, on the other hand, had looked like a mousey teenager who'd decided to go to the party as Shirley Bassey.

After pulling the thing off its hanger, I held it up and then glanced across at Gabriel.

'Perfect,' I said.

And it would be perfect. The ultimate revenge on Patrick, to make a boy wear the dress he'd forced me to wear. If he could only see. I imagined his face, the horror that would crease his male-model perfection, the sneer of intolerance that would curl his lips. Shuddering at the powerful emotions of loathing that the thought of him churned up, I thrust the dress at my houseboy.

Gabriel looked stunning in the dress. He swept back and forth across the bedroom carpet letting the bead-encrusted hem of the gown swish lightly against the legs of the bed. His little smile as he glanced in the mirror warmed my heart and I lay back on the bed in my tailored suit with my legs crossed at the ankle and one arm behind my head, feeling every inch the successful businessman who has bought a gorgeous hooker.

'Come to Daddy, sugar,' I said, enjoying playing the part. 'Come on over here and tell me who's the daddy.'

Gabriel shimmied over, his scarlet lips pouting and glossy, his eyes heavy with desire and pride. I slid my hand over the front of the gown, enjoying the slinkiness of the fabric over the firm leanness of his thigh. Underneath, I knew that the Directoire knickers were giving him absolutely no support whatsoever.

But when my hand reached his crotch, I knew that no support was actually needed, because his slender tool was flying high inside all that satin. Curving up, straining toward his belly button, I could feel the ridge of it under the material of the dress and it made me shiver with pleasure. He was fully loaded and ready to go, and all dressed up just for me.

Loosening the tie that I'd put on while he'd been dressing, I swallowed hard and pretended to rub the bristles that would have stubbled my chin had I actually been a man.

'So,' I murmured, 'how much is this gonna cost me?'

Gabriel fluttered his eyelashes in a moment of confusion, then caught up with me. 'For you,' he whispered, 'it's not gonna cost a thing, mister. For you, it's free.'

I raised an eyebrow and swept my gaze up and down the front of his dress.

'Mmm, nice.' I licked my lips. 'Very nice.'

I let my hand wander back over the front of the dress where his cock was making a lovely hard ridge through the fabric.

'Kiss me, sugar,' I said.

He leaned down, one hand pretending to push back the long hair he imagined that he had. His lips fluttered across mine and I sighed, relaxing back against the pillows. His mouth moved gently, tantalising and full of promise. Soft lips, so girlish that I was almost convinced. He slipped his tongue lightly over mine, then traced a line of gentle tingling over my cheek to my ear. He kissed me slowly, unhurriedly, his lips warm against my skin as I closed my eyes and imagined that I was a strong, rich businessman in an anonymous hotel room with a babe that was so hot she scorched.

He paused at my neck, his lips like soft butterflies against the pulse that thudded in my throat. I reached up and cupped his head, stroking his soft hair with my fingertips and revelling in the feel of the bead-encrusted dress as it moved lightly against my arm. The moment was pure eroticism, pure sensuality, and I wanted to make it last.

Still kissing me, his fingers slipped down over my stomach to the fly of my trousers. I rested my hand lightly on his in a subtle encouragement and cupped his as he curved his forefinger over the zip and under. There was a light pressure that made me press up towards him, needing more, then I sought his mouth with mine as I pulled him down on top of me.

I kissed him savagely. Hungrily. Desperately. I was so turned on that I could feel my white cotton knickers drenching with juice as I arched my hips up to his. The evening gown was taut between us now, his cock crushed inside it, all that manhood tight against my stomach. I fumbled with the tiny buttons that fastened the dress at the back.

'Oh, baby,' I murmured against his mouth. 'You make me so darn hot.' I suddenly realised as I said the word 'darn' that I wasn't just any old businessman seducing a willing woman. I was one businessman in particular and it gave me a curious flush of pleasure to realise that it was Max that I was pretending to be.

I wriggled a little and freed one leg so that I could wrap a thigh around Gabriel and imprison him further. Then I slid the gown off his shoulders and slipped my fingers across his tender skin.

'Mmm,' he shivered. 'That feels so nice.'

His lips sought mine again and we kissed for a long time, he with his hands cupping my face and me with my fingers playing lightly up and down his nobbly young spine. The kissing could have gone on for ever, we were both so involved with the sensuous dance of tongues and the flutter of lips, but as I let my fingers wander down Gabe's back, I felt the neat little parcel of masculine buttocks that he had under the satin dress and it made my pulse suddenly race.

I gripped him tightly in my arms and flipped him over so that he lay below me, his golden hair spilling over the pillow.

'Remember when we first started this, I said that there were three rules?' I asked, pinning him with my arms. He nodded. 'Tell me what they were.' I raised an eyebrow in challenge.

Gabriel pursed his lips, smearing a little bit of lip-shine across the soft stubble of his barely there five-o'clock shadow. He frowned and then met my eyes with his.

'OK,' he said. 'Rule one: you're not my girlfriend and there are no ties.' I nodded, smiling, as he carried on. 'Rule two: no penetration. Never ever.' He grimaced. 'And rule number three you were keeping in reserve.'

'OK, I've thought of a number three.' I smiled. 'Rule number three is that I can break the rules.' I frowned at him to emphasise what I was saying. '*You*, Gabriel, can't. But I can. Understand?'

He nodded demurely and I slid the dress down over his shoulders to reveal his chest. I dipped my head and flicked my tongue hard across one of his nipples, watching with satisfaction as it sprang to attention under my scrutiny. I licked all around it, savouring the taste of his skin and the flavour of his blond wispy hairs.

'Tonight I'm in a rule-breaking mood,' I continued, coming up briefly for air. 'And tonight I'm breaking rule number two.' I watched his eyes widen with surprise. 'Just this once.'

'Oh, Mrs Horton,' he breathed.

'Mr,' I corrected him with a grin. 'I'm a guy tonight, remember? But you can call me Max.'

211

'Max,' he murmured, his lips widening sweetly around the name. I bent my head back to his chest, almost purring as I lapped at the tight little nub of flesh. Gabriel moaned under me, his hips tightening and thrusting up to mine a little. I slid my hand down the outside of his flanks, stroking and teasing, then I grasped a handful of soft silk. I wanted the dress away so that I could feel his skin. Locking my stare with his, I grasped the fabric tight and gave it a sharp pull.

The renting noise as the fabric of Patrick's expensive dress tore was incredibly satisfying, as was the look of mild shock mingled with excitement on Gabe's face. I savagely wrenched the fabric some more, tearing it and freeing his thigh, then I eased the material up so that I could stroke his leg. Tenderly, I rubbed little circles with my thumbs, concentrating on his knot of muscle on the long lean length between hip and knee, then I slid down and caressed the back of his knee, gently easing his leg up so that he bent it and then hooked it around my buttocks, just like a girl would do if she was going to stay in the good old missionary position.

Gabriel's other leg came up and around and I felt him rest his heels against my trousered buttocks. I slipped my arms either side of his shoulders and rested on my elbows, then with little kisses and murmurs, I began to hump him, enjoying the feel of his bone-hard cock against the zip of my trousers. I rubbed and pressed, watching as he tipped his head back and fluttered his eyes closed.

I dipped my lips to his throat and sucked. Gently at first, but then with greater hunger as I felt his dick swell to even greater length under me. He felt massive, much bigger than his slim lankiness would have an observer believe. I felt myself soaking the crotch-seam of my trousers and felt suddenly desperate to cut to the chase and have him inside me. We'd been messing about with each other for months, so foreplay was hardly needed.

I fumbled with the zip of my trousers, wriggled, and then kicked them off. Then I sat up and slid my knickers down over my thighs, enjoying the cool air on my hot skin. Gabe, beneath me, lay there in the remnants of the torn evening gown, great swathes of crimson beaded silk bunched around his waist. His cock, barely contained by the silk Directoire knickers, reared up and peeked out of the waistband like some beast with a mind of its own. I cupped him briefly with my hand, revelling in the feeling of heat that emanated from his sex, then I tore my knickers off and jerked his downwards too.

He had shaved himself. His sex snaked, gleaming and denuded, from between his thighs, not a hair in sight. I goggled for a moment, then ran my forefinger over his soft skin, loving the sensation of bareness. He looked like a young boy. But a young boy with a man-size cock straining against the warmth of my palm. His swollen balls kissed the skin of his upper thigh looking for all the world like ripe apricots. As I gazed at him, I felt my cunt contract hungrily.

Placing my hands squarely on Gabe's lean chest, I raised one leg and swung a perfect arc over him to rest astride, my moist sex painting milky juice on to his belly. He moved his hands, cupping my buttocks and then stroking up to the curve of my waist, pushing my shirt up. Staring into his intense eyes, I rocked forward and moved my hips. Then plunged suddenly down on to him, slipping my juicy sex down over his shaft until his depilated groin was tight against my butt. He was big. He made me gasp as he moved a little, and I sat upright. Then, twisting my fingers around his nipples in a tight little pinch, I began to move.

I controlled our movements, flexing my thighs and easing myself up and down. Arching my body above him, I reached up to tug at my striped tie and pull it from the shirt collar. Reaching down, I gripped his wrists, twisted them up above his head, and wound the tie around him so that he was bound. In response, Gabe contracted his glutes and pushed further into me.

His movement made me start to slip more quickly up and down his cock. Through narrowed lashes I watched his face. I watched as he sighed and started to lose himself, his eyes becoming darker so that the irises were almost indistinguishable from his dilated pupils. A fine sheen of perspiration beaded his brow and his sinuous, boyish muscles undulated under the skin of his chest and upper arms.

As I watched him, I felt a sensual languor steal through my limbs, a heat that made me shudder as it stole up my spine. Electric shimmers pulsed over my skin. My pulse began to hammer more quickly and I could feel the pound of my own blood behind my temples.

We moved gradually faster, in perfect unison, and slowly the familiar sensation of bitter-sweet ecstasy prickled through my body as I neared orgasm. My nipples puckered against the smooth fabric of my bra, and poked through the fine poplin of my shirt. Gabe, his eyes fixed on mine, slipped his hands up and over the swollen mounds and began to knead them firmly.

I moaned a little, aching with need as I arched above him and then sat down hard on his straining rod. My skin began to tingle as I threw my head back and cried out. Wave after wave of pleasure broke over me and I snapped my eyes shut to savour the rhythmic pulsing, pushing down hard on to Gabriel as he became suddenly still inside me.

Realising that he was at boiling point and that I'd forgotten to even think about a condom, I raised myself up and sat above him, holding his stiff rig gently in the crook of my hand as he came. Great globs of spunk thrashed across the pale skin of his belly, and his hot cock beat a pulse against my palm, then became still. A faint sheen of sweat glossed his forehead, and his eyelashes made great shadows on his cheeks.

I laid my cheek on his chest and listened to the gradual slow of his heartbeat as he got his breath back, then I curled up in the curve of his arm and fell into a blissful sleep.

When I woke up, Gabriel had tidied away the evidence of our play-acting. There was a glass of fresh iced water on the bedside cabinet, and a note that said he'd gone over to Clara's bedsit. I sipped the water, smiled at his boyish scrawl, and curled back down under the duvet for another hour. Then I went for a run, showered, and sat in front of the computer to see if I could find Sam.

There was no mail. I went into the chat rooms and cruised for a while. Then I bumped into Eva.

Sapphire: Howdy girl. Long time no see.
Dominique: I know, sorry. What's going on?
Sapphire: Leon's out so I'm playing around. What about you?
Dominique: just looking. I was hoping to bump into SamUK. Haven't seen him have you?
Sapphire: no, lol, why don't you get yrself some variety? Try a new cock for size.
Dominique: lol, how do u know i haven't already?
Sapphire: well . . . nothing would surprise me at the moment, sweetness. You've changed so much the past few months.
Dominique: changed??
Sapphire: yes. you're different. you don't do as you're told any more. Even Leon's noticed it.
Dominique: that's good tho, isn't it? i don't want to be a doormat for the rest of my life.
Sapphire: no. the new you is a refreshing change sweetie. Oh, hang on for a minute.

She was gone for a while. I started chatting with a girl

calling herself Dizzy who was interested in swapping pics. Then Eva came back.

Sapphire: sweetheart I have to go. Leon's home early.
Dominique: okay, see ya soon.
Sapphire: I was meeting a friend in here, Devilish One, if he comes in will you chat him up for me? You'll like him, he's adventurous.
Dominique: sure, anything for a friend, lol. Bye now.

Devilish One rolled up around ten minutes after she'd left, by which time I was getting pretty tired of Dizzy's inane chat. Talking to Devilish One, I soon forgot how jaded I'd got with the net. He was funny and sarky and I found myself laughing out loud at a couple of the things he said. We swapped e-mail addresses and said good-night, then I cruised around again futilely looking for Sam for one last time before I logged off.

Eventually, I made a decision: I was going to have to ring him and sweet-talk him.

I opened a bottle of wine and drank two glasses to give me Dutch courage, then plugged the phone back in and dialled Sam's number with a shaking finger. It rang a few times, and then someone answered it, but I knew right away that it wasn't Sam. And it wasn't, thank goodness, Mrs Grey either.

'Hullo?'

'Alex?'

'Yeah?'

He couldn't have been less forthcoming if he tried. I took a deep breath and tried to charm him.

'Hi, Alex. It's Carrie here – um, Dominique?' I grimaced at my own reflection in the hall mirror. 'We met when I was staying with Sam back in the summer.'

'Yeah, I remember you.'

He remembered, but by the sound of his voice he

wasn't charmed. I wondered what Sam might have told him about me since our break-up.

'Alex, is Sam there?'

'Nope.'

'Oh. Well, do you know when he'll be back?'

'Nope.'

'Oh. OK. Um – could you tell him that I called? Tell him it was Carrie.'

'If I see him.'

'Don't forget, will you?'

'Is that it?' he asked with a patient sigh. 'I'm on my way out, so if you don't mind . . .'

'No. Sorry. That's all. Just let him know that I rang. Say that I really, really need to talk to him.' I bit my lip. 'And Alex? Tell him that I'm sorry, will you? Tell him that I realise that I acted like a bitch and I want to make it up with him.'

There was no response, just a bit of heavy breathing that told me he was still on the line. Then he grunted. 'Bye, Carrie.'

The severed connection hummed loudly in my ear.

I got mail from Devilish One almost right away and we chatted in the evenings for the next few days. When he suggested meeting up, I had no qualms at all. The stuff that I had enjoyed with Sam, and then with Virge and the group, had made me confident. I suggested the bar in a large, anonymous travelodge in Wells. Just in case Devilish turned out to be as gorgeous as he sounded, I thought with a grin, thinking of the cheap rooms and en-suite bathrooms.

I was early for the rendezvous, and curled myself into a red plush chair in a corner with a copy of Mark Harris's *Sins of the Flesh* on the table in front of me. The book had seemed the most obvious sign to use in recognising each other, and we'd laughed. By eight o'clock, I had become tired of checking out each new face that sauntered up to the bar, and was getting mightily bored of fending off hopeful businessmen with a stern 'no thanks' each time they offered to buy me a drink.

By eight-thirty I had decided that Devilish One wasn't coming, so I drained my cranberry juice and stood up. A firm hand gripped my elbow and I was steered towards the door of the bar. Twisting around, my heart in my mouth, I was shocked to see Leon close beside me, his pale eyes boring into mine. My heart kicked against my ribs and then plunged abruptly down into my guts with a sick-making finality.

Chapter Seventeen
a salve for every sore

'L-Leon. What are you doing here?'

'I could ... ask the same of you,' he countered, his voice tight and sounding as if it was loaded with grease. His habitual pauses mid-sentence had become more pronounced: that meant he was either nervous or angry. Probably the latter.

I swallowed hard and tried to wrestle my arm free of his slightly sweaty grip, but he was stronger than I remembered, and his fingers remained welded to my flesh.

'Don't try that,' he hissed, steering me in the direction of the lift. 'It wouldn't do to make a scene.'

'What are you doing? Where are we going?' I struggled some more and his fingernails bit my skin. I winced.

'Be quiet. We'll talk in privacy: I don't want everyone ... to know my business.'

'I don't want to talk to you.' We neared the lifts and Leon pressed the call button. 'Let me go, Leon, I'm warning you.' The lift doors slid open and he pressed me in towards the mirrored rear of the empty space.

'Warning me about what?' he sneered.

'This is as good as kidnap,' I protested as he pressed the button for the top floor. 'I'll scream.'

'Scream away,' he said airily. 'I virtually own this travelodge chain. So don't think anyone's going to take your word . . . against mine.'

He held my arm just above the elbow all the way up and I stared hard at the side of his pale, fleshy face. What on earth was he doing here? Had Eva told him about this meeting? I'd run it by her about it in the strictest confidence. And she'd never ratted on me about any of my other jaunts, so it was unlikely that Leon could have found out through her.

A cold sickness spread through my stomach as a thought occurred to me. Maybe she had ratted on me each and every time. Maybe my half-brother knew all about my new habit of picking up strangers on the Internet. My thoughts, never lightening sharp at the best of times, suddenly leaped ahead of themselves and I opened my mouth in disbelief.

'You're Devilish One, aren't you?'

Leon turned his pale, cold eyes on me, swept my body with them and then smirked, but didn't reply. A horrible thought wormed into my head as the lift doors pinged open.

'Are you –' I hardly dared say it '– are you the Huntsman?'

Leon's eyes were blank and nothing registered as he stared at me. I tried to evade his hand as he reached for my arm, but his fingers closed tight around me and I decided, with a tolerant roll of my eyes, that I may as well let him play master for a while.

He guided me towards room 656, slid the key-card through the slot and pushed open the door with his foot. The room beyond was sparsely furnished and anonymous in the extreme. Beige carpet, beige walls, beige bedcover. I stood just inside the door and watched as he locked it and pocketed the key-card.

'What do you want, Leon?' I said, when it became obvious that he wasn't going to speak. 'It's a bit of an effort to get me all the way down here just to talk to me. Why couldn't we chat next Friday? Or you could have come to my place.'

'I don't want to ... talk,' he said, turning and unbuttoning his jacket. 'I want to see what it is that makes you so damn hot these days. What makes all these guys chase after you.'

He dropped his jacket over the back of a chair, where it subsided with an empty rustle of silk lining. He turned to face me as he unbuttoned his cuffs. His eyes swept over me again.

'You're such a little mouse, Carrie. A pathetic little thing. Always have been. I remember you cowering in the corner at just about every birthday party I took you to.'

His lip curled with distaste as he looked at me, and I suddenly felt that I was that seven-year-old girl again, too terrified to even say happy birthday to my bouncy, popular hostess. He was right: it had been the same at every event, the only thing that changed was the outfits and the houses.

I had loathed it, hated knowing that I was only there because the mother of the birthday-girl felt sorry for me, or that I had been tacked on as a last-minute addition to make up numbers when someone else cancelled. It had been torture and, as soon as I was old enough to express a preference, I always said no. And after a while the jolly, pretty, popular girls stopped inviting me.

Dragging myself back to the present, I heard Leon continue, 'I can't begin to imagine what Patrick saw in you. Or Max,' he breathed. 'So I want you to ... show me.'

Gaping at him, I shook my head in disbelief and then tried to summon a laugh. 'This is a joke, right?'

His pale eyes regarded me without expression, then he began to unbutton his shirt. 'No joke, Carrie. I want to see you naked. On that bed. And then I'm going to see if

221

you can make me as hard as you seem to make everyone else.'

'Shit.' It was all I could say under the circumstances. I folded my arms over my breasts and frowned at him.

'Leon, you're my brother. If I made you hard it would be . . . unnatural.' I caught myself mimicking his pauses and knew that I was nervous. I took a deep breath before carrying on. 'Not to say criminal.'

He shrugged out of his shirt. 'Fuck natural, Carrie. And fuck . . . the law.' I noticed that his chest was as hairless as a fat baby's and probably as well-cushioned. I suppressed a shudder. 'And anyway, the only blood we have in common is our father's. Your slut of a mother, remember, came a long time after mine.'

He was right. His own mother had died of some horrible illness without a name back in the 50s when there weren't so many cure-all treatments around. Father had married my mother after almost a decade on his knees in the local church. Then they'd only stayed around long enough to have me before they were reversing down the motorway slip-road and into oblivion.

So that made Leon my half-brother. But that still meant it was incest, didn't it? I stared at him and rubbed my cold arms with icy hands, feeling sick and numb inside.

'Don't worry,' he grunted. 'I'm not going to . . . fuck you. I'll leave that to the studs. Get on the bed.'

I shook my head.

'Get on the bed, Carrie.'

There wasn't really any way out of it. I walked slowly over to the bed and sat on the edge of it, watching as he turned to stare at me. We eyed each other silently for a moment, each with our own private thoughts.

'Take your dress . . .' the pause was so long this time that I wanted to finish his sentence for him '. . . off.'

I bit my lip and smoothed the soft pink wool against my thighs. He couldn't make me, could he? I frowned hard and ran a finger across the stitching on my hem, thinking hard. I felt sick and cold. He couldn't make me, I was sure of that. But I did have a choice, here, I told myself eventually.

The choices were simple: I could let him call the shots. Or I could turn the situation to my own advantage. What would Dominique do?

I narrowed my eyes as I glanced over at Leon. He was getting impatient so I said, 'If I do this, Leon, I want a promise from you.'

'This isn't a bargaining thing, Carrie.'

'No, I realise that. I'm not bargaining, but I am asking you for something. A favour,' I said, keeping my voice reasonable. 'I'm asking you for something and I bet you can't even remember the last time I asked you for anything, can you?'

He thought for a moment, his pudgy hands tucked inside the pockets of his trousers, then shook his head.

'No,' he conceded. 'For a mouse, you're pretty damn self-sufficient.' His eyes met mine. 'What do you want?'

'I want you to set me free of these bloody awful dinners we do at your house,' I said, all in a rush. 'I don't ever want to have to come to one again. Ever. Unless I want to. OK?'

His expression lightened and I thought for a moment that Leon was going to smile. 'Sure,' he said. 'I hate them too. I was only doing them for you, to give you the feeling of . . . family.'

I gazed at him in surprise. 'Don't you – don't you want me to come to your house every month?' I asked.

He met my gaze and then shook his head. 'I find it a pain, Carrie,' he said simply. 'We have nothing in common. I have nothing that I want to talk about with you. The choices that you make puzzle me and your . . . lifestyle is beyond my comprehension.' He shrugged and I watched as the plump folds in his neck deepened. 'Now take off the dress.'

Our brief moment of communication was over. But I'd

223

got what I wanted, even if it did taste like a slightly odd type of victory. I pulled the dress over my head and sat there on the bed in my smooth black all-in-one and charcoal-dark stockings, fingering the narrow watch strap on my left wrist. Leon's eyes swept over me and the corner of his mouth twitched as he licked his fleshy bottom lip.

'Lie down,' he commanded. 'Lie down for me like you do your other men.'

There was a pause in which I sighed and then flopped back on the bed, determined to show him that this meant nothing to me, that I was completely uninvolved. I could feel a tight little tense knot at the base of my skull that said I was more involved than I wanted to be, and it didn't feel very nice. Leon stayed on his side of the room and I heard him drag a chair over and sit down.

'That looks pretty uninspiring,' he said after a while. 'Is that what you do for these guys you meet up with? Lie there like a rag-doll?'

'No,' I muttered.

'Can't hear you,' he said.

'No!' I said, loudly this time.

'Do what you do for them.'

'I can't. It's a two-way thing,' I protested. 'Having good sex is about two people who fancy each other getting together and doing what feels right.' I crooked my head to stare at him and he hurriedly covered his now-naked crotch with one meaty hand. 'Good sex is not about one person standing there while another one poses. Although,' I conceded, 'that could be nice too, if both their hearts were in it.'

'Get on all fours.'

I wondered if he'd heard my little speech, or whether he was just ignoring me to be bloody-minded. I rolled over and propped myself on hands and knees and then waited while he fumbled and grunted. Glancing over at him – quickly so that he didn't see me looking – I saw that my big strong bully of a brother was having trouble even getting it up. His face was pink and slightly pathetic, his white hands bunched around a very soft dick, and his forehead creased with a slightly despairing frown.

I felt suddenly very sorry for him. And something strange happened to me then, because I suddenly lost my fear of Leon. All my life, he'd been the one in charge, the one telling me what to do. Big, strong Leon, admired by his business associates as the one to watch, the dollar-millionaire with the acute financial brain. The man with the beautiful socialite wife, the biggest house, the fastest car, the most expensive holiday. All my life I'd obeyed him, feared him, and never been able to escape him. But, looking at him now, I realised he was just a fat man who couldn't get a hard-on.

I sat back on my stockinged heels and watched him as he cradled his tool in one hand as if it were a poor dead bird. For the first time in my life I felt sorry for Leon, and it made me do something that I'll never forget.

I got up and walked slowly over to where he sat in the beige-upholstered chair. Gently, I took his hands in mine and laid them on the arms of the chair. I bent down and kissed Leon softly on his mouth and then ran my fingers through his hair.

'Let me do that for you,' I whispered. 'Just this once. It'll be our secret.'

I kneeled beside him and slid my fingers around his soft sex. It felt strange in my hand, kind of defenceless. I looped a finger around it and slowly, gently, began to jerk him off. Nothing happened at first, but when I kissed Leon again, I felt a stirring in my hand, a soft flutter that began slowly at first but grew and swelled.

Leon fixed his eyes on my breasts. They were delicately swathed in the black silk of the all-in-one and I took a breath inward, letting my nipples swell out and pushing my ribs forward so that my cleavage looked full and rounded. He liked that; I could tell because his wiener twitched against my palm and I suddenly had a little more length to play with.

Shifting my position a little, I got between his knees, pushing his thighs apart and wanking him a little harder. Leon shuddered and let his head drop back a little, his pleasure lighting up his face and lending colour to his normally pale cheeks. He seemed to like the feel of my silk all-in-one against the inside of his thighs, so I let myself sway between his legs and moved sinuously, like a cat rubbing against him. I cupped his balls in my free hand. They were like clock weights: heavy and smooth. I caressed them gently, opening and closing my fingers around them as I carried on with the firm rubbing of his now-rigid cock.

I slid my fingers up and over the top, closing his loose foreskin around the bulbous head then slicking it back down. He groaned and shifted his hips, thrusting at me a little, and I paused for a moment.

'You like the silk, don't you?' I whispered. He nodded, unable to speak for the moment. I reached underneath me and unpopped the fastening of my all-in-one. Drawing it up over my head, I was aware of his eyes fastened first on my neatly trimmed snatch, and then on the joggle of my breasts as I wriggled free of the tight garment. His cock swayed against his belly and I caught it, held it, then wrapped the all-in-one around his meaty shaft.

'I'm going to jack you off with this,' I murmured. 'Does that feel good? Do you like that?'

He nodded dumbly, and I speeded up a little, watching his face as I wanked him harder and faster. The silk bunched around him, whispering against his solid todge, and I felt a sudden rush of sensuality, a gush of juice in my pussy as I kneeled there wanking the bully-boy Leon into my silk teddy.

He creamed off very suddenly, thin milky gobs of spunk oozing up and spitting out on to the jet-black fabric. There was much more of it than I had expected, and I used my other hand to cup him with more of the silk, absorbing every drop of it until the teddy was darkened in large patches and sticky to touch.

Leon moaned a little and whispered something. I thought he said my name, but as I leaned in closer and laid my cheek against his, I heard him say 'Eva'. I smiled, feeling the first wash of affection I'd ever felt for my half-brother unfold inside me. It was a delicate flower, and I didn't really want to nurture it, but the fact that our roles had so irreversibly changed, the fact that I was now the one in charge, made me more tolerant and I let the affection I felt take hold. Blood is blood after all.

I phoned Eva while Leon was showering and asked her to come to the hotel. She tried to demur, saying that she was busy and not able to just drop everything at my behest, but I insisted.

'Come here now, Eva,' I demanded. 'I'm here with Leon and I think he'd want you to do as I say.'

'Leon's there?' I had her full attention now; her voice sharpened and I could tell she had pressed the phone closer to her ear. Grinning, I let her stew for a minute.

'Yes,' I said, after a few beats. 'Leon's here. We've just had an interesting hour in a travelodge bedroom. I think you'll wish you'd been here when he tells you about it.'

She hissed through her teeth.

'He was supposed to tell me before he did it,' she said tautly. I raised an eyebrow and smiled into the phone.

'I don't know that he wanted to share the experience, Eva. But I think he'd want to see you now. And I know I do. I want to hear exactly how much you've told him.'

'Wait there,' she said abruptly. 'I'll be around forty-five minutes.'

'So, Eva.' I was sitting opposite her at a corner table in the travelodge's discreetly beige dining room. Leon was sitting quietly to her right. 'You told him everything?

227

Every time I met anyone?' My eyebrows were so raised with disbelief that I felt as though they might disappear up into my hairline at any moment. Eva, tapping the long ash off the end of her cigarette, merely pursed her lips and stared calmly back at me.

'You didn't say it was a secret,' she pointed out.

'No,' I conceded. 'But that's because I hadn't imagined that I'd need to spell it out. You said to me, when you first showed me the net, that I wasn't to tell him. I had naturally assumed that "not telling" meant it was a secret. Between you and me. And now I find out that it's only *me* who can't tell Leon stuff. You, by contrast, tell him the whole story. And then you set him up for me to chat with, too!'

'Leon is my husband,' she said defensively. 'We tell each other everything.'

'Oh, get on,' I scoffed. 'Why did you do it? Was it because you were jealous that Max turned you down but asked me out?' Her eyelids flickered slightly and I knew I'd hit the mark.

She didn't rise to it though; she simply repeated what she'd already said. 'We tell each other everything. Always.'

'That won't wash, Eva. You're the one wearing the trousers in this relationship.'

Eva leaned forward, flashing her small but perfectly formed breasts as she did so. 'Actually,' she hissed, 'it's an equal match. You seem to think that Leon controls his business life and I control our home life. But you have to realise that you are sadly outdated, Carrie. Modern marriages don't work like that. At least ours doesn't.'

'So tell me how it does work,' I said. 'And tell me about Marie-Therese.'

Eva's eyes narrowed at the mention of her maid's name. She crushed her cigarette in the ashtray, selected another one from the half-empty pack that lay next to her knife and spoon, and propped it in the corner of her crimson-painted lips.

'Leon?' she prompted, curving an eyebrow in his direction.

My brother, who had remained silent and slightly dazed-looking throughout the meal, looked from one to the other of us. 'What?' he said at last.

'Tell her about Marie-Therese.'

'Oh.' A tender smile washed over his face. 'Marie-Therese came to work for us about two years ago. She's a very loving person. I . . . we . . . like her a lot. And she likes us. It's an arrangement that suits us all very well.'

I nodded. 'Does it make you happy?' I asked, sipping my orange juice.

'Very,' they both chorused.

I nodded. 'Good.'

There was a long silence where each of us mulled things over in our heads. I thought about Eva telling Leon everything I'd ever told her. It should have made me angry, but strangely it didn't. It just made it much easier for me to say what I wanted to say next.

'OK,' I said. 'I'm going in a minute. You can pick up the tab, can't you, Leon?'

He nodded.

'Listen up,' I said firmly. 'From now on, I want to live my own life, the way I want to. Make my own decisions, make up my own mind about things. I won't be coming to any more of your Friday dinners, which I'm sure will please you both as well.' I stood up, feeling slightly amused at the nonplussed expressions on their faces. 'Don't call me. If I want to see you, I'll call you.'

I started to walk away, then had second thoughts. Turning, I looked at them for a moment, smiled, and bent down to peck first Leon on the cheek, then Eva.

'See you around,' I said. And walked quickly away with a light heart and a bouncing step.

* * *

229

The house was empty and peaceful when I got home. Gabriel had left a note pinned to the fridge with a magnet. He said he'd gone to Clara's, and that I had the rest of the night to sleep, eat, drink, do whatever I wanted. I smiled as I took the note down and held it briefly to my nose, flaring my nostrils around the delicate scent of his skin that still clung to the paper. Gabriel was such a sweetie, so caring once I'd got past that sulky exterior. I'd really enjoyed having him as my lodger-cum-house-slave, but I could tell that he was ready to move on. We both were.

It was extraordinarily pleasant, I mused, as I ran a hot bath and poured in scented oil, just to do what I wanted. To be my own master, or mistress rather, and not be beholden to anyone else for reasons of honour or filial duty. Now that I didn't have to see Eva and Leon any more, I felt almost fond of them.

I sank down into the steaming water and let it lap up under my chin, smoothing my hands over my bobbing breasts and closing my eyes. I was really relaxed, more relaxed than I had been for years. Maybe for ever. I let my mind play over my life, my relationships, my work and my new-found independent spirit. It was Dominique that had given me the strength to put my foot down. She'd given me the guts to say: 'Actually, no, that's not what I want.'

So now that she'd shown me how to have some backbone, how to see what it was I didn't want my life to be like, how was she going to figure out what it was I did want my life to be like?

I slowly smoothed a rounded bar of soap over my arms, lingering in the crease of my elbow and then the rounded curve of my shoulders. I rubbed and slipped the soap over my wet limbs until I was covered with a fine foamy lather, then glanced across at the mirror that ran the length of the back of the bathroom door.

I looked flushed, and my eyes shone almost feverishly

bright. My hair, caught up hastily into a knot on the top of my head, was damp from the steam that clung in the warm air, and tendrils of it clung to my cheeks and neck. I looked very happy and quite self-satisfied, like a comfortable cat that's just lapped up two saucerfuls of the best Devonshire cream.

I smiled at myself and then realised that it was not myself that I smiled at. The girl in the mirror was Dominique: vibrant hair, vivacious energy, lashings of self-confidence. I was her. I'd become her. In fact, if I really thought about it, I'd been her all along without realising it; it was simply that pretending to be someone else had given me the bravery to act in a way that had been suppressed all my life. Dominique was Carrie and Carrie was Dominique. We were one and the same person. We could make our own rules. *I* could make my own rules.

Smiling, I lay back in the bath and slid my hands lower over my body, caressing the undersides of my curving breasts and lingering for a moment on the rosy nipples that I could pull and elongate with soft fingers.

Making my own rules meant getting rid of all the things that irked me. Like Leon. Like my job. Closing my eyes and settling down to stroke myself to a languid climax with my fingers, I decided that the very next day I'd start looking in the appointments section of *Design Week*. And I'd contact Sam. And Max. And the Huntsman. They were three people I definitely *did* want in my life. I knew that without having to think twice about it.

The trouble was, and I realised this as soon as I switched on the computer and opened my mailbox, there was at least one of those three highly desirable males who didn't appear to want me. There was still no mail from Sam. He was proving to be far less submissive than I had thought he was. Pretty strong-willed, in fact. I bit my lip and stared at the 'no new messages on server' flag, full of admiration for Sam as I wondered what to do. Should I accept defeat gracefully? Or demand a fair hearing?

I decided to delay my decision and just penned an e-mail to Max instead. I asked whether we could get a pizza together sometime soon. Then I sent one to the Huntsman saying that unless I got to meet him in the flesh, I wasn't free or willing to come on any more weekends.

Max sent me a dry line about coming running the moment I whistled, but that I'd have to whistle loud because at that moment his laptop was plugged into a hotel room socket. In Dallas.

The Huntsman didn't reply immediately, but when he did he made it clear that the real-life face-off wasn't going to happen if he had anything to do with it.

Dominique,
Whatever happened to keeping a little mystery in our lives? Surely it's the ones you can't see who are the most exciting, and if you could see them then the excitement would turn to boredom in no time. I don't want to see you, so why on earth would you want to see me???
Regards, H.

I frowned as I read that. I did want to see him, and the stuff about mystery was a load of rubbish, just an avoiding tactic, I knew.

Dear Huntsman,
Hmm, mystery huh? Not very convincing.
And as for why on earth I'd want to see you, well, it might just have slipped your notice, but you HAVE seen ME. In Bournemouth. So it's only fair.
Dominique xxx

I got a reply from him at lunchtime when I checked my mailbox at work. He simply laughed at my reasoning

232

and said that it was his privilege to see who was coming on the weekends he arranged. I wasn't satisfied at that.

The thought of the Huntsman, of what he looked like, of the sort of man he was, of seeing him in the flesh, began to eat away at me. I worked through my lunch break, eating cheese sandwiches while frowning over some visuals, and by mid-afternoon sent him another e-mail.

Dear Huntsman,
You may well consider it a privilege to see me, but I think that's just underhand. I think it's my right to see who's manipulating me, surely? Please? Please, please, toe-sucking-please?
Dominique xxx

Dear Dominique,
Ha ha ha re: toe sucking. Now that's an offer I just might be tempted to take you up on. But really, why should I let you see me? I'm here for yr protection, remember? And, hey! I've never manipulated you, at any time. You do everything from yr own free will and you know it!
Regards, (resignedly) H.

Dear H,
Hmm . . . Why can't I meet with you? You have me intrigued. Are you a hunchback with a tiny schlong? Or maybe you're not really a man at all?
Yours sweetly on bended knee,
Dominique xxx

Dominique,
On bended knee? Now that I like. But what's with the sweetly submissive act? I know that's not the real you! lol. And I'm not rising to the bait about the man thing. At all.
Regards, H.

Dear H,
Such a shame. You're going to miss me then.
D xx

After that, I let him stew in his own juice for a while.
Although, to be truthful, it was probably me who did the
most stewing. He sent me a few more e-mails which I
didn't answer. I tried to ignore my curiosity, but meeting
up with this man who'd kept me amused and intrigued
for nearly six months was becoming a bit of an obsession
for me.

I couldn't concentrate on my work for the rest of the
day, and on the train home I buried my head in *Design
Week* looking for jobs that would take me away from
where I was at the moment. But every lurch of the
carriage and every cough from the person sitting next to
me brought me out of my concentration and threw my
mind back into the spin that it had been in since the
Huntsman had first replied. I had to see him, by fair
means or foul. But he didn't seem to want to play the
game.

Design Week wasn't helping. The only jobs I could see
that I even remotely fancied were based in London; and
while weekend trips to the capital were great fun, I
wasn't sure that I really wanted to move there full time.
If I was going to move that far, I may as well uproot my
life wholesale and go abroad.

The idea made my pulse-rate suddenly race with
excitement. I frowned at the floor and thought hard. Why
not? Why not just sell up and ship out? I had nothing to
tie me here any more. I was freer than I had ever been in
my life, if you didn't count a relationship with a man I'd
never seen in the flesh, and a once every few months
session of unadulterated lust with Max. And if Sam was
going to keep up the silent treatment, there was nothing
for me to hang around for.

I hugged my idea to myself with glee and mounting

excitement. This could be the start of something good. A new life for the new Carrie.

I stepped off the packed train and elbowed my way through the commuter throng with my head held high and my heart still knocking against the inside of my ribs with tantalising feverishness. Numerous dark-suited, Crombie-coated men eyed me with pointed interest, but I ignored them. I had a plan and I needed to get home and put it into action.

That evening, I e-mailed an old college friend that I had kept in touch with sporadically over the years. Catherine Fanshawe had married into a Green Card and got herself a partnership in a design consultancy in the States. I asked her what the opportunities were in the wild wild west, and pressed send.

Catherine wasn't all that helpful. Either she was protecting her own interests, or there really was no need for British designers across the Atlantic. I suspected the former, so I mailed Max and asked him what he knew. He sent me a long e-mail all about me needing a hard-to-get H1 visa to work legally in the States, but that he knew enough lawyers to get around the problems that that threw up. That night he called me and I shivered with pleasure to hear his deep, velvet tones spilling out of the ear piece and into my mind.

'Hi, Carrie. So, do you want to come work for me?'

'No.'

His laughter boomed out and I grinned and held the telephone receiver away from my ear.

'Why not?' he said at last when he'd finished laughing.

'Because I don't want to owe you anything. I want to be my own person. If I'm going to make a fresh start, then it has to be just that, doesn't it?'

'Carrie, I'm not going to do you any favours that I wouldn't do for anyone else. Why don't you just come out here for a couple of months? We can see how things pan out. You could do worse, you know.'

'I don't want you to give me a job!' I protested. 'I want to do it on my own! I want to be employed because I'm good at what I do, not because I'm screwing Mr Big who runs the damn corporation!'

'But you're not screwing Mr Big,' he pointed out. 'You haven't darn well screwed Mr Big in weeks.'

'No, but then whose fault is that?' I smiled as I twisted the phone cord around my finger. We were back on familiar territory here, the old jab and thrust that made me feel so excited when I was with him, the teasing that almost went too far but never did. Whenever I threw down the gauntlet Max was always ready to pick it right up, slip it on his hand and smack my bottom with it. I licked my lips slowly. 'You're the one who's always out of town.'

'You're darn right I am.' He laughed. 'I have to make an honest buck somehow. But, listen, I'm in London tomorrow. One night only. Come up. Have dinner with me.'

'I can't just drop everything and go to London!' I spluttered, feeling extremely flattered and just a little bit tempted. It would certainly be the perfect way to take my mind off my yearning to meet up with the Huntsman.

'Sure you can,' he pressed. 'I'll even reserve a ticket for you. You won't have to do a thing except turn up at the right time. I'll have a car waiting at Paddington.'

'Do you do this for all the potential employees you're trying to seduce into working for you?' I laughed.

'No, never have before,' he said with a smile in his voice. 'But I might make it a habit if it's successful.'

'It won't be successful,' I murmured. 'Because I don't want to work for you, so just accept it. But I might – and I said *might* so don't get too excited – enjoy watching your attempts to coerce me. But you have to know that you'll lose in the end. I won't work for you, Max. I couldn't; it just wouldn't be right.'

'That's fine, Carrie. If you took the easiest route, then you wouldn't be the person I thought you were anyway.'

He paused while I thought about the kind of person he had me pegged for. He made me sound as if I had integrity streaming out of every pore. Could I live up to that? I grimaced at myself in the hall mirror and silently hoped that I could. Then I took a deep breath and then spoke again.

'I can be free for dinner. But I have to be home the same night so I don't miss work. It's already difficult enough at Richardson's, without me going AWOL.'

'I'll have you back at the train station by midnight, Cinderella.'

Chapter Eighteen
decision time

'*A*re you wearing any underwear?' Max said softly, as the waiter left our table and moved silently among the other diners. A small smile curved the corner of his mouth and his grey-eyed gaze held mine.

I squirmed against the smooth leather of my seat, took a tiny sip of wine and nodded. In fact, I'd worn my best matching set, hot pink to match my tight suede jacket. The little black dress underneath the jacket was so tight that I'd debated wearing knickers at all. But then I'd remembered that the matching set also had a thong option, so problem solved.

'Take them off,' whispered Max, a devilish twinkle lighting his eyes as he leaned forward a little. 'Take them off and give them to me.'

'I can't,' I said, laughing. 'Not in here!'

We were having dinner at a fashionable London restaurant which overlooked the Thames. I smiled and gazed across the table at Max. He looked very well groomed: a crisp white shirt stretched across his muscular chest. I shivered at the suggestion of the dark hairs that shadowed through the fabric. They covered his skin like a wiry fuzz. He was so full of animal magnetism, it'd been all I could do to stop myself from demanding that we had sex in the back of the car he'd arrived in at Paddington Station. But I'd restrained myself and simply held his hand tightly, revelling in the sense of erotic anticipation that I could feel burning in my sex.

I caught my bottom lip between my teeth and widened my eyes at him, then glanced towards the waiter. He was busy at a table across the aisle. Far enough away to make it probably safe for me to extract my knickers from under my dress, but near enough to make it tantalisingly possible that he would turn and see me in the act.

I smoothed my skirt up over my thighs and dropped my serviette lightly across my lap. Max, moving more quickly than I had ever seen him move before, leaned over and lightly scooped it up, crushed it into his palm and held it tight in his own lap.

'No covers.' He grinned. 'You have to do this in the open.' He glanced sideways at the waiter. 'Go on, Carrie, or are you chicken?'

'I'm not chicken!' I protested, laughing. 'I simply don't want to get thrown out of here.'

'Worse things have happened here, darn it.' He chuckled. 'If the stories in your tabloids are anything to go by. The rich and famous get away with it. It all blows over and everyone's forgiven when the next scandal hits the headlines.'

'But I wouldn't be forgiven, because I'm not famous,' I pointed out. 'I'd probably spend a night in the cells for indecent exposure.'

He crooked an eyebrow and made a chicken-cluck noise. I grinned and surreptitiously flipped open a couple of the tiny buttons which fastened my dress all the way up the front, keeping half my attention on the waiter and half of it on Max's reaction.

I wriggled and slid down a little in my chair. I smoothed my fingers under the elastic lace edges and slipped the fabric over my hips. Slipped it over my thighs. Then caught the slightly damp gusset with my thumb and wriggled it out from between my legs. The thrill of perhaps being seen was exciting, and the look on Max's slightly flushed face was a real turn-on. He looked as if he'd like nothing better than to slide under the table, prise my knees wider and press his tongue to my pussy. I slipped my shoe off, lifted a foot and ran it lightly up his thigh to his impressively bulging fly. His face remained impassive but his eyes spoke volumes.

'Give me your underwear,' he growled at last. 'Pass it under the table.'

I looked at him, my foot still in his lap, then calmly lifted my lacy thong to my own nose and inhaled deeply. Max's eyes widened in surprise and he shot the waiter a glance, but no one was looking our way. I crushed the soft lace in my left hand, then tossed it lightly across the table where it landed neatly between Max's glittering silver knife and fork.

'Carrie!' he protested. I simply smiled, watching him as the knickers disappeared into the palm of his large hand and were tucked under the table. I kept up the slight pressure on his crotch with my stockinged toe and watched in amusement as his blush deepened.

'Carrie, stop it.'

'You started it,' I said with an innocent smile.

When we'd eaten, I sat in my curved leather seat and gazed out of the wide window, chin in hand, thinking how lucky I was. I had my whole future ahead of me. I could make any choices I wanted about what I was going to do with it, and who I was going to spend it with. Max sat opposite and watched me, a cigar in one hand and balloon of expensive brandy in the other.

'You're quiet, Carrie,' he said at last.

'Was I? Sorry,' I said. 'I was just thinking about what I was going to do. Where I was going to go.' I gave a small smile. 'I feel so free.'

240

'I want you to come with me,' he said, leaning forward and crushing the cigar into a crystal ashtray. 'You know that. Come back with me, Carrie. Be with me.'

'I don't know,' I murmured, smiling. 'I don't know if I want to be with just one person right now. I want to keep my options open. I might even quite like to be by myself for a while, I'm not sure.'

He nodded, his eyes fixed on mine. 'I can understand that,' he said. 'Just don't go too far away from me. I need you.'

I stared at him in surprise.

'You do?' I laughed a little to hide the nervous flutter of excitement in my belly. 'Wow. No one's ever said that to me before.'

'No, I know you've had a rough time in the past. Leon told me a bit about Patrick and what you'd said about him.'

'Leon did?' I was surprised. 'I always imagined that he thought I was exaggerating.'

'No, I think he knows deep down that Patrick wasn't the right man for you. Leon cares about you, Carrie. He doesn't understand you, but he does care.'

I blushed a little and bit my bottom lip. 'Well,' I said, 'I don't want him to care for me. I want him to leave me alone. I have some new men around, some that I particularly want to be around, ones that I want to get to know more. And there's no room for Leon.'

'Is there room for me?'

I smiled across the table at him. 'Max, there'll always be room for you. I love being with you.'

'Then let's be together all the time.'

I watched his hands move across the pale damask of the tablecloth and thought how much I enjoyed being with him, how he turned me on. I was so tempted just to say yes. To go with him. It would be so easy. I took a deep breath and sighed lightly.

'I want to,' I said. 'But I'm not quite ready for a

commitment like that. Not yet. I want to stay free for a little bit longer.'

'You'd still be free,' Max said, sitting back easily in his chair. 'I'm not going to put any boundaries around you.'

'Good, I'd hate that.'

'So, who are these other guys?' he asked with a smile. 'You sound as if you have a whole stable of willing studs out there.'

'No, I haven't!' I protested, laughing. 'There's just you. Plus another guy who I seem to have lost track of. Plus someone else whose real name I don't even know.' I laughed again and watched him pour me some more wine. The clear pale fluid shone like watered gold in the elegant-stemmed glass and I took a tiny sip before setting it down carefully on the table-top.

'Three men?' He widened his eyes in mock horror, grinning.

'Yes. Bad, isn't it? But I'm making up for lost time. And I may never even know who one of them really is, so maybe he doesn't count anyway.' I twisted the stem of my wine glass. 'Do you know, I thought it was Leon for one horrible moment the other night. But the Huntsman's far too much fun to be Leon.'

'I think you do Leon down too much, Carrie. But listen,' he leaned forward and laced my fingers with his own, 'I'm glad you think I'm fun. That *it* was fun. I liked it, too.'

He looked at me with an intensity that seemed to make his eyes even darker than they already were. Grey that eased into black. Charcoal. Almost black.

I watched him without blinking as the meaning of his words sunk in.

My heart stilled to a low fifty.

I felt suddenly suffocated. The room was too hot. There was no air. I couldn't speak. All I could do was sit there while my panicking brain pressed the fast-forward button through all the chat that I'd had with the Huntsman,

242

and all the things I told him about myself. All the things he'd watched me do on the CCTV. All the things he knew about me from talking with the Snow Queen.

I jumped up, dashed the contents of my full wine glass in Max's surprised and suddenly pale face, and marched swiftly away. By the time I reached the door I was almost running. Behind me I could hear the frantic scrape of Max's chair as he shoved it back. He started to come after me. The waiters surged around him in a murmuring throng and began to dab serviettes at him. He roughly brushed them aside, then threw his credit card on the tablecloth.

He was on my heels by the time I got to the door. I wheeled round to face him, both my hands flung up to ward him off.

'Back off, Max. Don't come near me!'

'Carrie –' His face was white and horrified, his eyes full of shock at the unexpected violence of my reaction. He reached for my hand.

I jerked it back out of his reach.

'Carrie, please –'

'What the hell did you think I would do when you told me?' I gasped, nearly choking on my own venom as I spat the words at him. 'Open my arms to you and say "Oh, how wonderful! What a jolly jape"?'

'Carrie, I'm so sorry. I thought you knew it was me! I thought it was part of the darn game we were playing!'

'Game? What game?'

I stamped my foot, rage swilling through my guts and bursting into my head like molten lava. I was so angry. So frustrated. Yet somehow so impotent. I felt as though the world had swung on its axis around me and I was somehow expected to walk across a landscape that was tilting. Swinging. Trying to push me off. How dare he? How could he?

And how could I not have known?

Max took a tentative step forwards, one hand outstretched, palm up. I knocked it hard away from me and tried not to see the pain in his eyes.

'I thought you knew it was me,' he whispered again, the rejected hand cramming deep into his pocket with a familiar action that made my heart feel as if it had a knife twisting in it.

Teeth clenched, I shook my head as I swallowed the huge, gravelly lump that had formed in my throat. I ignored his pleading, horrified eyes and turned away to push out of the slowly revolving doors of the glass-fronted restaurant. I didn't know where I was going, or what I was going to do, but I had to get away.

I plunged out into the orange-drenched darkness of the city at night.

I don't know for how long I walked, or where I went, or what people thought when they went past a striding girl with a blank face and a dazed look in her eyes. I kept my hands jammed in the pockets of my pink jacket, and my head down against the wind as I walked. Little snippets of conversation that I'd had on the Internet with the Huntsman kept replaying in my head and I felt my slow-burning fury slowly subside into sadness.

I should have known. It should have been obvious, I chided myself. I recalled what Max had said that night when we'd sat in his car after dinner at Leon's. He'd talked about family, and making new families. As the Huntsman, he had a whole new family which consisted of people like Virge and the Snow Queen.

I knew that the family that he had made around him was almost perfect in its simplicity, its common – erotic – purpose, and in its loyalty to him. I almost envied him that, but I couldn't forgive him for pretending to be someone else, not yet. Maybe never. Even though he had thought that it was a game I was playing. Me! I stopped on Westminster Bridge and stared up at Big Ben. Why on earth had he thought that I had known?

I strode on, over the bridge and on to the South Bank, walking with no particular purpose but to clear my head and stop the sick sadness that was trying to creep through my being. I eventually wound up outside Mrs Grey's townhouse with my forefinger pressed impatiently on the bell.

'Who is it?' The voice sounded curiously disembodied as it issued from the intercom set in the wall of the porticoed entrance. I leaned forward and said my name.

'I'm a friend of Sam's. I need to see him,' I added, biting my lips nervously.

There was a long silence and I thought for a moment that she was going to just leave me out there on the doorstep and not deign to acknowledge my presence any further. But then I heard the safety chain rattle, and then a loud click as she unlocked the heavy front door.

'It's very late,' she murmured, eyeing me with curiosity through the gap.

'I need to see Sam.'

She must have seen the intense determination on my face because she suddenly held the door wide.

'I think you'd better come in.'

Mrs Grey was wearing a long silky robe that clung to her elegant curves with the fluidity of water. Her silver-blonde hair was caught at the nape of her neck in a velvet ribbon and her face was devoid of make-up. She looked relaxed, content and very beautiful. I twisted my hands and stood still in her hallway, suddenly aware that it was nearly eleven at night and I had probably roused her from her bed.

She closed the door behind me.

'Carrie,' she said, looking me up and down with a little frown. 'You seem a little disturbed. Is there something I can help you with?'

'No.' I shook my head, biting my lips again to stop myself from doing something silly like weeping. 'I just need to see Sam.'

Mrs Grey stepped forwards and laid a cool hand on my arm. I shivered and held on to my tears, but the soft sympathy in her eyes and the firmness of her palm against my skin made me lose my self-control. A solitary tear plopped on to my hand.

'Ssh, don't cry,' she whispered, moving in a little closer. Her arms enfolded me and I leaned forward, almost falling on to her neck as she swept me into a deliciously warm, soft, Dior-scented embrace. It felt so good just to let someone comfort me, that I let the tears go and they soon darkened the front of her silky robe. I drew back slightly and saw, as I wiped my smeared mascara from under my eyes, that her breast pressed against the wet fabric and that her nipple was as hard and taut as a piece of ripe fruit. I stared at it, mesmerised, and she gave a soft, low laugh.

'Want to suck it?' she murmured, her fingers light and quick as they drew back the edges of the robe. I gazed at her without speaking, astounded. She cupped my chin and drew my face to hers so that her lips played lightly across my mouth for a moment. 'Come on,' she whispered. 'Come to Mummy. I'll make it better.'

She slid her hand to the back of my head and I felt languorous and heavy-limbed. Powerless to resist. Her perfume and the deliciously dark personal scent that rose from her naked breasts seemed to mesmerise me, and I let her guide my mouth to the nipple that she proffered. My legs faltered beneath me, and I let her hold me close as she sank into a chair. She pressed me down on to my knees in front of her and I leant forward against her, my legs curled under me and my own breasts rested in her soft lap.

Mrs Grey's breasts were round and full, but not as firm as perhaps they'd been when she was younger. The skin felt smooth against my lips, and as I touched the tip of her nipple with my tongue I tasted her dark signature scent. My sex gave an involuntary squeeze. She cupped her breast and let her fingers play over my chin as I slid my lips over her rosy teat and latched on.

I suckled there, like a baby, feeling safe and warm as I let her nipple slide over my tongue and felt it harden. She sighed softly, her free hand coming up to sweep away the tendrils of hair that had slipped down from their fastenings during my walk through the streets. Her fingers felt warm and soft as she gently stroked my hair back from my face and tucked it behind my ear. I sighed a little and licked around her areola, making her breast wet with my saliva so that I could slip more easily back on to her.

Her hands left my face and hair, and I felt them move slowly down to the buttons that fastened the front of my dress. She popped first the top one, then more, until the dress flapped open and I heard her sharp intake of breath at the sight of my breasts encased in the pink lace bra, and no knickers. My pussy contracted again as she ran a finger over my naked belly and underneath me. She slid a finger easily into my wet hole and I gasped against her breast as she began to frig me with a single finger. There was a slick, squelching sound as my juices suddenly flooded her fingers and I knew we could both hear how turned on I was.

'So wet,' she murmured. 'So juicy on my hand. Oh, you dirty little girl, Carrie.'

I sobbed slightly as I gobbled harder at the taut peak of her nipple. She strained against me, pushing further into my mouth. I gave a low moan as she found my clit with her thumb and applied a sweet, insistent pressure. She began to grind my sex with her hand, her movements firm and sure. Her thumb coiled and rubbed around my clit, sending little tingles rushing out from my cunt that seemed to race along all my nerve endings. All my passion and emotion, all the upset of the past hour suddenly drained out of me and I gasped, sliding slickly off her tit as I came on to her hand, flooding her palm with sweet sticky pussy juice.

She gently stroked my hair and let her cool fingers smooth across the flushed skin of my cheeks while I recovered. Then I sat back on my heels and began to button my dress with trembling fingers. Mrs Grey sat still, smiling serenely, her breasts still swollen and exposed. She made no attempt to cover herself and I glanced up at her.

'Fuck me now, Carrie,' she murmured softly.

I shook my head. 'No,' I said. 'I just need to see Sam.'

Her face became a mask of irritation. 'Fuck me,' she insisted. 'You came, didn't you? I made you come, you ungrateful little bitch.'

'I'm sorry,' I said, standing up, feeling slightly unsteady on my feet. 'I have to see Sam. I didn't mean for you to do that to me. I didn't ask you to.'

She stood up, her face angry and tight as she belted her silk robe closed.

'He's not here.' She didn't look at me, but I thought I saw a look of triumph twist across her face.

'Well, I'll wait. That is . . .' I felt suddenly embarrassed and very rude '. . . if you don't mind.'

'You'd have a long wait, my dear.' She raised her cool eyes to mine, her face studiedly blank. 'Sam's gone. He doesn't live here any more.'

I stared at her. It was there again, just for a moment, that strange look of triumph in her eyes, and my only thought was that she was lying to me. I pushed past her and took the stairs two at a time, ignoring her when she angrily called me back. I threw open the door to Sam's room and stopped two paces in.

The books were gone. The computer was gone. Sam's stetson was gone. And in their places were piles of colourful Benetton jumpers and a very surprised-looking girl who sat up in the bed and stared at me. A magazine lay open on her lap and a hairbrush rested on the duvet cover. We stared at each other, open-mouthed. I'm not sure who was the most shocked.

Mrs Grey, still polite but with a distinctly frosty edge to her voice, came close up behind me and said, 'As you can see, Carrie dear, Sam's room is now Rachel's room. Sam left about a month ago.'

'Wh–where's he gone?' I could barely force the words out and I knew I sounded like a particularly sick frog as I croaked at her. 'Tell me where he is!'

'I'm sure, Carrie, that if Sam wants you to know where he is, he'll tell you.' She swept her eyes coolly up and down my body. 'Now, let me see you out.'

'Mrs Grey –' began Rachel.

'Thank you, Rachel,' interrupted Mrs Grey firmly. 'I'm so sorry you were disturbed.'

Her hand closed around my elbow and she steered me back out on to the landing and down the stairs. I let her, my movements slow and my head bowed weakly. I felt as though a great sliver of ice had taken up residence inside my heart, and I knew that the future that had seemed so rosy only an hour or so before was now looking like a great wasteland of missed opportunity.

Mrs Grey didn't speak again; she simply closed the door behind me. The key turned in the lock with a very final-sounding click.

I stood outside the house for a few moments, looking up at the windows as if I thought clues would somehow miraculously reveal themselves to me. But the only thing that I saw was the light flicking off in the window of Sam's room. Rachel's room. I turned and dug my hands deep in my pockets, frowned hard and began to walk slowly up the road.

I had reached the corner when she caught up with me. Rachel, her long hair streaming back over her shoulders and a huge fisherman's jumper thrown on in haste over her striped pyjamas.

'Excuse me!' she called.

I turned and looked blankly at her.

'Sorry,' she gasped, stopping and pinching her side with one hand. 'I'm not used to running.' She thrust a piece of paper at me. 'Sam did leave a forwarding address. I know because I heard him talk about you with Mrs Grey. He said if you ever got in touch, or if you ever phoned, then she should be sure to give it to you. He was very definite about that.' She smiled, her face open and friendly, her green eyes shining in the darkness. 'When you catch up with him, say "hi" from me, won't you?'

She turned and was gone as quickly as she had come, her slippered feet just audible as she trotted back up the way she'd come. I held the piece of paper in one hand and tried to steady my racing pulse.

'Thank you!' I yelled. And looked down at the address that Sam had gone to:

Bruton's Waterhole Ranch
Saltfork Creek
Texas

I stared at the piece of paper in my hand and then burst out laughing. Sam, my original Internet cowboy, had followed his heart's desire and gone off to be a real cowboy out in the Lone Star State. My heavy heart lifted and I stuck my arm up at an approaching black cab.

'Paddington Station,' I said to the driver, grinning happily.

'You going home, little lady?' The driver grinned back at me.

'Yes,' I said. 'Home. That's where I'm going.' And I settled back against the cracked vinyl seat and folded the piece of paper carefully into my pocket.

The next morning was the usual rush-hour chaos but for once I didn't mind. I dressed carefully in a blue two-piece suit and made sure I had on a pair of stockings that had no ladders for once. I piled my hair up on top of my head and secured it with a few pins. When I got to work, I checked my reflection in the mirror that hung behind the tastefully underdecorated Christmas tree in the reception area at Richardson's.

'Hi, Carrie, you look smart. Got a client meeting?' Posh James was at my elbow almost as soon as I was through the studio door.

'In a way,' I said. I nodded curtly to him, and strode through into Don Richardson's office without knocking.

'Carrie.' He frowned. 'What's with the suit?'

'I just wanted to look smart,' I said with a breezy smile. 'Don, I have four weeks holiday a year, don't I?'

'Yeah,' he said, still frowning but more warily now, his eyes fixed on mine.

'And is it fair to say that you've been unhappy with my work lately?'

'Well, not unhappy.' His frown deepened. 'Let's just say that there's room for some improvement. Your heart's not been in it.'

'Oh, I see.' I smiled disarmingly. 'But you said my design concepts were weak. Which they are. So I'm taking my four weeks' holiday in lieu of notice so that you can find someone with much better design concepts than mine.'

His eyes bulged. 'What?'

'I'm leaving,' I repeated.

'You can't do that.'

'Oh yes, I can,' I said as sweetly as I could, trying to quash an irrational feeling of glee at the dumbstruck look on his face. Don hated to be outmanoeuvred.

'But, Carrie –'

I held up one hand to interrupt him.

'Goodbye, Don,' I said. 'It's been lovely working with you. I'll let you know where to send my P45 when I have a forwarding address. And Don?' His head jerked up a little. 'Have a very Merry Christmas!'

The rest was easy. I rented the house out to Gabriel, Clara and four of their university friends for a decent monthly amount. They paid me more than I would have got if they'd been a family or a professional couple, because there were three of them in the upstairs rooms, and two of them used the sitting room and dining room as bedrooms.

I sat down with Gabe and wrote a list of instructions like what to do about the heating, and which day the recycling vans came. Then I hauled out the box of Christmas baubles and left it in the middle of the kitchen table next to my lists. Gabe pursed his lips and made a cryptic comment about being the angel on the top of the tree if I'd just stay until New Year, but I ruffled his hair and shook my head firmly. I was going, and nothing could stop me.

I packed up and put a lot of things into the attic, leaving my precious stuff with Laura who cried and scolded me, and said that if I wasn't back in time for her wedding she'd personally come and hunt me down. When I booked my flight I found that I didn't need a visa for the States, just so long I was planning to stay for less than three months and had a return ticket. I had plenty of money to support myself during my stay, and I had the addresses of three good hotels, four cheap hostels and Bruton's Waterhole Ranch.

I stopped the rented pick-up, clicked off the radio, and got out, using my hands to brush the road-dust off my jeans and red flannel shirt. A light wind had started about an hour ago. Little eddying swirls of dry, orange earth had been whipped up and then blown into the open window of the pick-up as I had driven along.

The coppery sun sat low on the wide horizon. I had to

shield my eyes with my hand a little as I squinted across the high-fenced pasture that stretched out away from me. Bruton's Waterhole Ranch was vast. At least six thousand acres according to the man who'd given me directions on the outskirts of the last town I'd driven through. I could see the big ranch house from where I stood, and the lodge which nestled on a hilltop behind. There were barns, a windmill and a lot of livestock pens, while coming towards me across the pasture-land was a lone cowhand on horseback.

'Howdy, miss.' He reined in and squinted down at me from blue eyes which twinkled out from a crease of leathery skin. 'Can I help you? Name's John Franklyn. I'm the steward here. This here's Bruton land you're on. Were you lost or just passin' through?'

'Actually I'm looking for someone who I think works for you.' I hooked my hands into the pockets of my tight jeans and gave him a friendly smile. 'A friend of mine. Sam Bronson. Do you know him?'

'Sure, I know Sam.' He laughed, a deep rumbling which came from somewhere inside his well-filled plaid shirt.

John Franklyn was a solid man nearing middle age. He had powerful arms with knotted brown musculature that told of long days in the open air working horses and tending cattle. 'Sam's one of the new boys. I nearly didn't take him on, but when I saw him up on my second-best roping horse, well, he's got a mighty fine seat, miss. And he has a good way with the cattle. Knows when a cow's sick. You can be mighty proud of yer friend, miss.'

'Oh!' I was pleased, and it must have showed because the benign blue twinkle flashed out from John Franklyn's face again.

'Say,' he said. 'Why don't you come on down to the ranch house and Mrs Franklyn'll fix you some coffee? I'll tell Sam you're here.'

'Thank you.'

I followed the road down to the ranch house and pulled in next to a battered brown pick-up. After getting out, I followed Franklyn's distant horse with my eyes. He took a short cut on a track that led through the pasture and disappeared out of sight in a dip. Mrs Franklyn appeared on the stoop, wiping her hands on a piece of chequered towelling.

Within ten minutes, I was sitting up on a sturdy gate with a deliciously steaming mug of black coffee in my hand. Sam trotted down the slope towards me and reined in nearby. His face was exactly the same, but I saw immediately that his hair was longer. Soft curls of it waved out from under the rim of the familiar black stetson and nestled against the collar of his shirt. Longer hair suited him, made him look more relaxed, more laid-back if that were at all possible.

I balanced my mug next to me on the top of the gate-post and smiled at him tentatively. I was still not sure about how pleased he'd be to see me, despite Rachel's reassuring words on the street that night in London. I felt my pulse flip nervously and a pack of little butterflies scooted around the inside of my tummy as I squinted against the sunset. Sam's face was in shadow, and all I could see were his hands tight on the reins. His knuckles seemed a little white against the tanned skin of his hands and forearms, but that was the only sign that he might be tense at seeing me.

'Hi,' I said.

As openers go, it was probably the most inane, but I couldn't come up with anything better, even though I'd had almost a week to think of the most brilliant greeting. I had imagined the moment when Sam and I said 'hello' so many times, fantasised about the things we'd say. But now that the moment was here everything was just very simple. One word was all I could muster.

Sam dropped out of the saddle without speaking and came over to stand about two feet away. He swept off the stetson and wiped his hot brow with the back of his hand, smearing dirt there. I smiled and held in check an intense desire to reach up and wipe him clean. I so desperately wanted to feel his skin under my fingers, taste his sweat on my lips. My emotions and desires were like a fever rising to boiling point inside me and I suddenly wondered what I was doing there. Out in the middle of nowhere. With the slimmest chance of getting back together with someone who I'd been so careless with.

'Hi yourself,' he replied. It was hardly the dialogue of a Hollywood blockbuster, but it made me feel all warm and gooey inside. With the stetson off, I could see his eyes, and his eyes said so much more than his words.

'Sam, I am so sorry,' I breathed. 'I was a complete and utter idiot and I don't deserve to be forgiven.'

He frowned, hitched his hands on his hips and took a step towards me.

'No, you don't,' he said. 'But maybe we can sort that out with the help of a harness and a riding crop. I think a little punishment would suit you for a change, Carrie.'

I felt a flicker of erotic pleasure twist in my guts at the thought of my sweet Sam trying to tame me with a riding crop. I grinned down at him, and he moved in close, grasped my waist, and swung me off the gate. Instead of standing down, I twisted my legs around his hips, enjoying the feel of his leather chaps against my bare skin, and he held me close, his erection pressing hard against the gusset of my jeans.

'I am so glad to see you,' he whispered, rubbing his nose against mine.

'And I you,' I replied.

I closed my eyes as Sam's arms tightened around me. I felt as if I'd arrived in his embrace for the first time. It felt like home.

Chapter Nineteen
home

A week into the New Year, John Franklyn said that a group of businessmen from the corporation that owned Bruton's Waterhole Ranch would be paying a visit. I didn't take much notice, but when their big white station wagon pulled into the yard, I felt a prickle of premonition surge up into my hairline.

The first man out of the vehicle was Max.

He thrust his hands into his trouser pockets in that familiar way he had, and I felt my face flush a deep red as I tried to control the frantic leaping of my pulse. He greeted the Franklyns as if they were old friends, slapped a couple of the cowhands on the back and then strode over to where I'd gone to sit.

I was in the shade on the stoop, one hand gently stroking one of the ranch dogs that I'd become fond of. Without speaking, Max sat down on the swing seat next to me and watched the movement of my fingers as I stroked Sheba's rough fur.

'I trusted you,' I murmured, as if it was only a day or so since we'd last been speaking. He took my free hand in his and held it closely between his warm, strong palms.

'I know you did,' he said. 'And I never did a darn thing to betray that trust. I never meant to hurt you, Carrie.' He sighed. 'If anything, I wanted to protect you. I thought that if you were on the net with me then, by my reckoning, you were less at risk from other people who might be out to hurt you. I'm sorry.'

I looked away, out to the far horizon. A dust-cloud had risen where a couple of cattlemen were bringing in some Brahmans. Far above in the wide blue space of the midday sky, a single hawk wheeled and circled, keeping an eye out for wildlife that might have been disturbed by the hooves of the cattle. I watched the bird dip and soar freely as I thought hard, trying to ignore the powerful magnetism of Max's hand on mine.

I had thought about him a lot, and talked about it all with Sam in the long, dark, hot nights that we'd spent up in the lodge on the rise behind the ranch house. I realised that part of my own new-found freedom was because of the Huntsman. He'd made me a part of who I was now. He'd given me the courage to go along to the weekends that his friends attended. He'd made me laugh and given me something to kick against when I was feeling irritated by Sam's submissiveness.

Sam, seeing Max gently stroking my fingers, sauntered over and slowly came up the steps of the stoop. He sat down on the other side of me, not speaking, not touching, just comfortably close. I took his hand and held it in mine, and then pressed both of their hands together in my lap, savouring the warmth of their skin against mine. There was a long, studied silence, and then I spoke.

'I think,' I said with a small smile, 'that the three of us should be able to work something out here. Together. Don't you think?'

I felt Max lean in towards me, and felt the pressure of Sam's thigh against mine. Then I leaned back in the seat as I happily closed my eyes.

Visit the *Black Lace* website at

www.blacklace-books.co.uk

Find out the latest information and take advantage of our fantastic **free** book offer! Also visit the site for . . .

- All *Black Lace* titles currently available and how to order online
- Great new offers
- Writers' guidelines
- Author interviews
- An erotica newsletter
- Features
- Cool links

Black Lace – the leading imprint of women's sexy fiction.

Taking your erotic reading pleasure to new horizons

BLACK LACE NEW BOOKS

Published in February

STELLA DOES HOLLYWOOD
Stella Black
£6.99

Stella Black has a 1969 Pontiac Firebird, a leopardskin bra and a lot of attitude. Partying her way around Hollywood she is discovered by a billionaire entertainment mogul who wastes no time in turning Stella into America's most famous porn star. But the dark forces of American fundamentalism are growing. The moral right-wing are outraged and they're out to destroy Stella any which way they can.

How will she escape their punishing clutches?

A sexy saga of guns, girls and grit!

ISBN 0 352 33588 2

UP TO NO GOOD
Karen S. Smith
£6.99

Emma is resigned to the fact that her cousin's wedding will be a dull affair, But when she meets leather-clad biker, Kit, it's lust at first sight and Emma ends up behaving even more scandalously than usual. They don't get the chance to say goodbye, though, and she thinks she'll never see her mystery lover again. Fate intervenes, however, and they are reunited at yet another wedding. And so begins a year of outrageous sex, wild behaviour and lots of getting up to no good!

Like *Four Weddings and a Funeral* with explicit sex and without the funeral!

ISBN 0 352 33589 0

DARKER THAN LOVE
Kristina Lloyd
£6.99

It's 1875 and the morals of Queen Victoria have no hold over London's debauched elite. Young and naïve Clarissa is eager to meet Lord Marldon, the man to whom she is promised. She knows he is handsome, dark and sophisticated. He is, in fact, louche, depraved and consumed by a passion for cruel sexual excesses!

This tale of dark, Gothic debauchery is a Black Lace special reprint.

ISBN 0 352 33279 4

Published in March

SIN.NET
Helena Ravenscroft
£6.99

Carrie's life changes when she discovers the steamy world of adult Internet chat rooms. Naturally shy Carrie assumes the identity of the sexually confident Dominque, and she's soon having a series of X-rated online liaisons. Suddenly she's having more fun than ever before. Is it submission or strength she wants in a lover? And can she blend all the qualities of Dominique into her own personality?

ISBN 0 352 33598 X

TWO WEEKS IN TANGIER
Annabel Lee
£6.99

When Melinda Carr inherits property from her Great Aunt Laura there are some surprises in store for her. Her new business affairs manager, the enigmatic Khalil, is very keen to bring out her wanton side and test her voracious sexual appetite to the limit. She's soon transformed into the creature of pleasure she's always wanted to be. But what will her strait-laced boyfriend do when he finds Melinda is following in the footsteps of her scandalous great aunt.

ISBN 0 352 33599 8

THE TRANSFORMATION
Natasha Rostova
£6.99

Three friends, three lives, one location: San Francisco. This upbeat story of complex relationships is a dazzling fun-packed story of three women at the sexual crossroads in their lives. Exploring their sensual selves in that most liberal of American cities they discover things about themselves – and their friends – they never knew existed.

This is a Black Lace special reprint.

ISBN 0 352 33311 1

To be published in April

HOTBED
Portia Da Costa
£6.99

Disaffected journalist Natalie is on the trail of an exposé. Her quest for a juicy story leads her to discover that her staid academic hometown has become a hotbed of sleaze and hidden perversity. Quickly drawn in, Natalie soon falls under the spell of Stella Fontayne – a glittering drag queen at the centre of an erotic underworld. Her sister and rival Patti is in on the action, too, and nobody is quite who or what they seem in this world where transgressing sexual boundaries is the norm.

ISBN 0 352 33614 5

WICKED WORDS 4
Ed. Kerri Sharp
£6.99

Black Lace short story collections are a showcase of the finest contemporary women's erotica anywhere in the world. With contributions from the UK, USA and Australia, the settings and stories are deliciously daring. Fresh, cheeky and upbeat, only the most arousing fiction makes it into a *Wicked Words* anthology.

ISBN 0 352 33603 X

THE CAPTIVATION
Natasha Rostova
£6.99

In 1917, war-torn Russia is on the brink of the Revolution and princess Katya Leskovna and her relatives are forced to flee their palace. Katya ends up in the encampment of a rebel Cossack army. The men haven't seen a woman for weeks and sexual tensions are running high.
This is a Black Lace special reprint full of danger, sexual tension and men in uniform!

ISBN 0 352 33234 4

If you would like a complete list of plot summaries of Black Lace titles, or would like to receive information on other publications available, please send a stamped addressed envelope to:

Black Lace, Thames Wharf Studios,
Rainville Road, London W6 9HA

BLACK LACE BOOKLIST

Information is correct at time of printing. To check availability go to www.blacklace-books.co.uk

All books are priced £5.99 unless another price is given.

Black Lace books with a contemporary setting

DARK OBSESSION £7.99	Fredrica Alleyn ISBN 0 352 33281 6	☐
THE TOP OF HER GAME	Emma Holly ISBN 0 352 33337 5	☐
LIKE MOTHER, LIKE DAUGHTER	Georgina Brown ISBN 0 352 33422 3	☐
THE TIES THAT BIND	Tesni Morgan ISBN 0 352 33438 X	☐
IN THE FLESH	Emma Holly ISBN 0 352 33498 3	☐
SHAMELESS	Stella Black ISBN 0 352 33485 1	☐
TONGUE IN CHEEK	Tabitha Flyte ISBN 0 352 33484 3	☐
FIRE AND ICE	Laura Hamilton ISBN 0 352 33486 X	☐
SAUCE FOR THE GOOSE	Mary Rose Maxwell ISBN 0 352 33492 4	☐
INTENSE BLUE	Lyn Wood ISBN 0 352 33496 7	☐
THE NAKED TRUTH	Natasha Rostova ISBN 0 352 33497 5	☐
A SPORTING CHANCE	Susie Raymond ISBN 0 352 33501 7	☐
TAKING LIBERTIES	Susie Raymond ISBN 0 352 33357 X	☐
A SCANDALOUS AFFAIR	Holly Graham ISBN 0 352 33523 8	☐
THE NAKED FLAME	Crystalle Valentino ISBN 0 352 33528 9	☐
CRASH COURSE	Juliet Hastings ISBN 0 352 33018 X	☐

TAKING LIBERTIES	Susie Raymond ISBN 0 352 33357 X	☐
ANIMAL PASSIONS	Martine Marquand ISBN 0 352 33499 1	☐
ON THE EDGE	Laura Hamilton ISBN 0 352 33534 3	☐
LURED BY LUST	Tania Picarda ISBN 0 352 33533 5	☐
LEARNING TO LOVE IT	Alison Tyler ISBN 0 352 33535 1	☐
THE HOTTEST PLACE	Tabitha Flyte ISBN 0 352 33536 X	☐
THE NINETY DAYS OF GENEVIEVE £6.99	Lucinda Carrington ISBN 0 352 33070 8	☐
EARTHY DELIGHTS	Tesni Morgan ISBN 0 352 33548 3	☐
MAN HUNT £6.99	Cathleen Ross ISBN 0 352 33583 1	☐
MÉNAGE £6.99	Emma Holly ISBN 0 352 33231 X	☐
DREAMING SPIRES £6.99	Juliet Hastings ISBN 0 352 33584 X	☐
STELLA DOES HOLLYWOOD £6.99	Stella Black ISBN 0 352 33588 2	☐
UP TO NO GOOD £6.99	Karen S. Smith ISBN 0 352 33589 0	☐

Black Lace books with an historical setting

INVITATION TO SIN £6.99	Charlotte Royal ISBN 0 352 33217 4	☐
PRIMAL SKIN	Leona Benkt Rhys ISBN 0 352 33500 9	☐
DEVIL'S FIRE	Melissa MacNeal ISBN 0 352 33527 0	☐
WILD KINGDOM	Deanna Ashford ISBN 0 352 33549 1	☐
DARKER THAN LOVE	Kristina Lloyd ISBN 0 352 33279 4	☐

Black Lace anthologies

SUGAR AND SPICE £7.99	Various ISBN 0 352 33227 1	☐
CRUEL ENCHANTMENT Erotic Fairy Stories	Janine Ashbless ISBN 0 352 33483 5	☐
MORE WICKED WORDS	Various ISBN 0 352 33487 8	☐

WICKED WORDS 3 Various
ISBN 0 352 33522 X

Black Lace non-fiction
THE BLACK LACE BOOK OF Ed. Kerri Sharp
  WOMEN'S SEXUAL ISBN 0 352 33346 4
  FANTASIES

- - - - - - ✂ - - - - - - - - - - - - - - - - - -

Please send me the books I have ticked above.

Name   ....

Address   ....

          ....

          ....

          .... Post Code ....

Send to: **Cash Sales, Black Lace Books, Thames Wharf Studios, Rainville Road, London W6 9HA.**

US customers: for prices and details of how to order books for delivery by mail, call 1-800-805-1083.

Please enclose a cheque or postal order, made payable to **Virgin Publishing Ltd**, to the value of the books you have ordered plus postage and packing costs as follows:

UK and BFPO – £1.00 for the first book, 50p for each subsequent book.

Overseas (including Republic of Ireland) – £2.00 for the first book, £1.00 for each subsequent book.

If you would prefer to pay by VISA, ACCESS/MASTER-CARD, DINERS CLUB, AMEX or SWITCH, please write your card number and expiry date here:

....

Please allow up to 28 days for delivery.

Signature ....

- - - - - - ✂ - - - - - - - - - - - - - - - - - -